"This woman is going to be the death of me."
—KHAN

PART I

n.tetterton

KHAN
PART I

N. TETTERTON

Copyright © 2020 N. Tetterton All rights reserved

The characters and events portrayed in this book are fictitious. Any similarity to real persons, living or dead, is coincidental and not intended by the author.

No part of this book may be reproduced, or stored in a retrieval system, or transmitted in any form or by any means, electronic, mechanical, photocopying, recording, or otherwise, without express written permission of the publisher.

Library of Congress Control Number: 1-9171839464

Printed in the United States of America

Warning

For the majority of the books that I write one can assume that they contain sexually explicit scenes, adult language, and violence that may be considered offensives to some readers.

For this reason my books are intended only for those 18+.

Also contains dark themes that some may find triggering.

MIDNIGHT SYN MC BOOK ORDER:

KHAN PART I
KHAN PART II
F*CKING CHAOS
TREAD Carefully
TILL The Day I Die
BOOK 6 - TBD

BLURB

WHY DO THEY CALL ME KHAN?
IT'S THE ROAD NAME I GOT WHEN I CAME TO THE MIDNIGHT SYNDICATE MC.
AFTER GENGHIS KHAN VICIOUS RULER, LOVER OF WOMEN, WHAT CAN I SAY
WE MAY HAVE SOME THINGS IN COMMON.

I NEVER WAS ASHAMED OF THE NAME UNTIL HER... UNTIL I HAD TO HAVE RESPONSIBILITIES.
ONE WOULD THINK THAT TAKING IN MY GODDAUGHTER WHEN HER FATHER WAS ARRESTED WOULD HAVE CHANGED MY LIFE THE MOST, BUT NO IT WAS WHEN BILLIE SAXS CAME INTO MY LIFE. FLIPPING MY WORLD UPSIDE DOWN.

EVEN IF SHE'S MARRIED I WILL DO ANYTHING TO PROTECT HER. EVEN IF THAT THING TO PROTECT HER FROM IS HER HUSBAND OR EVEN MYSELF... WHAT CAN I SAY? SOME SAY I HAVE A HERO COMPLEX...

CHAPTER ONE	11
CHAPTER TWO	21
CHAPTER THREE	35
CHAPTER FOUR	46
CHAPTER FIVE	58
CHAPTER SIX	65
CHAPTER SEVEN	80
CHAPTER EIGHT	86
CHAPTER NINE	96
CHAPTER TEN	111
CHAPTER ELEVEN	119
CHAPTER TWELVE	132
CHAPTER THIRTEEN	145

CHAPTER FOURTEEN	156
CHAPTER FIFTEEN	164
CHAPTER SIXTEEN	176
CHAPTER SEVENTEEN	189
CHAPTER EIGHTEEN	202
CHAPTER NINETEEN	218
CHAPTER TWENTY	232
CHAPTER TWENTY-ONE	244
CHAPTER TWENTY-TWO	249
CHAPTER TWENTY-THREE	259
KHAN PART II	271
MIDNIGHT SYN MC BOOK ORDER	283
ABOUT THE AUTHOR	285

CHAPTER ONE

...his intense stare should be frightening but it brings out a sense of excitement.

KHAN

How is it that I can pull the trigger ending someone's life and not even blink, no hesitation? Yet here, in this room, I'm sitting nervously in this chair. Almost twitching, at least twitching on the inside. Not even the barrel of a gun to my temple makes me twitch on the outside anymore. Maybe I've just become complacent about near-death experiences.

This is fucking weird. Rubbing my hand down my legs trying to smooth out my dress pants over my legs. Why did I have to wear a fucking suit? Oh right, because walking into this place in my jeans, t-shirt, and my cut would send any chance for Ella to be able to come here right out the window. I try to not make any eye contact with the women who shuffle around me in the room even though they all keep glancing over towards me. I can deal with their looks and any other time I wouldn't even think twice, but this isn't about me... this is about Ella.

"Davis," well, that's me... here goes nothing.

As I walk towards the room that the woman is standing next to, I can hear the sharp intake of breath that she sucks in, *at least it's good to know that it isn't just my normal clothes that draw women to me*. I watch the blush begin to form in her cheeks the closer I walk towards her, but she looks away, refusing to make eye contact. She is most likely around 22, so this all makes sense. She's just old enough to be in the column of 'women I would fuck'… which is pretty much anyone over the age of 21. But she isn't sure what to think of me. My appearance intrigues yet also terrify her and she can't quite figure out why she immediately thinks about fucking me.. I'm sure at first she notices my build, I'm taller than most men and I take care of my body. Between working on my bike and the hours I spend at the gym I make sure to stay in shape. I nod my head and give her a small smirk as she motions for me into the room. As I pass by her I can't help but smirk and wink.

"Ms. Saxs will be with you shortly." Her words are barely over a whisper as she closes the door behind me, blush still consuming her face. Rubbing my hands together as I walk towards the chairs which sit in front of the large wooden desk. There is a computer that sits on the right side of it. On the left side of the desk, there is a stack of folders, and three left haphazardly between the pile and the computer. There is also a container to hold the pens on the desk but at least 5 or so just dropped on the desk. At the front of the desk, there is a large wooden nameplate which reads 'Billie Saxs, Principal'. Behind the desk is a large window and I'm sure that during the school year she can see the kids walking around the campus. On the wall to the right, there is a dying plant and a cactus. There are photos, but they are slightly too far away for me to get a good look at to see the faces, or exactly what is happening, and honestly, I'm too nervous at this moment to be daring enough to get up and go look at them. Who would have ever thought that I could ever be nervous again, but as I sit in this extremely fancy private school, me the guy who dropped out of high school? Yes, I am nervous. To break these nerves, I start to try and gauge the woman with whom I will be meeting shortly. The woman who uses this office is someone who tries to break her character, she tries to be perfect; which shows with the perfectly placed file folders on one side and the pen holder with the majority of the pens in them, the plants to the side and the photos. From afar the office looks perfect, almost like a photo-worthy of a magazine; however, the files are strewn across her desk, the pens which have been dropped in no particular order, in fact, one of the pens is missing its cap, and the dying plant tells me that her real self, breaks through and she can't quite help it.

The door behind me pops open and I stand up assuming that the woman that I am meeting with will be standing there, but the same flustered woman is standing at the door and her words come out quick. Without meeting my eyes she rambles out, "I'm so sorry, Ms. Saxs is running behind it should only be a few more minutes." I wish that I could just go ahead and get this over with. The young woman mutters some more words that are incoherent as she shuts the door. Running late just further proves my theory on her. She can't help but let her true colors breakthrough. I hate people who pretend to be something that they are not.

There are two built-in bookshelves behind me on each side of the door. The books bring back memories of when I was a kid, my mother reading to me as I fall asleep, and I can't help but walk over and check out the titles. I smirk as I take in the titles and wonder if she has actually read all of these or if they are just for show. There seems to be no particular order of the books on the shelves. Except that one set of shelves is reference books while the shelves I'm looking at are all fiction books, I wonder if she tries to organize them. Gauging by the rest of the office, I bet she does. She organizes them, and within the week they are out of order again. She seems to have a wide array of novels, classics as well as some more modern novels.

Anna Karenina

The Alchemist

The Hunger Games

Gatsby

Catcher and the Rye

Divergent

Fahrenheit 451…

I pull the book out of the line when another grabs my attention. This book sits sideways on top of a few other books on a different shelf, something quite out of place with the rest of the books that sit on the shelves.

"The Anarchist cookbook?" I can't help but whisper the words out loud as my fingers graze over the spine, whoever this woman is I'm not sure if I've ever met someone quite like her. Bringing my attention back to the book in hand I open it up and flip through the pages, noticing the little words that are scribbled along the spine and the dog-eared creased corners... either she bought this book second hand or she has read it... more than once. When the door opens, my nerves from before taking ahold of me again, and I shut the book quickly and put it back onto the shelf... slightly out of place, much as I am in this room, but still almost into its place.

The energy seems to shift when she walks into the room, it's a mix of stress and something else that I recognize but given the woman standing in front of me, I cannot seem to believe it. There's a folder in her hand. I can see her gaze as she scans the pages.

"Mr. Davis." Well, let's start this awkward interview already.

"Not exactly, but I can understand the confusion" my words come out condescendingly, there's nothing new there, but as soon as she looks up at me, I internally kick myself. She stops in her spot, which is mere inches away from where I stand and her bright green eyes look up at me. She is a head shorter than I am, even with the tall black heels that she is wearing. She looks to be maybe twenty-six and I'm not sure how she could have made it as a principal of a school like this so early in her career. Her dark hair flows down and over her shoulders and it manages to contrast with her creamy porcelain skin. Her black skirt stops right below her knees but the way that it fits tight to her I can tell that without it, her legs would be hard to take my eyes off of. She's wearing a black and white plaid blazer with a black silk blouse underneath it. I expect to hear the same intake of air as the woman from earlier did, but she doesn't, which manages to surprise and disappoint me at the same time. Even if outwardly she doesn't show her attraction to me I can see the small ways that she is trying to push it down. I can see her pupils dilate just slightly. I watch as her free hand moves up to smooth out her hair. Not that I think I am God's gift to women or

anything, but I just know how women react to me even women who try to be as prim and proper as Ms. Billie Saxs is trying to make people believe that she is.

You don't get a certain reputation without being able to sense these things.

BILLIE

How did I fuck that up? I force myself to look away from the man standing in front of me back down to the folder. Flipping through a couple of pages I then remember all of the notes which I have for this meeting. This is the meeting that I was not looking forward to, but with already running late this morning and then traffic, I am more flustered than normal and forgot. I glance back up at the very intense man standing in front of me. His deep blue eyes take me by surprise and they cause me to quickly look back down to the folder which sits in my hand.

I have to look up to him to be able to get a good look at his eyes and can't help but wonder how tall he is. I'm judging by my 5'4 frame with 4-inch heels on and the still head that he has on me he is probably around 6'4. His dirty blonde hair is nearly shaved on the sides but much longer on the top, he has styled it with gel, combing it straight back. He's wearing a suit, but I can tell that he feels very uncomfortable, well if this man could possibly be uncomfortable about anything. Even with the suit, I can still see the tattoos which peek out from over the collar of his shirt. They bring out a sense of curiosity in me that makes me think about pulling the collar back so I can get a better look at them.

Hmm, this man is not like the ones I'm used to meeting with every other day. From looking at him I can tell that he's full of masculinity, almost like a modern-day Viking, not like most of the fathers and administrators that I deal with day today. His entire demeanor starts a throbbing that I haven't felt in some time. The ones who have softer hands than I do. No, this man… he knows how to work with his hands and he's not afraid to get them dirty. Even though the suit conceals what exactly his body would look like underneath something tells me that it would not disappoint. The scar right along his cheekbone contradicts the rest of his face, it's the only flaw on his face that I can find. Yet does things to me that I'm not so sure about. It screams to me that there's something dangerous about this man… something dark and for some reason, it excites and at the same time terrifies me.

"Daxton Wessex," he extends his hand to me, "I'm Ella's legal guardian. It's been very recent. I sent over the paperwork last week." I reach out to shake his hand and have to repress all of my emotions that threaten to boil up. The throbbing increases and I have to look away from him quickly to sustain the sensations. Clearly, it's been too long since I have had sex. I pull back my hand after I can gauge my previous assessment of his rough hands was correct, as I glance back to the paperwork in my hand and flip through a couple of pages. Of course, I remember all of my notes to this particular meeting now, after I have made a complete idiot of myself.

"Yes, I do apologize. I see it right here." I mutter, seeing one of the books on the shelf is out of place… interesting, this man does not strike me as one who reads. "Please have a seat" I motion to him as I walk around my desk. I can still feel his eyes on me, setting my skin on fire wherever they land, as I move to my chair. Which causes all of my nerves to be overly aware of the situation.

"Mr. Wessex-," I begin.

"Please," he cuts me off and leans forward looking straight at me, "call me Dax." The way he says his own name seems foreign to him, almost as if he isn't used to saying it either.

Nope, don't want to do that.

I can tell that by the way he looks at me, the way that he talks, and the way that he carries himself he is used to women doing whatever it is that he has in mind. I smile up to him again, politely. "Mr. Wessex." I insist, sternly, without breaking eye contact until I have made my point across to him then looking down at the paperwork which sits in front of me, "Ella's grades are incredible. She's an A+ student, top of her class, with no disciplinary actions. She participates in after-school activities. On paper, she looks like a perfect fit for the school." This is the part of this job that I hate. I

emphasize the word *she* and when I look back up at him I can see the look on his face is not what he wants to hear. The playfulness that his eyes were just holding is now dissipated and a more serious look replaces it.

"But..." he trails and I have to look back down to say what I need to say. If I look him in the eyes I will not be able to form the words.

"...But," I pause again as I can still feel his eyes on me even without looking up to him just yet. "Let me clarify that I am not the deciding vote here. I am simply here as an initial interview, mostly to weed the majority of the kids who have nowhere near a chance of being here." I pause again letting myself look up to him, knowing exactly how I can say what I need to say without making it seem so blunt. Deep breath, "How is it that Ella came into your custody so suddenly?" I ask him maybe if I walk through the situation it will become apparent.

"Her father is..." he pauses for a second, I know that he is trying to find the right words to say to me.

"Incarcerated?" I ask him in a small voice and he glances away. Everyone has heard of Oz Davis and his arrest. As well as, his association with the Midnight Syndicate MC.

"Pending trial," He cuts his eyes and stares at me, hardening his stare. "and her mother took off, abandoning her when she was 6, Ella is my goddaughter." I can see the love he has for Ella. When he speaks of her mother leaving his eyes to fall down and I wish I could do something for this girl, not even meeting her and I want to protect her from having a messed my life myself. As big and scary as Dax is sitting across from me when he claims her as his goddaughter his eyes are full of pride, "I want nothing but the best for her."

"And what is it that you do?" I ask him. There are rumors about Oz Davis... all around this city, but Daxton Wessex I, nor anyone that I know, has heard of any sort of connection to the Midnight Syndicate or for that matter even heard of him.

His smile confuses me and I'm not sure if he smiling at me or if he smiling because he's practiced this enough that he knows exactly what to say. "I'm a business owner."

17

"Oh," I look at him a little surprised. "Which business do you own?" I ask him. I have my suspensions of which business he owns, if he's the legal guardian of Ella, who is Oz's daughter, the chances of him not being a part of the club are highly unlikely.

He raises his eyes and looks straight at me, testing me, trying me, his intense stare should be frightening but it brings out a sense of excitement. "I don't understand how that's any of your fucking business." He continues to stare at me and my breathing increases. I'm not sure if it's due to the anger, from the way that he is speaking to me, or if it's the fact that him speaking to me like this is somehow turning me on more. It's clearly just because I need to get laid and that this man is a primal definition of what a man should be.

"Mr. Wessex," I mutter and I match his intensity, "I don't think you understand how all of this works."

"I don't need you patronizing me," he begins to push himself up out of his seat, leaning his large frame overtop my desk, bringing himself closer to me, trying to intimidate me, "just because you think that you are better than me, Billie." His voice continues to rise and continues to push himself closer to me with each word he says and with the last word, my name, he flicks his hands towards my nameplate which sits on my desk. But why is it when he uses my first name somehow it causes the tension between us to rise if that is even possible? He's leaning almost all the way over my desk, hands pressed firmly on the wood. Screw him and him trying to intimidate me.

I slam my hands on the desk and push myself up, matching his stance, his tone, his volume, and his demeanor, "It's. Ms. Saxs." our faces are closer than I intend for them to be and for a flash of a second I see a sense of surprise and maybe intrigue to his eyes and the corner of one side of his lip pulls up into a small smirk, but it disappears just as quickly as it appears. Once he gets his expression under control, his eyes become more intense, differently than the intensity they had before. This time he looks at me like he wants to devour me. "Now, Mr. Wessex," I lower my voice to a normal volume and stress his name, still not wavering in my stance, "what I was saying is that at this private school, not only are the students evaluated but so are their families." I pause as I sit back down and he begins to take his seat once more understanding what I am

meaning, "my recommendation is on the students themselves, and forgive me if I am wrong I am under the impression that you may not be too familiar with the private school system," he nods that he is not, "ok, I am trying to help you because all of this is going to be under review with the board of directors. Once she gets her approval from me. And those questions will be expected to be answered." I pause once more. "Even with Ella's fantastic record, Oz Davis's pending manslaughter trial will have an impact on her being approved. So, unless on paper" I make my point by holding up the folder that sits in front of me, "you can have a way that not only counterbalances it but pushes it over for a positive look on the school. I'm sorry Mr. Wessex, but as much as it pains me to say it… it doesn't look good." I stop and his lips press into a firm line. "Now, I will pass along her application with my seal of approval," I lower my voice because I'm not supposed to reveal the next piece of information, but not only do I feel bad for this girl, but because I can also see how much he wants to give her what he can, "you could get a call, but I will tell you that they will do research on everyone before they call you and Ella in for an interview."

He looks down at his hands and mutters, "So, it doesn't look good."

"I'm sorry." I shake my head, "believe me I wish that there was more that I could do." if there was I may hate my jobless.

"Thank you," he looks genuinely disappointed for a second, and then his face turns almost playful, "Billie," he's tempting me to correct him again as he gets up and strides towards the door pausing at my bookcase, and looks back at me picking up the book which sits out of place on the shelf, "You mind if I borrow this?"

The question takes me off guard and I mutter, "Ye-yeah, sure."

"Thanks," I hear the words as he walks out of my office. Sighing, I sign my name to the folder and put it in the yes pile. Hopefully, for once this school will give a kid a chance without digging her entire family through the mud.

I glance at the countdown on my computer's home screen… 14 days… thank god… I don't know how much longer I can go without sex. I can't help but think about Daxton Wessex and how much he set me on edge. I spin around in my chair facing the window now and close my eyes, feeling the sun on my face, but it doesn't make the prickling all over my body go away.

10 days left...

"CRAP," I hit my steering wheel, "no, no, no, no." I continue to hit the wheel as I watch the smoke rise from my hood. Popping the hood, I get out from the driver's side of my 2010 Camry. As I open the hood more smoke begins to pour out of the car "WHY?" I scream, dramatically, as I kick the bumper of the car. I hear a rumble of what I can only assume is a motorcycle in the distance and then the rumbling is gone. I spin around, leaning against the car, fishing my phone out of my back pocket, and look at the screen. I swipe on the screen until I get to my roadside assistance and press the send.

"Billie?" I hear the voice, and before I look over I see those blue eyes I can already feel on me. When I finally gain the courage to glance over I see him and I have to force my mouth to stay closed. When his black leather vest, which is covered with patches, everything makes much more sense.

CHAPTER TWO

...The article about which tampon is best for your vagina is mentally stimulating for you?

KHAN

Four days later as I ride to the shop from my "meeting" I see legs, holy shit legs, that trail up to the most perfect ass that I have ever laid eyes on. The legs are standing on the side of the road, bent over, in front of her car, hood up, black smoke coming from her engine... that's not good. I slow my bike down and kick the stand down pushing myself off of the seat. I need to help whomever these legs are... it's not until I see her spin around and lean against the front of the car that I can't help but release a laugh. I should have recognized those legs, but with her shorts that she is wearing I can now see much more of them. So. much. more. of them. They may even be able to show a small amount of her ass. And I can feel my dick slightly press against my zipper because all I can think about is that mouth attached to those legs and the way that it stood up to me, putting me in my place and... I'm in trouble.

When Billie stood up to me for a second there was nothing I wanted to do more than to pull her across her desk and fuck her, especially since her top happened to open as she leaned over the desk, and due to our height differences I got a little bit of an eye-full of her lacy bra covered tits, of course, I couldn't look down to fully appreciate them, but the image of them have played in my head a couple of times while I was fucking the girls from the club.

That was hot, I'm not sure I have ever had a woman stand up to me and refuse to back down. It's why I borrowed the book because that fucking woman is something special and now I haven't been able to get her out of my head. I've already read it before, a couple dozen times at that, but if I borrow it, then I have a reason to see her again. It's the same way that a girl *accidentally* leaves her ID or her purse. I only didn't think that it would be this soon before I saw her and apparently I didn't have to set up a reason to see her again.

"Billie?" I call out to her, my dick hoping that she will put me in my place about using a name that she has already told me not to, but what I don't see at first is that she is on her phone as her eyes widen before she even looks to me. I try to let the fact that I cause this sort of reaction out of her go at least for now. "Tow truck?" I ask her and she nods her head. "How long is it going to be?" I ask her because I know as I look at the smoke rises due to the color and the rate at which it is releasing that there are a few things that could be wrong and all of them are not good.

She sighs defeated, looks over at me, and as dramatically as she can say, "Three hours," her head falling backward so she's staring up to the sky. I pull out my phone and make a couple of texts, then return it to my pocket.

"Cancel it," I tell her as she looks at me shocked. I reach over, grabbing her phone away from her ear, and say, "Hello, yes, could you cancel that tow truck?" The woman on the phone is as confused as Billie is in front of me and then I hang up.

"Mr. Wessex, What are you doing? I need someone to tow my car." She's fucking pissed now.

"It's fine. And call me Dax."

"How is it fine? It just crapped out on me… and I have things that I need to do." She's flustered, stomping her flip-flop-covered foot, which may be the most adorable thing that I have ever seen. I try not to smile at her.

"Billie," I say trying to calm her down or trying to take her mind off of this. "I called someone they will be on their way shortly to come and get it." Her eyes widen as she looks over at me and calms down nearly immediately.

"Oh," her voice is a whisper.

"I'll give you a ride to the shop." I can tell that she wants to protest. So, I reach over and put my hand against the small of her back in an attempt to lead her over to my bike. For some reason, with this move, women tend to just go with whatever is happening.

"On that?" She asks, pointing to my bike, and I nod my head. She shakes her head again and says, "I can just wait for the truck." And as much as I don't want to, I laugh.

"Come on, it's not far. And you don't want to just stand out here for the next 30 minutes until they get here. It's hot, but I guess on the positive side you could make some extra money." I joke with her and her jaw falls open.

"Did you just say I look like a hooker?" She says the words between small giggles.

A grin forms on my mouth that feels unusual, one that I haven't felt in some time as I playfully shrug my shoulders, "Those words never came out of my mouth," and then I tease her as I let my voice drop leaning into her ear to say, "you know you want too." The shiver that is barely noticeable makes me feel like I have won.

"I'm married." The words blurt out of her mouth and I'm not sure if that should excite me or disappoint me. Because she only shouted it out because she can feel the tension as much as I can, but she shouted it out to make sure that I know that she is married. Although, from what I have learned in my life being married is not a deal-breaker. I can't help but chuckle and she's covering her face while attempting to figuratively back-pedal, "Oh my god, I'm so sorry... I didn't mean to assume that you wer—" I stop her but I'm still chuckling, pulling her hands from concealing her face.

"It's fine, trying to get you on the back of my bike isn't me propositioning you." Well, not completely, "I'm just trying to help someone out who is obviously having a difficult day." It's only a small white lie. "Just because you will have to be wrapped around me on it doesn't mean you have to be wrapped around me off of it."

"Hrmp," she makes a strange noise falling over her words, and stares off eyes wide, before she takes a deep breath and looks at me again, "um okay… I guess." I feel like I've won this battle. But she pauses and I glance over to her. "You know, even with you helping me I can't do anything more for Ella's case."

I nod my head as I state, "I figured," I pick up the helmet off of my seat and place it onto her head clasping it underneath her chin and tightening the strap. I bring my leg over the bike and reach for her hand. She clasps it and nervously kicks her leg over the bike and slides behind me… kind of… she has kept so much distance between us that she is barely even sitting on the seat. She is more like sitting on the fender over the back wheel. On second thought, maybe I shouldn't have made the joke about her being wrapped around me.

"You ever been on a bike?" I ask her and she thinks for a second and bites the inside of her mouth.

"A couple of times, but that was a really long time ago."

"You see this." I point to the exhaust pipes on the side, she nods her head. "Do not let those pretty legs touch it." She cocks her head to the side and I smirk, "it gets very hot and you're not exactly dressed to be on the back of the bike, but we aren't far so should be okay."

"Should be…" She mutters causing me to laugh.

"Nothing in this life is guaranteed," I say and crank the bike up.

"Dax, where's your helmet?" She asks before I slowly start walking the bike forward a bit. Looking over my shoulder partly to make sure that traffic isn't coming, but mostly to look at her.

"On, your head, Billie. You are way more important to society than I am." I can see her smile in my mirror. "Okay," I reach behind me and grasp her legs pulling them closer to me; feeling her pressed against my back now. "Hold on tight, Billie. I don't want you to fall off." I then feel her reserved arms wrap around me.

"Is this okay?" She asks me and I chuckle.

"That's perfect."

BILLIE

I feel so weird having my arms wrapped around Dax. I can feel the hardened muscles that are underneath the jacket, as he drives down the road. I can't help but look at the patch which takes up the entire back of his jacket. There's a large skull with what looks like a sight marker cross on its forehead. Above the logo, the top rocker reads Midnight Syndicate, and underneath the bottom rocker says, Sonston End. The vibration of the bike from underneath me is strange and I look around as we begin to slow, pulling up into a parking lot but I don't see a garage.

"Dax, why are we stopping?" I ask him as his heel kicks down the stand and he lets the bike rest on it.

"I was out running errands, and I need to finish them before I head back to the shop." He tells me and for a second I feel bad about keeping him from what he was needing to do. "Come on." He stands up holding out his hand for me to use, I take it, and then carefully get off of the bike. He then lifts his own leg over the bike. He doesn't start to walk until I do keeping one step behind me until we reach the door, then using his long arms, he reaches around me to open the door. As we cross the threshold of the store all I can hear from behind the register is, "KHAN! It's been forever since I've seen you." He nods to them without smiling or letting his face change at all.

"Dax, I really need to get my car." I pout at him causing him to smirk and shake his head I'm sure at my actions. I watch him as he walks down the aisle of the auto store and I can't seem to see much emotion on his face. Unlike a few minutes ago when he made the joke about me looking like a hooker, where his playful smile took up his entire face.

"Billie, they have to go get it, then get it back to the shop, and look at it. We have plenty of time. It's going to take a little bit. If you need me too I can take you anywhere you need to go." I can't help but look down and bite the inside of my mouth nodding my head. He definitely would not want to go with me on my errand.

"Khan," the same guy comes up to him and they do one of those weird man handshakes and I take the time during their conversation to look over the patches on his vest and notice a patch that says V. President. I can almost hear the news anchor from the night before, who was talking about the arrest of Osbourne "Oz" Davis, who was the president of the Midnight Syndicate Motorcycle Club. The one that really makes me question him is the small patch that reads 1%. I know what the 1%er stands for, meaning that they are a part of the 1% that is a part of some sort of criminal activity. The name that the clerk called him *Khan* makes me think and I'm pretty sure that I have heard mummers of someone named Khan within the club, but can't seem to place them.

"Billie," he says to me and I look over pulling me out of my thoughts.

"Khan?" I ask him and I swear for a second I see him become uneasy.

"It's a long story." He mutters not really looking at me this time.

"Well, apparently we have time." He shakes his head as if he isn't going into that. "Oh-kay."

I drag the word out and look at him again "VP?" He shrugs his shoulders. "You look a little young to be a VP." And he laughs.

"That's the first thing I thought about you. How you got your position when you are so young?"

How dare he… "Are you insinuating…"

He cuts me off, putting his hands up, and says, "Oh, no… I was just saying you're what 26 and already principal, that's impressive." I can't help but smile.

"I'm 31."

"Oh yea?" he raises his eyebrow and looks surprised. "And look at me thinking you were almost too young for me," He looks to me for

a few more moments, as I can feel the heat radiating through me before he abruptly turns to walk down the aisle shifting the mood of our conversation slightly. I follow behind him before I nearly barrel into his chest when he spins around abruptly, "Where was your *husband* that he couldn't come to get you today?" *Do I detect a small sense of jealousy?*

"Um, he's..." I pause, not sure if I should tell him where he is or not. I see the 1% patch and now am curious about what type of crimes he is involved in.

He follows my gaze to his 1%er patch and I'm sure connects the dots to my thoughts in his head.

"So, he's out of town... where is he at?" I shrug my shoulders. "What do you mean you don't know?"

"He's somewhere in the pacific right now." He nods his head understanding now.

"Navy?" He asks

"Yeah, how'd you know?" I ask him as he reaches over and picks up some of those weird blue paper towel things. I'm not really sure what the difference between the blue ones that I have only seen at the auto stores and any other ones.

"Dad was a Marine."

I'm sure I look shocked for a second and before I can stop myself I blurt out, "What does he think about all... " I pause before I pick up my hands and wave them in front of him, "This?" He actually smiles causing his entire face to soften.

"Wouldn't know, he died when I was 15." I suddenly feel like an asshole and maybe he can sense it, he leans into me and whispers, "It's not your fault." Then letting his voice return to a normal volume, "He was a fighter pilot," his thought trails for a second and he looks like he's thinking about something, he sudden shakes his head slightly and continues, "anyway the bird went down never found the body..." he trails for another second, "Best thing that ever happened."

"What?" I ask as my voice kicks up an octave.

"He was a real dick. Had a drinking problem, especially the few years leading up to his death. Still convinced that he was drunk when the bird went down."

"What about your mom?" I can't help but ask.

"She died when I was 10." How does my heartbreak for this man who most likely has some sort of record and is as tough as they come? And I think I understand that his dad drank about his mother dying. "Again, not your fault don't feel sorry for me." His last words are almost a plea. I understand this request wishing that I could have asked many people the same things. He turns suddenly and starts to walk up to the register.

"What did you do after that?"

"My uncle took me in. Never around… blew all the life insurance money that I got from my dad's death. I found the MC later that year." I nod my head understanding why someone in that sort of situation would want something like the MC. Orphaned, shit for a guardian, he was looking for a family. It also makes sense to me why he's so determined the get Ella into the school, having being orphaned himself, he needs to make sure that she has a decent guardian.

"How long has the husband been gone?" He asks and I actually smile

"6 months, he comes home in a little over a week."

As the guy, whom he was so friendly with earlier, rings up his items as Dax starts to speak again, "how long have you been married?"

"Ten years." His eyes widen, completely turning to the side and looking at me. I can see the kid who is ringing up the items, his eyes widen as well and they are both looking at me.

"No shit, seriously?" His statement is a serious shock. I nod my head and then he continues, "Better than me, I think I only made it 3 years… and that's included the year that we were separated."

"Sorry," I don't know what else to say in this situation and he shrugs his shoulders. "What happened?" I ask him before I can stop the words from coming out of my mouth.

"Shit just happens." He pauses and contemplates saying more. "It didn't work out. I moved on. So did she. Haven't seen her since." He hands the kid behind the counter a handful of bills and doesn't wait for his change, saying, "Thanks, Chris." As he grabs the bags off of the counter I try to reach for one. "Stop it." His words sound more like a growl than words. Turning around he nods towards the door.

"Kids?" I ask him

"Nah, we were just kids… probably got divorced about the same time you got married. She left town and we've never spoken again." Strangely, he doesn't speak a bad word about his ex-wife. Most men would instantly trash-talk an ex especially an ex-wife, "But learned my lesson on that shit." He says the last statement and reaches for the door. I jump ahead of him and instead open it for him. He stops and just stares at me. We stand in the strangest standoff, him standing about a foot back from the exit as I hold the door open for him waiting for him to walk through. When a man walks through the door without saying a word to me or acknowledging that I'm holding it open, I watch as Dax's eyes follow him, and then he rolls his eyes and walks through the door.

"Marriage isn't always bad though," I try to convince him letting the door shut as we walk back over to the bike.

He shrugs his shoulders as he places the bags that he got from the store into a saddlebag, "I dunno about that." He pauses again before getting onto the bike and adds, "I've never known anyone who has had a happy marriage… plus no matter what you do someone always ends up hurt." I look to him questioning because that statement almost makes me have a completely different opinion about him, "Come on, just think about it. Either one person hurts the other… and you break up. Which one or both people get hurt… or someone dies." I try to find the words to argue his point but he isn't technically wrong. He grabs his helmet and puts it on my head, again.

"The same can be said with just dating though," I say to him as he reaches under my chin, lifting it up to give him a better angle to tighten the strap.

"That's why I don't date." He says as I feel his fingers tap my helmet. As I process his words I watch him kicking his leg over his bike and sitting down waiting for me to get on behind him.

I can't help my naivety when I say, "Then how do you... you know..." as I reach for his hand and straddle the bike.

"Fuck?" He asks and laughs, I'm sure he's laughing at my question. I nod my head even though he can't see me. He doesn't answer the question instead says, "Where are we going next?"

"You don't have to take me," I tell him and I swear I can feel his eyes roll as he swears under his breath.

"Where are we going? I can sit here all day." I groan as I tell him where to take me. When he cranks the bike I can feel the vibrations underneath me. He pauses for a moment then growls, reaches back, I can't stop the gasp that comes out as he grabs me by the legs and pulls me close to him as if I know what his next words are going to be I grab ahold of him. "And Billie you don't have to be committed to someone to fuck them." I'm sure satisfied now that he set me on edge again he moves the bike out of the spot.

KHAN

How in the fuck did I get myself into this...

I sit down as Billie goes and checks in. As I flip through whatever magazine that was on the table, I picked up, I try not to laugh when she whispers to the woman behind the desk her name.

One would think, that if someone whispers their name to you there would be an unspoken understanding that you speak quietly back, at least that's what I am assuming Billie was trying to do. Instead, I swear to God, if I was deaf I still would have heard the girl behind the counter say, "Okay, you have a 3:30 with Rebecca for a full Brazilian." I could have played the entire situation off like I never heard it. Until that is, I saw Billie's reaction in my peripheral. Her head snaps to look over her shoulder at me and I just lift up my magazine as I laugh behind the pages. Fuck, now all I can think about is her hairless pussy.

"You know, I can see you laughing," she mutters under her breath as she sits down next to me.

"What? Did you say something this article is really good?" I say from behind my magazine.

"Oh yeah," she leans back looking at the article, "the article about which tampon is best for *your vagina* is mentally stimulating for you?" She quips her words at me making sure to exaggerate the words 'your vagina'. I have to try very hard not to laugh because her comment takes me by surprise and is slightly out of what her forced character lets her be.

"Yup," I stand my ground letting the magazine fall away from concealing my face and she rolls her eyes and laughs again, "real riveting stuff here." I see the girl behind the counter look over to us and smile.

"Billie, hey girl," A small blonde-haired woman comes around the corner. Billie gets up and walks over giving the girl giving her a hug and the woman stares at me over her shoulder. I must remember to ask her about being friends with the woman who rips hair off of her pussy.

I sit, flipping through a different magazine patiently waiting for her to finish. I wonder how long a thing like this takes to do. Taking out my phone I check my texts, replying to a few of them, and then send a text to Ace asking about the car. He doesn't respond which causes me to press my lips into a firm line.

"She should be done soon." The girl behind the counter tells me. "Rebecca is very quick. She's the best waxer that we have."

"Thank you," I nod to her, politely, and she smiles. I contemplate asking her for her number, she is cute. I'm going to need a way to erase Billie from my mind after this day anyway, and with her giggles and glances over to me, I can tell that she wants to say something else. I'm sure that it wouldn't be hard to get her to come over later.

"Let me go ahead and pay for her. How much is it?" The words come out of my mouth before I realize what I'm doing and as I approach the counter and I'm not sure why I do it. It's kind of fucked up if you think about it. I'm paying for another man to enjoy this waxing. Whatever, being nice to her. She's nice and has had a bad day.

"$60." She tells me.

"Jesus Christ," I mutter as I pull out my wallet, "do you know what she normally tips?" She shrugs her shoulders so I just pull out a hundred and hands it to the girl behind the counter. "Can you just give her the rest as a tip?" She nods her head and I smile, "Thanks." I'll wait for a few more minutes and then I'll get her number, I don't want her talking to me any longer than I have to.

I walk back over to the chair, sitting down, maybe I'll wait until Billie comes out of the room and before we leave I'll get the girl behind the counter's number. I wonder if Billie would get jealous?

"You and your wife are cute together." *Oh, shit wasn't expecting that to be what she was thinking about.* I start to correct her when she starts speaking again her words coming out quicker this time, "She's been coming in here since before I started here. I love her. She's always so sweet. Rebecca loves when she comes in as well." I start to open my mouth again but Ms. Talkative doesn't give me a chance to speak, " I don't see many men coming in with their wives, but it's nice to see that some men are secure enough in their sexuality to come into a place like this." Fucking kill me, now.

"She's ac-" I try to tell her the truth but she cuts me off and continues.

"Not only come with her but pay for her. It's really sweet you know she only does it for you but it's still really sweet. I mean, I knew Billie was married. Obviously, I could see her ring and all, but no one had ever seen you. It doesn't surprise me that you're…" I try to step into the conversation in her trail of thinking of the right word but how do I correct her now without completely embarrassing her and making myself seem super weird for being with another man's wife as she gets waxed and I paid for it? "It doesn't surprise me that

you're hot. Please don't tell her I said that. I don't want to get into trouble, but you're really hot. But that's not a surprise because she's gorgeous…"

Oh, thank god.

I think as I see Billie round the corner and jump up walking over to her. I toss my arm around her shoulder, "Come on, I gotta get outta here." I mutter into her ear, trying to keep her from pushing out of my body.

"I gotta pay." I wave her off

"It's already taken care of," I say pushing her to the door and start to open it.

"You paid for me? Why?" She asks me.

"Oh," the girl behind the counter nearly squeals, we are almost out of the door completely as she finishes her sentence. "you guys are such a cute couple."

"A what?" Billie almost shouts as I shove her the rest of the way out of the door and make sure it closes. Billie stares up at me, waiting for me to explain.

"She got the wrong idea. I tried to tell her," Billie looks at me confused.

"You tried." She asks raising one eyebrow at me.

"She just kept talking. I couldn't get a word in edge-wise. I tried to stop and correct her a few times but she would just cut me off and then the longer she went on the more awkward it got and I couldn't correct her then." Billie starts laughing. Her reaction surprises me.

"What did she say?"

"I don't even know how it happened. It escalated so quickly. Sorry though, I should have stopped her." I look down grabbing my helmet and placing it on her head.

She looks up to me with a smug look on her face, "I guess it's okay… this time." I smile back at her and clip the strap and make sure it's tight, but not too tight.

I slide onto the bike and reach my hand up for her to hold to stabilize herself, "So, how are you super friendly with someone who rips hair off of your pussy." At the word, I hear her gasp a little, which I'm sure is at my choice of words.

"I've been coming to her for years. We talk about things while she's doing it."

"Oh yeah? Like what?" I chuckle as she clutches my hand.

"Well," she starts as she steps on the peg and tosses her leg over, "she may have made the same mistake that Michelle made. That's why I was laughing so hard. The same thing happened to me. I couldn't correct her before it got really awkward." I start the bike about to slide her forward again, but she slides her body until it's right against me, wrapping her arms around my body, and leaning her head against my back, which causes my body to react.

This girl may just be the death of me.

CHAPTER THREE

...You feel this tension between us too, don't you?

BILLIE

I'm a little surprised when he pulls the bike into the parking lot of the garage, which according to the sign is called Pistons, instead of stopping somewhere else, again. He parks it in the spot which has a sign that says *Khan* and helps me up off of the bike and then gets off of it as well. He places his hand on the small of my back and escorts me through the garage all the way to the left side where the only hydraulic lift sits… where my car sits with the hood up and three men working underneath it. I turn and look at Dax, "Do you guys only work on bikes?" Overly aware of his hand on my lower back.

He shrugs, "Mostly, but we work on the cars that the club owns as well." I nod my head understanding. "So, we have the means," he then turns to the men working on my car and speaks louder, "Ace," the man who turns around is just as tall as Dax, with dark features, "how is it looking?"

"Khan!" He smiles, still curious about the name, and the tall man walks over towards us, he looks over to me and I watch him as his eyes trail over my body before Dax clears his throat and breaks his attention, "Man, it's not looking good." Both men turn and Dax walks without moving his hand, towards the side of the building that we just came from. I walk with them into an office I watch as Dax sits behind the desk. I sit in the chair in front of the desk and Ace lean against the filing cabinet against the wall. The man, Ace, looks to me again and asks "your car?" I nod my head. "Makes sense now." Dax clears his throat again. "Oh yeah, so we are still running some tests, but as of right now it looks like it's a cracked block." Dax then groans and runs his hands over his face.

"What does that mean?" I ask and Ace again looks at me.

"It means the car is toast." I can't stop my groan then. "You might as well buy a new car." Ace tells me honestly, and my eyes fall

"I can't afford that right now." I'm more or less saying it to myself and look down at the floor, fighting with the tears that are threatening to spill from my eyes.

"Ace, fix it, whatever is wrong with it." Ace groans, rolling his eyes. Someone yells for *Khan* and Dax gets up from behind the desks and follows the voice into the garage.

"I know Khan says to fix it but it's going to take some time if it is a cracked block. We basically have to rebuild the engine. Probably going to take a week and a half until we can get it up and running." I nod my head, understanding but not really have an option at this point.

"Whatever it takes," I pause and then look back to Ace as he begins to straighten himself. "Khan?" I ask him and he smiles knowing that I'm asking about where the name came from.

"Genghis Khan," Ace states, I stare back at him not really understanding what he means. He rolls his eyes and then continues "They say that 1 in 200 men are descents of him. Cause he fucked so many women." There's a growl from behind us and as I look back I see a glare coming from Dax's face. Ace's eyes grow wide as he moves from the office and I can only assume back into the bay where my car sits. Dax walks from the doorway, shutting the door, sitting down in his chair behind his desk again, and looks at me. I can't help but smirk at him.

"That's not the whole story," Dax growls yet I can't help but look at him intrigued. "And I'm not telling the whole story," He leans in resting his arms on his desk, "yet. You have to gain that level of trust." He stiffens back up and starts again, "Billie, we'll get your car fixed, don't worry about it, it's going to take a little while, though. You have another car at home?"

"Yeah, I just have to go and get it out of storage."

He shakes his head, waving off that thought, "Don't worry about it, you can borrow mine until we get it fixed. It's right outside."

"Dax, I can't just borrow your car until then," he glares at me and I shake my head again throwing up my hands to make more of a point, "you barely know me."

"I know enough." He laughs.

"You've only met me once. As you said have to gain that level of trust."

"Bil," the use of the nickname that I only let a few people get away with calling me makes me fidget in my chair. I'm not sure why I don't correct him. "You are a private school principal whose husband is in the military. You are like a living, breathing perfect fairy tale princess, who could not ever do anything bad. I'm sure you're not going to run off with my car. Plus, your car is still here and all I have to do is run your VIN and can find your home address." I have a sinking suspicion that he has other means to find my home address. "Plus, your husband is about to come home and I remember how busy spouses are right before homecoming."

"I'm not perfect, but I understand your point," pausing, I look up to him and he's trying to persuade me with his stare, "OKAY," I say the word reluctantly. He then holds out his hand and asks for my phone. "Why?"

"So, I can put my number in your phone to call my phone. So, I can let you know when the car is ready." I reluctantly hand over my phone. I watch as he types a few buttons and hands the phone back over to me. We sit for a few more minutes and he looks as if he is contemplating something. "Question," Dax states, and I look back up to him, and he is sitting with his elbows on the armrests of the chair and his fingers touching by his face "hypothetically, if one was to make a sizable donation to the school," I put my hand up to stop him.

"That's bribery," I say to him which causes him to toss his head back and laugh. He stands up from the chair and walks around his desk, leaning on the edge and bending down closer to where I sit.

"Oh, you really are a perfect princess if you believe that no one at that school has ever taken a bribe. Plus 100 thousand dollars can accomplish a lot" He pauses and smirks again leaning in right next to my ear and whispers, "bribery is nowhere near the worst things that I have done. Nor is it the worst thing that I have done for Ella." Holy shit, a hundred thousand dollars he can afford just like that. The knock on the door eases the tension and he tells them to come in without really moving back at all. Ace walks through the door slightly disappointed until he sees the situation which is currently unfolding in the office, now he seems much more intrigued.

"Blocks cracked. Already ordered the parts." Dax nods and tips his head as if telling him to get lost. And I'm assuming as quickly as Ace takes off that is exactly what his head nod meant. Dax grabs the keys off of his desk and nods to the door for me to follow him.

"It's going to be at least a week before it's done. I'll make sure they get it to you as soon as they can."

"Just send me an invoice," I mutter to him and he shakes his head.

"No, don't worry about it." He stops at a large black Land Rover with dark tinted windows, so dark that you cannot see in the car at all. "Here it is. Let me know if you need anything or if any lights pop up," I nod my head.

"Bil," he mutters as I reach for the door handle and I turn around just as two hands plant on both sides of me on the car windows. My breathing quickens and he lets his head fall so that his nose trails my chin, "You feel this tension between us too, don't you?" I don't say a word. "Just nod if you do," he mutters as I half nod my head, only once. He moves his head slightly bringing his lips closer to mine and I can't help but lick my lips. He smirks at my response before pausing for a second, "And you want me just as bad as I want you?" He whispers and I can feel the breath that holds his words on

my lips. My breathing quickens more and I nod my head one more time. His lips turn up in a full smile, "I thought so," he leans in closer to me, his lips are hovering over mine. I can feel his breath on my own lips.

I manage to straighten my thoughts out and pull my hands up pushing against his chest. He looks up at me even more amused.

"I can't do this. I'm married. My husband is deployed."

KHAN

"I can't do this. I'm married. My husband is deployed." I can't help but find her comment comical. Although, it's slightly shocking.

"You forget I grew up in the military. I have met plenty of wives." I leave out the part of losing my virginity to the neighbor when I was 14, while her husband was deployed. She looks at me like she's disgusted with me and pushes me further. "I'm okay with the few days that we can have. In fact, that's perfect." She shoves me, harder, pushing me even further away.

"Are you kidding me? I'm not that kind of wife. I have never and will never cheat on my husband. I love him and I'm loyal." Her voice wavers only slightly when she says 'love him' which makes me wonder about her words, "And yes, there is some sort of sexual tension between us, but that's probably just because I haven't had sex in 6 months." Her statement is slightly shocking to me. I don't know many women who wouldn't cheat on their husbands when they are gone for so long. "If you're letting me borrow your car because you think I'm going to sleep with you then screw you. I'll find my own way." She shoves the keys into my chest and moves away from me and begins to walk towards the road. As mad as she is I can't help but chuckle at her screaming *screw you*

"Bil, I'm sorry. Come back." I say to her amused and reach for her arm spinning her back around. "That's not why I offered to let you borrow the car." I pause trying my best to backpedal while simultaneously trying to keep my laughter under control. "There are no strings attached to it.-" she cuts me off

"Why are you laughing at me?" she shouts at me.

"Because no one has said, 'screw you' to me since I was 12" Admitting it to her causes whatever hold I had on my laughter to start to break down as I hold my hand open to her with the keys in them.

"Shut up," she playfully smacks me and my laughing takes over now. As she takes the keys from me again. She climbs up into my Land Rover and I take a second to watch her as she climbs up inside and cranks the truck. I begin to turn around and walk away, *Shit.* I remember the handgun that sits underneath my driver's seat and grabs the door as she tries to shut it and reach inside. "Dax," she exclaims. As I lean in close to her, head down close to her lap. "What are you doing?" In the same tone but with slight panic in her voice as my arm reaches between her calves, with my head even closer to her legs, I can see her wiggle as if to create more of a distance. I yank the gun out of its holster and pull it out from under the seat. Her eyes wide when she sees what I was reaching for. In one motion, without standing up, I pull it from under the seat and place it into the waistband of my jeans. "Any other weapons that you're forgetting about?" She smirks over at me.

I think for a second, just to play along with her statement. "Nope," I pause, bluntly so she knows that I'm looking, takes in her legs one last time as she sits in my truck. I can only imagine running my hands up them meeting what is in the middle. Looking up to her smirking while playfully saying, "All 9s are currently safely stowed away, at my waist." I hear her gasp, indicating to me that she knows exactly what I'm implying. I imagine her pussy becoming wet. "Let me know if you need to borrow one." I wink to her as I stand up and step back for her to be able to close the door. Her eyes widen for only a second which lets me know that I got to her and then her grin grows wide.

"Oh, I'm sure you will have no problem finding someone who wants to borrow one, Khan." With that, she shuts the door and drives away. *Oh Billie Saxs, you are trouble.* For some reason with Billie's use of the name, for the first time in my life, I'm actually kind of disappointed in my reputation.

I can't help but watch after her as she drives off with my Land Rover.

What am I thinking?

"Khan, did you let her take the Land Rover?" I hear Ace ask from behind me, I nod my head still watching her drive away. "Wow, what does this girl have a golden pussy? You don't let anyone drive that." He asks and I glare over at him.

"Shut the fuck up, she's the principal at the school I'm trying to get Ella into."

"Oh, okay… so you're trying to bribe her?" Ace asks and I shrug my shoulders.

"Ace, I have no fucking clue what I'm trying to do with her." I pause and look over to him as I see him walking away back towards Pistons. "Ace," I shout loud enough to hear me and watch as he turns around, walking back closer to where I stand watching her drive off and ask him, "you know any woman who would wait 6 months for their husbands without fucking anyone else?" He shakes his head, looking back at me.

"Yeah, my mom," He laughs.

"Yeah, me either," I understand what he's trying to say, in a nice way, he's saying that he's never met a woman who would remain faithful to their husbands when they are gone for an extended period.

"Not a single woman that I have dated though. Hell, most of the women around here take off as soon as there are cuffs on their man. Before the trial even begins. Why do you ask?"

"Just wondering," I still stand watching the backend of my Land Rover disappear into traffic. "I'll cover whatever it costs to fix her car." He nods his head slowly looking at me like I have lost my mind.

"Boss?" He asks and I just shrug my shoulders.

"Just do it." Looking back to him I look at my watch and notice the time, "Shit, Ace, I gotta go meet with Chik." Tom Chikatilo is the club's attorney.

I pull up to his office a few minutes later and walk into the building. "Hello, Lisa." The words come out to Chik's secretary and she smiles up at me.

"Hey, Khan," her smile has an underlying meaning to it and I watch as she sticks her chest out a little bit more and I can see her unbutton her top button as I glance around the room. When I look back at her I can see the black lace from her bra peeking out from her top. "Chik will be right with you. How have you been? It's been a little bit since I have seen you." I nod my head and for some reason, I cannot help but think about Billie and how completely different from Lisa that she is. This is exactly why I need to forget about perfect little Billie Saxs and her perfect legs.

"Lisa, how long you think he's gonna be?" I ask her. She smiles and looks down at her computer screen.

"Probably 15 minutes." I contemplate for a second and then ask.

"You need a break?" I ask her and she smiles grabbing my hand and leading me to a storage closet in the hallway. She pushes me in and unbuckles my belt as she kneels down and finishes freeing my dick from my pants.

"We don't have a lot of time." She looks up at me and I smirk at her.

"So, you need me to hurry up?" I ask, she smiles, "Are you able to make me cum in a couple of minutes?"

"Baby, I can make you cum in seconds." *Doubtful, you don't happen to have those green eyes.* I think to myself as she takes me completely into her mouth. I close my eyes and lean back against the shelving, in my head seeing Billie's face when I was leaning into her trapping her against my car. Thinking about my hands on her thighs today. I don't even try to hold back when I feel my release threatening to come. "I told you." She smiles at me as she stands back up and I shrug. I can't tell her that the real reason I came so fast is that my

head and my body were swirling with pent-up aggression called, Billie.

"You told me to hurry," I say to her as she opens the door. As we turn to walk back to the front all I can hear is Chik from the doorway of his office.

"Goddamnit, Khan," he looks at me as he motions for me to come in and shuts the door, "How many times have I told you to stop fucking the help?"

"I didn't fuck her, Chik. Promise" I hold up my hand in a Boy Scout salute.

"Khan," I groan as he says it. "Okay, so it doesn't look good. The DA sent over a plea agreement." He says to me and I look more interested to him. "20 years. 15 with good behavior."

"Chik, what the fuck is that?" I'm fucking pissed. The president of our chapter is behind bars and they are offering him 20 years.

"Khan, the case is airtight... there's nothing I can do. This deal is a godsend..."

"A godsend?" I'm shouting now, "A fucking godsend," I think before yelling so other people can hear what I'm about to say next and I drop my voice to a lower level, "we spend good money to these sons of bitches to make sure that shit like this doesn't happen." And he nods his head.

"I know, that's the only reason why we got a plea agreement. Well, between that and Jeff pulling some strings. We take it to trial and we're looking at life. If he takes this deal he may still be able to walk his daughter down the aisle at her wedding."

Fuck, why'd he have to bring Ella into it?

"Okay," I say to him and he looks back up at me. "I'm sorry Khan, I need you to go to the jail with me to talk to him about it though." I nod my head.

"Of course, when?"

"Now?" He asks and I nod my head once more. We get up from our chairs and head to the door. I leave before him mostly because it will take me longer to sign in and be able to go and get back to see him.

"Bye Khan," Lisa looks to me and smiles, "call me sometime." *That's not going to happen.* I don't even look back at her as my phone buzzes and I look down at it to see a text from Billie,

Billie: I'm sorry, thank you for helping me today.

I smile at the message

"I'm serious Khan, call me." She says as I look back at her and somehow she has unbuttoned another button on her blouse. I try not to roll my eyes in front of her and wave a weak goodbye, then look back to my phone and type back.

Me: Anytime, I'll let you know when I know more.

I crank up my bike and head towards the county jail where Oz is being held. Chik gets there shortly after I do, tells them that I am with him, and we are taken back to see Oz. Seeing him in the orange jumpsuit always depresses me.

"Prez," I cheerfully say to him and he smiles back.

"Khan, my man."

"Oz," Chik starts and Oz holds his hand up,

"Chik, we will get to that in a second. First I need to hear about my daughter." Chik quiets for a second, "How did the interview go?" He asks me and I nod my head.

"It went really well." I don't want to tell him the 100% truth, "The principal told me that on paper she is a perfect fit for the school." His smile turns up. "But we still have a couple of interviews."

"I knew she would be?" He asks me and I again only tell a partial truth. Almost as if he can read me like a book his demeanor changes. "And did they say anything about our current situation?"

"Don't worry about it. I'll figure it out. "

"Shit," he mutters under his breath before looking at me, "how is she handling everything?"

"To be expected. I don't want to lie and tell you that she's perfect, but she's handling things." He nods his head and adds

"I don't want her to come to see me yet, not until we know one way or another." I nod my head somehow understanding that.

Oz decides to take the plea agreement. But we all agree that it would be best if we could try and push it back until Ella is accepted. As Chik and I get up to leave Oz calls up to me, "Khan, can I talk to you for a second?" I nod as I look to Chik and he nods and walks over to the other side of the room, in a hushed voice Oz leans in and says, "I'm not getting out any time soon." I look down at my hands as guilt flows through me, "Fuck out of here with all that Khan, we all knew the risk… it could have just as easily been you in here instead of me," and he sighs, "look, man, the club needs to be ran, you already know how to do it. Shit, with everything I've been going through you, have been running it for the past couple of years."

"Oz, I haven't been…"

"Khan," his voice raises and I know that this is his serious voice, "you have been more of a president to that club in the last 3 years than I have been in the last 10. This is your club." He tells me and I nod my head because his words mean too much.

"It's still up to a vote." The words come out hoarse because this is the most important thing that has happened to me.

"I don't see a problem there."

CHAPTER FOUR

... I promise, I'll be good. Look my hands are in my pockets.

KHAN

I head home, pull into the driveway, and can already see the slew of cars in the driveway. My house has recently turned into a mini clubhouse even if the clubhouse and my house are on the same grounds... which is nice since then I can head to the clubhouse while Ella is home. Since I got custody of Ella, all the brothers have been helping me out. A lot of responsibility was thrust on me last month when Oz got arrested. I had to step up into his role within the club and for Ella.

"Hey, Fury," I call out as I walk into the kitchen and pull some water out of the fridge.

"Hey Khan, she's upstairs." He nods towards the stairs. "Hasn't wanted to talk to anyone all day. Told us that she hated all of us."

"Fury, we need to have church in an hour. Can you send it out?" I sigh at him and he nods his head, feeling bad for the kid. I grab a soda for her, water for me, and I walk upstairs. Knocking on Ella's door she yells.

"Go away."

"Ella," I call to her, "come on, it's me." The door opens slightly, "Thank you" I smile at her handing her the can I'm holding in my hand.

"Uncle Dax, I hate all of them." I laugh as I sit down on the floor next to her bed that she plops down on.

"I can understand that…" I pause, "You know between you and me, sometimes I hate them as well." She giggles. I remember when this kid was born Oz couldn't have been prouder. When Tina took off he was crushed and she wouldn't come out of her room for months… I had many of these conversations with her at that time as well. The guys and I have helped raise her ever since. I feel bad for her most days because not only does she have a super big, scary-looking biker dad, but she has a dozen big scary biker pseudo-dads as well. The older she gets the more I start to feel bad for whatever guy she ends up dating… even worse, for the one, she marries. And I also feel like this is somehow the universe getting back at me for my life full of debauchery is that I get guardianship of a 15-year-old girl.

"Uncle Dax, can you be honest with me?" She asks and I am dreading the next 10 minutes of my life.

"I always have been" which is true. I have always figured out a way to tell her an honest take on whatever she is asking.

"Did he do it?" I pause not exactly sure as to how to answer her question because did he do it? Yes, he fucking kind of did, but he had a reason too, yet we cannot tell the courts why he did that. I groan and rub my hands over my face, "I will take that as a, yes" she says quietly.

"El, it isn't that easy as did he or didn't he." She turns her head to the side as she looks at me. "Okay, you can never repeat this, nor can you ever tell your father that I told you." He nods her head. Then she holds out her hand with her pinky extended, doing what we have done since she was 6 when I promised her that I would never leave her as Tina did, I take it, and we pinky promise. Something that neither she nor I have ever broken. "Technically, yes he did do it; however, the man who was killed…" I trail trying to figure out how to say everything in a way that will not freak her out but will also make her understand, "we found out that he was threatening you." Her eye widen. "El, I want to stress to you that you never have to worry about anything ever happening to you. All of us all of those guys… your dad… me… you are like a daughter to all of us, and what your dad did, what we all did… we would do it a million times over again, knowing well and good that what is happening to your dad could potentially happen to us."

"I know," her words are quiet. "I haven't ever felt unsafe." She admits.

"There isn't any thanks needed." She smiles again. I get up and tap her leg with the water bottle in my hand as I walk towards the door her little voice starts again,

"Uncle Dax," I stop and turn to look at her, "I kind of feel bad for being mean to everyone today."

"Don't, they deserve it," I say between laughs. "El, I'm going to head over to the clubhouse for a little bit if you're okay with that"

"Yeah,"

"I'll be back as soon as possible. Text me if you need anything"

"It's okay Uncle Dax, I know that I've been cramping your style,"

"El-" she stops me, shaking her head.

"No, I know I am, my dad used to do the same thing. I feel safe and you will literally be like 500 feet from here." I smile, still feeling slightly bad, but for whatever reason, but yet I go anyway… making sure to lock the doors and walk the feet to the clubhouse. When the house was built outside of the clubhouse we made sure to first soundproof the clubhouse. When I walk through the door Roxy, the house girl slides a whisky to me and I smile at her.

"Thanks, Rox" she's probably the only girl that is frequently in the house that I have never, will never mess around with. I'm not really sure why, we have always just had a friendship.

I walk into our 'war room' and I sit down in my chair… how in the fuck are we going to fix this. I rub my hands to my temples as the

rest of the officers file in. Ace, treasure and Fury, the sergeant at arms, and Tuck our Road Captain.

"Khan!" They all shout and I just glare back at them. "What's up man"

"I met with Chik and Oz." Tuck and Fury both look shocked as they look up at me and the rest of the club comes into the room. The 16 men all sit around and I stand up at the front with everyone still talking to each other and the room sounds like a school cafeteria. How and when did the club get so big? I take a sip of the whiskey and try to clear my throat. Nothing... I've had a bad fucking day.

"SHUT UP," I yell at the room and it instantly goes quiet. "I met with Chik and Oz this afternoon. He has been given a plea deal. Chik says it's the best that he's gonna get. If we go to trial he will most likely get a life. If he takes this deal..." I stop and take another large swig of whiskey in my cup. "He takes this deal and he will get 20 years... 15 with good behavior." The room actually stays quiet longer than I have ever seen it go and then Ace speaks up.

"I met with Oz last week. He told me when this happens we need to vote for a new president." I glare at him and he pauses, "Technically he is still the president... for now. But he told me that his vote is for you, Dax." I know when Ace, or any of the guys, use my real name that they mean what he is saying. Everyone beings to speak saying that he had told them all the same thing. And how they agree... I'm floored. I finish my whiskey as I figure out the words to say.

"Shut up. Okay I get what you guys are saying and I appreciate it," I pause, "but not until the plea is accepted. Which we are trying to push back until Ella gets accepted into this school."

"How's that going?" Ace asks.

"Could be better, that's something else that I wanted to talk to you guys about," I mutter. "On paper, Ella is perfect for the school... in reality, they research the family." Everyone groans because we know what that means, "I've talked to some of our contacts whose kids go there who have informed me that many times you can get them to overlook the research into the families for a small donation."

"Fuck yeah," Blaze from the back yells, and Ace and I both glare at him.

"How much?" Ace asks.

I down the rest of my whiskey and look at them, "100 thousand, now I know that technically this is my responsibility-"

"Fuck that, she's all of our responsibility," Blaze yells again from the back and everyone yells in agreement.

"Yeah Prez," Ace says at my side, I glare at him telling him not yet and everyone roots around him, "You may be legally responsible for her but her school any of that shit, the club will pay for it."

"I can afford her tuition," I tell them not wanting to tell them about Oz's off-shore account that I will be pulling it from but I can't get ahold of the 100k for the bribe.

BILLIE

5 days

I meet with Lucy for our weekly dinner date but dinner date is really just code for drinks. I pull into the parking lot and jump out of Dax's car and walk into the bar to meet Lucy.

"Did I just see you pull up in a Land Rover?" I shyly look away as she grins. "You finally got a new car?"

"Not really, mine shit the bed a couple of days ago… needs work. It's kind of a loaner."

"Kind of?" I've known Lucy for so long that I don't remember a time when she wasn't a part of my life.

"Okay, remember the guy I was telling you about the other day who-" she cuts me off

"You mean 451, the sexy one who, made you wet, and is suddenly the legal guardian of his goddaughter?"

"Lucy!" I shriek, "I only said one of those things."

"Oh, I could tell the other two by how you were talking about him. Does he fall into this whole thing?" She asks me and I smile and wrinkle my nose at her question. "Holy shit, how?"

"He saw me and stopped when I was standing on the side of the road. He canceled my tow I was going through with my roadside assistance and called his *guy* to come and get it. He gave me a ride back to his shop but ended up making a stop and then took me to my waxing appointment."

"Did you have a date?" She asks me and I revolt.

"No, I'm married, Lucy"

"Whatever, Brad is a dick." She has never been very fond of my husband.

"Still, I'm married. Anyway, I have a cracked block, whatever that is, and he's having his shop fix it." She looks interested.

"He owns a shop? Maybe I'll take my car there." She wiggles her eyebrows. Knowing my friend I know that she's just trying to catch a look at the man who has made me flustered.

"He says that they really only do bikes, but they work on the club's cars there."

"The club?" She asks when the recognition hits and she, "Midnight Syn?" She says which is what the locals call the Midnight Syndicate. I nod my head. "Oh, sexy, works with his hands, and an...." She pauses and lowers her voice, "An outlaw. I bet you he knows how to handle some torque." I can't help but laugh mostly because her comment doesn't even make complete sense. She and I suck up the remaining of our drinks and ask for another.

"That's not even the best part." He stops mid-sip and looks back over to me.

"Well, spill it."

"He tried to kiss me." My eyes are wide as I spit the words out and continue to sip the drink.

"Do what?" She asks me as she coughs on her own. "Tell me everything. I mean you let him right?" She mutters at me and I laugh then make myself glare at her in response.

"I feel so bad," I deflate as I'm talking to her. "I'm married." I hold up my left hand. "And my husband is going to be home in 5 days and I'm here telling you a story about some biker trying to kiss me."

"I don't give a fuck you have got to tell me everything." Lucy was in a relationship for a while, but after they split up she has refused to be in a relationship since. I'm not exactly sure what all happened and I never pressed her to tell me everything. I just know that he was abusive.

"He walked me out to his car and right before I got into the truck he put his hands on the side of me and I was trapped against the car." I reenact the scene for her and tell her the story of my almost kiss with the only man, besides my husband, in the last decade.

"Holy shit, Bil, I bet you that man fucks like a..." she wiggles her eyes at me causing me to roll my eyes and laugh

"You know they call him Khan around the club."

"What?" She laughs, then her face falls as the name strikes some recognition as well, "Khan?"

"I dunno. One of his guys at his shop said that it's because Genghis Khan fucked a lot of women, but Dax told me that there's more to the story."

"Well, when you find out... you have to tell me... but if there's one thing that I know... is that if a man has fucked that many women... he knows how to fuck."

"Luc isn't that like...?" I ask her, not finishing my question, and she laughs.

"Bil, you were so much more fun before Brad came along, but as long as everyone practices safe sex who the fuck cares."

1 day

Dax: Princess, your car is ready.

The text comes through and I jump up from my desk... not really because I want to give up the Rover for my shit-box Camry, but because I don't want to answer questions from Brad when he gets home tomorrow.

Me: THANK YOU

I type back in all caps.

I pick up my phone and my bag as I rush out of the door. Everyone has been gone for a couple of hours already, I needed to stay a little later to finish up some things before this weekend when Brad gets home.

Me: I'm leaving school now, are you still open?

Dax: Technically no, but I'm still here. Just knock on the door if it's locked.

When I arrive, I see my car sitting in the parking lot, but all of the doors are shut and the lights are off except for a dim glow that I can see from the glass door that shows from the hallway. I bang on the door and am startled as one of the bay doors opens. "Bil, over here," he mutters. I walk towards the open door. I cannot see Dax until I get to the door and gasp when I look at him. He standing in a bay, standing above his bike, clearly he has been working on it, shirtless while sweat streaks down his chest. I could tell from when I rode on his bike that he had some muscles, but I don't think I have ever seen muscles on a man, in real life, quite like his. His arms are covered in tattoos, as well as up his neck. He has a few tattoos on his chest, but those tattoos are not what takes my breath away it's the lines that I can see from his abs... but more importantly it's the abdominal lines that form that "v"... and for some reason, I cannot stop myself from imagining running my tongue down those lines until it reaches the ultimate destination. *I wonder how big...*

I shake my head as the door comes sliding back down behind me. He releases the button that he has pressed with his finger to close the door and turns walking back to the bike, I see the large tattoo of the MC logo across his back. I cannot help but step up to look at it more closely when he turns around and we are face to face towards one another.

"Billie," his eyes drop to look at me and I can smell the sweat from the work which he was doing before I got here. "Like what you see?" He asks me as he steps closer to me and for some reason I feel like I cannot breathe. *What the fuck is this man doing to me.* We are standing so close that I can feel his body heat, but we are not touching. I can't help but lick my bottom lip and drag my teeth across it. He smiles and he steps back breaking our tension. His actions send confusion all over my face and he laughs. "Ms. Saxs, when you're ready… I'll be here… but I can wait and figure out whatever this chemistry is going to result in until you're ready. 'Cause Princess, this tension here, is going to explode and honestly, I'm not even sure if I'm ready for that." I stare dumbfounded as he laughs again and tells me to follow him to his office, to grab my keys. "How was the Rover?"

"It was fine." He grabs his shirt off the chair slipping it over his head, an audible sob accidentally comes from me, and I can see his smile he has on his face once the shirt falls into its place.

"Here you go." He hands the keys to me as we walk out into the lobby, as he unlocks the door and holds it open for me.

"Shit, I left my bag in the truck," I mumble the words as spinning around in the direction of the Land Rover. Nodding he clicks the fob that is in his hands and I walk over to the passenger side and grab it out of the seat. "Bye, Rover, I'll miss you." When I turn around he stands silently laughing. "What?"

"You want to keep her?" He asks me and I stand shocked continually blinking as he continues to quietly laugh.

"Um," I pause and try to force the words out. "I couldn't do that." His slight laugh ceases.

"Sure you could, I'm not using it."

"But it's so nice," I mutter and he nods.

"I know, it's sad really… I have a truck back at the house… this one usually stays up here." He pauses looking at me, "She doesn't get the attention she deserves either, you two have something in common, you could keep each other company."

"Dax, that's like a 70k dollar truck" ignoring his last statement.

"More like 90 after everything." I can't help but look back and forth from my shitty car to the Land Rover sitting in front of me; my mouth slightly agape.

"I wouldn't even know where to being explaining that tomorrow." His lips pursed I watch as he nods his head in an understanding gesture. When he steps forward to grab my bag I can't help but take a step back, protecting myself from the gravity in which his body seems to have over mine.

"I promise, I'll be good. Look my hands are in my pockets." He holds his elbows out, to make a point. He takes his hand out for just a second to reach for my bag, tossing it over his shoulder, and then pushes his hand back into his pocket. I step next to him as we walk towards my car.

"Oh, I almost forgot to ask, how much do I owe you." Feeling like a complete idiot and making sure that he doesn't think I'm trying to take advantage of him.

"You're good." He shrugs, but I can't help but see him roll his eyes at my question.

"No, it had to have been expensive." But he just shakes his head and makes a zipper motion with his hands to his mouth. I'm dumbstruck as we continue to walk to my car. When we reach it I find myself wishing that the parking lot was longer. He walks past me as I reach the car, the lights on my car flicker once signaling that the car has unlocked. He opens the door and tosses my bag into the passenger seat. I don't know how to act or what to do to repay him. I cannot come up with anything so instead, I wrap my arms around his neck and I hug him tightly. I can feel his arms cautiously wrap around me and hold me tightly against him. Feeling his rigid body relax against mine. I feel his arms release and I wish he would hold on longer, but instead, I take his lead and let go as well. "Thank you, Dax." I place my hand on his chest, and I don't want to leave.

"No problem, princess, let me know if you need anything at all." He turns and starts to walk back towards his shop.

When I pull into my driveway I am surprised to see the lights are on... that can only mean one thing... that Brad is home early. Turning off my car I exit the car and walk up to the front door, fighting with the conflicting emotions of happiness and sadness at the exact same time.

KHAN

I hear someone call out my name as I am opening the door and watch as Ash comes up to meet me... "Was that just a 5 thousand dollar hug?" I glare at him since I am clearly not wanting to talk about that. "Oh, shit dude. What is going on with you?" I grumble some nonsense and he laughs as he follows me into the lobby of the shop and I lock the door behind us. He follows me into the bays as I walk back over to my bike and begin to work on it. I start to feel weird as he just continues to look at me. "Need help?" He asks as I shake my head no. "Wanna go to the club?" He asks me. I stop for a second.

"Yeah, I need to go check on the club anyway." Sirens is the strip club that the MC owns. I need to work Billie out of my head... although much of the last two weeks my thoughts have seemed to be consumed with Billie Saxs. It's only 8 o'clock which means that the nighttime dancers will be coming in for their shifts. I finish up with my bike and we head over to the club.

When I walk into the club the energy changes instantly and there's a hum in the air. "The words spreading already," Ash whispers into my ear and I shake my head at him. What he is trying to say is what he always says, when I come here, that the girls are spreading the word that I'm here.

"Chell," I greet the bartender and she smiles at me handing Ash and I both a glass of whiskey. I walk towards my office, enter it, and push the door almost all the way closed. The light rap on the door brings my mind back from the thoughts of what I actually need to be doing. When the door opens wider I see Stormy standing in the doorway wearing a cross top that I'm sure ties in the back and a skirt that doesn't cover her entire ass, with the straps from her thong pulled up over her hips making her ass look larger than what it is. From where she stands I can see that the skirt is short enough to see that her thong is so small that you can almost see the top of it from the bottom of her skirt.

"If it isn't Khan." She coos as she shuts the door, walking through the office, and sits down on my desk. I lean back in my chair, not saying a word to her, but letting her know that I may be interested in what she is thinking about. She slides herself across the edge until she is sitting in front of me, placing her feet on each side of me on the chair. "Where have you been hiding?" I feel one side of my mouth curving up into a smirk in response to the smile that sits on her face, while she reaches behind herself and unties her top letting her tits pop out. I reach up to her, grasping her by the wrists and pulling her onto my lap. I'm going to fuck Billie Saxs out of my system.

Hopefully this time it works.

CHAPTER FIVE

...You've gotta go...

BILLIE

Lucy and I skipped last week's dinner since Brad had only been back for a couple of days. He told me to go but I still felt like it was wrong. So tonight, I am catching her up on everything.

"How did the homecoming go?" Her words are flat and I can tell by her words that she really doesn't want to know but that she's only asking out of obligation. I pause mid-sip not making any eye contact with her. "Oh, well that can't be good."

"No, it was fine... it's just." I pause looking around, not wanting to admit the next words that I'm going to say, "We haven't had sex since he got home." Her eyes widen, sitting her glass down slowly and carefully, and turns to me. "And it's not like I haven't been trying... because believe me I have been... but it's like he's not interested... and..." I trail and grunt out in frustration. "I went 6 months without sex... and then we did... once, and now he's good... I swear before he left," I stop and she nods...

"Don't even start with that Bil-," Lucy drops her eyes to me.

"What?"

"Don't try and pretend with yourself that everything was great before he left." She puts it bluntly to me. "He was being distant before as well. You didn't realize it but you would complain about characteristics that told me he was."

"No, he wasn't."

"We had this same conversation but in reverse." She continues in a tone that is supposed to mimic me, "Lucy I don't understand. He's getting ready to leave soon and he's never here and when he is it's like he wants nothing to do with me." She makes me remember the conversation. I glance down and pick at my nails as I sigh. "Okay, Bil." She snaps to me, and I'm not sure what's going on with her tonight. "We'll play like we don't remember before he left." He clears her throat, nodding to the bartender that we need another drink, and then starts again, "I'm sure you've been trying with him. Since you are all tied in knots about a certain sexy biker."

"Lucy!" I gasp as she laughs finally.

"Seriously though, Brad won't fuck you, just go fuck the infamous Khan." She said as she leans over sipping her drink.

A month later, I am sitting in my office, as I receive an email from the board of directors about the new students coming to the campus this year. There are only 5 students who are new to the system, and I smile whilst the name Ella Davis stares back at me. Wondering how exactly Dax was able to get her into the school and knowing that I also don't want to know.

Thinking about Dax makes a tightness in my stomach happen, Brad and I still haven't had sex since the night that he got home…which makes it very hard for me to stop imaging Dax standing in the bay of Pistons, shirtless. My eyes close as I start to daydream about him lifting me up as his lips crash down to mine… taking me back to his office and doing terrible things to me there. I feel a presence in my office as I open my eyes and I feel like my dreams are bleeding over into my reality.

"Do you need me to come back later?" He mutters as my eyes flutter open coming face to face with his complete amusement.

I clear my throat and quickly say, "What?" And I shake my head which makes his amusement grow on his face and I see the corner of his mouth turn up. "What are you doing here?" I ask him, standing up and rushing over to the door to look out into the lobby since not one other person is there.

"Yeah, I would have checked in, but no one was out there." I groan, closing the door hoping to hide me from the embarrassment of anyone else hearing the jokes that I'm sure he's going to make. "Oh, do we need privacy?"

"With you, there's no telling. Plus you had to come in here wearing your cut." He looks equi-parts hurt, may be offended, yet maybe impressed that I knew the term for his vest. "What?" He shakes his head and rolls his eyes "What?" I say louder this time.

"I came to return your book, I'll go through."

"Wait," the word is barely above a whisper as I reach out touching his arm. "I'm sorry, I just don't know how the directors will feel if they come in and see all of this," I say as I motion with my hands him standing in front of me.

"Those guys, they love me." He mutters as he finds the place on the shelf where it belongs and slides it in. This act surprises me, the fact that he put it back in the exact place where it took it out of.

"What?"

"I told you 100-"

"Ah, I don't wanna know." I cover my ears and walk over to my desk leaning on the edge of it.

He chuckles saying, "You know I was looking at your bookshelf when I was here and this was actually the most surprising book I found." He pulls it out and shows it to me The Anarchist Cookbook.

"Oh, I confiscated that one two years ago and I guess someone put it up there before I got a chance to throw it away." He looks at me

like he doesn't believe me with the smile that was lingering on his face growing. He steps forward and stops. "What?" He continues to look at me with a disbelieving look and takes two more steps forward as if playing a game of chicken and the lie. "Okay, fine... I was curious." He lets the laugh that I know he has been holding in out.

"You don't need it, I can show you how to make everything in here." My mouth drops open and he laughs again, "Well not really, but I have a guy who can." he closes the remaining gap between us and whispers so if someone else was in the room only he and I could hear. "I told you, princess, bribery is nowhere close to the worst things that I've done." I can't help but chuckle as he takes a couple of steps back and sits down in the chair. "So, how was the homecoming?" He asks me and I realize that I haven't spoken to Dax since I left Pistons.

"Good, he was actually home when I got home with my car from your shop." His face falls to a confused look as if he wants to say something but knows that he shouldn't.

"What?" I ask him. He doesn't respond verbally, just brings his hands to the air, shaking them along with his head, as if he's telling me that he's not going to walk into that trap, "No, you're thinking something. Say... it." I make sure to emphasize each of the last words.

"He didn't want you on the pier when he got back." I shrug my shoulders and kind of look away. I feel some sadness wash over me and hear him shift in the chair and say, "I didn't want to say it," there's a strange silence between us until he breaks it and says, "Oh, we got word on Monday that Ella is going to be coming here."

"Yeah, I just got the email now." He nods his head.

"So, I guess you'll be seeing a lot more of me."

"Yay," I wave my hands in the air but say it in a voice that doesn't have any enthusiasm. He laughs.

"Anyway, the real reason why I wanted to stop by is to ask if you could maybe look out for her. She's gone through a whole lot in general... I just want to make sure that she's okay... and she doesn't have really any good women to look up to." Although I'm not sure how good I am to look up to as I was just fantasizing about her godfather when I'm married to another man.

And I look over to his vest seeing something different from before "Dax, did you get promoted?" I say pointing at the patch that is now in place of the VP patch that was there before and now says, President.

"Doesn't really work like that, but I guess if you want to call it that then, yeah."

"Congrats" he laughs, most likely at the fact that I have no idea what I'm actually congratulating him on.

"Well, we've been missing one for a little bit so."

"Say no more I understand," I say putting my hand up.

At that moment there is a knock on my door and we both look at each other as my assistant, Abby, opens it without looking up at first and says, "Ms. Saxs, Brad is here to see you." Her eyes finally look up to see Dax sitting in the chair, me sitting against the edge of my desk directly in front of him grinning like I'm an idiot. "Oh," she says quietly and then pauses and says again, "oh, my." her eyes are wide and at the recognition of the name my eyes go just at wide looking back at the man sitting in front of me.

"Abby, I'm with a parent right now, tell him I will be right with him." When the word parent comes out of my mouth I see Dax do a full-body cringe. Abby stands at the door, mouth wide open, staring at him for a few more moments before I clear my throat and say, "Abby," in a loud enough voice to get her attention and snap her out of her trance and she shuts the door quickly. "Let Brad know I'll be finished in a moment."

"I guess that is what I am now huh, a parent," and he cringes once again. "Who's Brad?" He asks.

"My husband..."

KHAN

"You've gotta go," she points at me. I stand up and she grabs my arm starting to pull me to the door.

"Wait," I plant myself into the ground so that even if she uses all of her body weight that she won't be able to move me. I turn my body to look at her, reaching out and touching her arm. I don't say anything at first just let us hang at this moment for a little longer, maybe longer than I should have, "Let me know if you need anything, at all." I look her straight in the eyes as I say the words and I can visibly see her inhale sharply, and bite her lip. She swore that the reason why there was sexual tension between us before was because she had gone so long without sex. Either that was complete bullshit or she's still not having sex, or maybe a combination of the two, which if he's home and not fucking her, then he's a fucking idiot. I turn quickly closing the remaining distance to the door.

Before she opens the door she says, "Why don't you bring Ella by so I can meet her before school starts." I nod my head and am secretly curious if she's just using it as a means to see me, to actually meet Ella or a mixture of both. Then she makes sure to speak in a manner so everyone in the office can hear her while she opens the door, "It was very nice to see you again Mr. Wessex, I cannot wait to see Ella in a couple of weeks, I'm sure that she will love it here." She says forcefully pushing me out of her office.

"Brad," she calls and I see a man, who was just previously staring at me as I had clearly just come out of his wife's office, get up and walk past me. He is probably around 5'10 which doesn't make him particularly short, but definitely shorter than I am. As he approaches me, he's glaring at me, but the closer he gets, and I'm sure the more he realizes the size I have on him he hangs his head and hurries past. I can't help but smirk and the whole scene. That's right, man, because let one thing slip in that marriage and I will be right there to pick her up and whisk her away... whoa, what?

"Abby," I say as I lean onto the counter where she is sitting. "How are you doing today?" I ask her and she just stares up at me not saying a word but sitting with her mouth hanging open... having women ogle over you is fun, but when they are like this it takes all of the fun out of it. I don't want to leave just yet because I want to see how this whole thing plays out. I'm curious as to how her marriage is actually. If it's great and everything is perfect. If it's the magical bullshit that people say marriage is, I try and convince myself that I'll back off, but if my intuition is correct, which it normally is…

Brad is only in her office for a few minutes before he comes out and leaves, he definitely looks over at me first before he leaves the office though. I glance back to Billie to see her rubbing her temples. She looks at me one last time, with a strained smile before she turns around and walks back into her office. That's probably not good. I debate going back in to talk to her some more. When I walked out of that office she was smiling, but now she's stressed. I just want to see her smile again before I leave.

Instead, I decide against it and walk out the front of the school.

CHAPTER SIX

...You fuck that up, and I'll be right there making sure you never get it back.

KHAN

Later that night, I am at Sirens again watching the business starting to wind down for the night, as I see a familiar man sitting across the room whispering to a woman, but staring at me.

Well, this is probably not going to end the way that he thinks it will.

I motion to Fury to watch my back as Billie's husband comes up to me, I love men when they get drunk, cocky, and think that they are invincible. "Are you fucking following me?" He yells at me over the music.

"What?" By the way, my favorite part about owning a club is being able to fuck with people when they are drunk.

"You heard me" he screams at me, "Are you following me?" He yells again and I can't help myself, after two whiskeys I like to fuck with drunk people that's about the only difference.

"Have we met?" I motion my index finger between him and me.

"I saw you at my wife's school today. You were coming out of her office and now magically you're here." He's pissed. Staring at me and pointing his finger into my chest, actually touching me. "Did my wife hire you to follow me?"

"Oh that is you, sorry sometimes I don't get a clear look at people when I can see clear over their heads." I don't let even a slip of a smirk form on my lips but this is fun. I can see his fist, ball up "I would advise you not to do that."

"Oh, yeah, fucking why not?" He says, finger still in my chest, smirk on his face. Also, I'm not a fan of people touching me in the first place. "I'll just say that you started it, I was defending myself, they'll believe me because I'm in the military whereas you are just some thug who runs around trying to fuck every woman he sees." Oh, and here. We. Go. See I hate when people assume that what they do makes up their personality. People see me and they assume that because I'm an *outlaw* that it means I have a certain type of personality. While Brad here thinks that just because he's in the military that makes him a good person, but people can still be pieces of shit and in the military.

I smack his finger out of my chest, "I don't give a fuck who you are, but it's pretty much an automatic ban for life from a place when you try and punch the owner in the face, or maybe that just… my rule… for my club." I see the smirk on his face start to fall as he looks around seeing everyone in the club staring at him like he has lost his fucking mind. "And there's no trying to fuck every woman I meet because I don't need to try to do that, it just happens. And at least I'm not like you, sitting here in *my* club" I can't help but emphasize the word my, "whispering sweet nothings in some slut's ear while my extremely sexy and sexually frustrated wife is at home." I hear Fury's laugh come out from behind me. "My advice to you," now reaching over and poking my finger into his chest, "is to leave, right the fuck now, leaving your girlfriend in the parking lot and go home to your wife… because let me tell you this, your wife, is not only fucking gorgeous but she is one of the smartest, funniest, and toughest women that I've ever met, and I'll promise you this… you fuck that up, and I'll be right there making sure you never get it back." Fury's laugh is roaring louder than the music now. I turn and walk back into my office slamming the door behind me.

Fury comes in a few minutes later still laughing. And looks at me. "He's gone. Who was that fucking dick."

"Billie's husband," I mutter to him and I glare at my phone trying to decide what to do. Do I call her and tell her what just happened, or do I keep it a secret?

"Oh shit, you mean like, The Billie." I nod my head. "The 5 thousand dollar hug, Billie."

"Yeah, that one," My words are bitter over the whole hug situations that Ash had to go and run his mouth about.

"The Billie that you can't stop-" I begin speaking before he can finish that sentence.

"Yes, okay... yes... her. Happy now?" I snap out causing him to jump back a little, eyes wide.

"So, like I-we all thought that you were just fucking with that guy, but you're serious about that last part." I don't say a word but just glare up at him and then he continues to speak, "Are you going to tell her?" Fury asks, actually serious and I finally make up my mind as I toss my phone onto my desk.

"I can't tell her... it can't come from me." She is well aware of some of my intentions.

"So, what are you going to do?" He asks seriously.

"I guess the only thing I can do... just wait it out." I pause and look to him again, "because something like that, someone like that, is bound to fuck it up sooner or later..."

When her name flashes up on my phone half an hour later I answer it before it fully rings.

"Billie?" My voice is hurried as I think about her husband leaving earlier pissed the fuck off.

"Dax, I'm really sorry to bother-," I can hear her panicking as I search for my keys on the desk getting ready to go to her house...

that I may or may not have scoped out already a couple of times. I'm heading out the door.

"What is it?" I say loud enough so she can hear me over the music still pumping in the club.

"I think someone is in my house, Brad is out of town, can you just stay on the phone with me until I figure it out?" There's a crash that I can hear and then a man's voice as a door hits the wall. "Oh, thank god. It's just Brad, now I really am sorry to bother you. Thank you."

"Billie, wait, He may be pissed-," but the phone disconnects before I'm able to say it all.

BILLIE

What in the world? I wonder as I hear the front door slam shut.

Someone is in the house... I push myself up in my bed slowly. My heart is pounding so hard that I can hear it in my ears. When I look at the clock on my nightstand it reads 2:00AM. Brad is supposed to be out of town for a couple of days... it can't be him. I reach for my phone... what do I do? I should call the cops... but who knows how long it would take them to get here and I don't know anyone who would be up at this time. Well, I do know one person, but... I can't bother him, I don't know him enough to bother him.

A crash comes from the other room and my hands are sweaty and the phone is ringing before I even realized that I dialed.

"Billie?" I hear him come through the phone. I almost expect him to sound groggy, but he doesn't he is wide awake.

"Dax, I'm really sorry to bother-," my words are coming out quickly as I am panicking.

"What is it?" His voice is loud and I think I hear music playing in the background.

"I think someone is in my house, Brad is out of town, can you just stay on the phone with me until I figure it out?" There's another

loud crash this time closer to the bedroom and then I watch as the door to my bedroom swings up and for a split second, I think that I'm going to die. But then a sense of relief washes over me as I see Brad standing in the doorway. "Oh, thank god. It's just Brad, now I really am sorry to bother you. Thank you." I say hanging up as I hear the sounds of him saying something but not able to make it out as I pull the phone away from my face. "I thought you were out of town?" The words are just a whisper as I am still trying to calm my over-pumping heart.

"Who was that?" He shouts at me.

"Uh-," I can't tell him who it actually was, because that would definitely look suspicious, talking on the phone to another man at 2 in the morning even if the call log would only show for a few seconds. "It was Lucy," he accepts my answer, I'm positive that it's only because he is very clearly drunk and it's not that far of a stretch that I would be on the phone with her.

"Who the fuck was that guy today?" He is shouting and now I can see the anger forming in his eyes. Now, I'm even more glad that I didn't tell him who was really on the phone.

"Wha-what?" I'm not sure if I'm still reeling from just thinking I was going to be murdered or not, but this is insane.

"You heard me, who the fuck is he?" I'm stunned… I have no idea who the "he" is that he speaks of. Clearly, he cannot be asking about Dax, he only saw him today and didn't even give a fuck about who he was before he left.

"I have no idea who you are talking about." I'm only slightly lying.

"That fucking biker who was in your office when I got there today?" He's yelling and his eyes are looking crazy.

"Wessex?" I say trying to downplay the entire thing.

"Yeah," he comes closer to me and I can smell the tequila on his breath, "THAT. FUCK."

"He's a guardian of a student who was just accepted." I pause and his eyes grow even more with rage, "Real sad story too, he just became her guardian. Her mother left and now her father is-" he cuts me off and storms up grabbing my wrist and bringing me closer to him.

"I don't give a fuck about all of that," he's in my face now and I pull back slightly which only makes him tighten his grip on my wrist and brings me in even closer, "who is he and why was he looking at you the way he was today? Better yet, why was he looking at me like he had some huge fucking secret on me." And I stop trying to pull them away.

"You're hurting me," I mutter and he laughs. He lets my wrists go as his eye widen.

"I'll show you what fucking hurting you are." He screams at me as I feel the knuckles of his closed backhand, come across my face. I stand in shock as I stare at him my shaking hand covering my face where he made contact. Then he grabs my arms again and snatching me closer to him. "Shut up, that's not the whole story and you fucking know it." Did something happen after Brad left my office? Dax was still talking to Abby when he left, but I'm not sure how long he stayed after that.

"Nothing happened, Brad. He helped me out when my car broke down a few weeks ago before you got home." And he laughs, pulling me in tighter.

"And you fucked him? As a form of a thank you" He asks yelling even louder. Who does he think he is and where the hell is all of this coming from?

"What?" I'm furious now, how could he even think that in the ten years that we have been married it has never even been an issue, and now all of a sudden. "No, I haven't fucked him." The word feels weird in my mouth as I say the word *fuck*. And Brad laughs out, bringing me in tighter, even after me thinking that he wouldn't be able to, and he looks down at me.

"You expect me to believe," his words are methodical and he lowers his voice into a tone which frightens me, "that this biker, who has a pretty fucking big reputation for fucking every woman whom he meets, want's to fuck you, helps you out with something, and you didn't fucked him." And I laugh finally pulling my wrists free.

"Yes," I shout as I put both hands on his chest, pushing him away, "That's exactly what I expect you to believe, because I'm your wife and I've never given you any reason to doubt me," I walk up to him and push him away once again, this time shoving him out of the door, "I haven't touched any man like that since before we got together, even when you don't want to fucking touch me," I yell the words and slam the door after I shout them into his shocked face, making sure to lock it. I then climb into my bed and lose the battle of trying to sleep. My hands shake for the remainder of the night, and I have to fight the urge of walking out and suffocate him with a pillow while his snores trail back into the bedroom.

The next morning I start to leave the house before Brad wakes up. I'm still furious as I get out of my shower and pat dry my hair. The sun is barely up when I put on makeup, trying my best to conceal the bruise still forming at my eye, and pull up my shorts. When I make it into the kitchen I can see Brad asleep on the couch, I don't know why he didn't just sleep in the spare bedroom. I hear his phone buzz on the coffee table and walk over to make it stop when I flip it over I see a slew of text messages, only the one that catches my eye is the one from an Ivy which I can see by the first couple of lines,

Ivy: **I can't believe you left me in the parking lot, we were supposed to spend the entire weekend together.**

My heart stops for a second. I walk back into my bedroom, pack a bag of clothes, my makeup, and toiletries, and leave my house. But not before leaving a note, underneath Brad's cell phone that says.

> *Ivy, is mad at you, hope you can make it up to her.*
> *-Billie*

I'm driving through town trying to figure out something, anything to do so I don't have to go back home. When I pull up into Lucy's driveway and walk up to the front door. I have a key but I don't want to just let myself in at this time of day anyway. So, I knock a bunch of times. Until I can hear the tired, cranky steps of Lucy coming to the door.

I can see her shocked face as she opens the door to me standing on her doorstep with luggage. She gasps a little "Bil," and for the first time since Brad got home last night, really since Brad got home last month, I break down and start to cry. "Shh, come here." She opens the door and ushers me into her house and into the living room. She sits me down on the couch. "What happened?" Her words are barely above a whisper and I relay the entire story to her. Not letting one detail out. She looks down at my wrists when I tell her about him grabbing them. And I quickly pull them away. She then looks at my eyes, when I confess that he hit me. She's angry and gets up walking into the kitchen, coming back with a washcloth, and wiping the makeup away to show the bruise. Crossing my arms making sure to hide the dark bruises on my arms. "Bil, stay here as long as you need. Fuck Brad." She sighs and smiles at me, "Want me to take you to a lawyer's office later on today?" And I laugh through my tears, "I'm serious Billie, not only does it sound like he is obviously cheating on you, but he physically hurt you." I contemplate what she is saying. Two things that I have always said I would never tolerate. I look down at my arms seeing the varying shades of purple on my wrists.

"I guess that it wouldn't be such a bad thing to talk to someone," I say in the smallest voice and she nods her head.

"We'll go see him this afternoon" she pats my leg, "until then go get some sleep," and she picks up my bags and walks with me into the spare bedroom that over the years I have drunkenly passed out in too many times to count. And for the first time since last night, I can fall asleep, quickly after she leaves the room. At some point in the day, she reenters the room and I barely remember the door opening and Lucy walks over to me, "Bil, I'm going to go out for a little bit, I'll be back in time to take you the lawyers office." I nod my head, but my eyes close again before she leaves the room. When she comes back she has all of my clothes from my house.

My phone buzzes throughout the day, but I don't check it. I don't even get out of bed. I just lie in it staring at the ceiling or actually sleeping.

"You have a missed call and a text from Dax." She says the name confused, but I don't respond I just roll back over and go back to sleep.

I fiddle with my hands as Lucy and I drive back from the lawyer's office and she suggests that we stop and get a couple of drinks. I would like a drink or 17 to numb the pain that surges in my heart. "Lucy, you don't think I'm overreacting about all of this?" I ask her and she shakes her head to let me know that I am not. "I mean we've been married for 10 years. I need to try and work it out," Lucy puts her drink down suddenly and pushes up the sleeve on my shirt to reveal the dark bruises still on my wrist.

"The fact that you are wearing a long sleeve in the middle of the fucking summer pisses me off." She swallows and sighs. I know Lucy's past and know about her ex who was violent towards her. "As soon as they realize that they can and you will come back they will continue to do so, and it will get worse."

"I just don't understand what happened, he has never been violent before. It's almost like he's a different person." I say to her. She pauses as she takes a sip and I'm positive that she rolls her eyes, "What?"

"He may have not been violent but that doesn't mean that he wasn't abusive. He has treated you like shit for years. He has tried to dull your shine. I tried to be okay with it because I thought you were happy and maybe you wanted to change, but deep down I don't think you really wanted to." She pauses maybe realizing that maybe it's too much truth for the moment and then starts again, "Also, he may be on drugs, just be careful, if he is, when he gets the papers Wednesday he's going to be pissed. Call Dax if you have to," I try to argue with her about how she's being ridiculous and when I look at her I roll my eyes knowing that she is only joking about the last part. I sigh as I look down at my phone and I hear her sad voice ask, "Has he tried to get ahold of you?" I just shake my head no and she reaches out to me "Oh, Bil. Don't cry over him."

My attorney texts me Wednesday morning to let me know that Brad got the papers as well as to advise me not to talk to him when he calls. Not if he calls, but when. It surprises me that he hasn't tried to call me since I left Saturday morning. I turn in my chair at my desk and wonder where did it all go wrong. I try to think about before he left for this deployment, I mean we were okay… but it probably hasn't been great in a couple of years. I just thought that we were in a slump, but maybe I have just been blind for years. Was Lucy right, that he had been emotionally abusive for years but I was just too blind to see that?

There's a knock on my door towards the end of my day, "Ms. Saxs," I glance at my calendar, double-checking that there isn't anyone scheduled and then I hear a familiar low voice talking in the lobby. "Okay, Abby, send whoever it is in and then you can go ahead and go home." She looks at me and smiles, nodding her head. I don't have anyone else on my calendar but from the flustered look on Abby's face and the low grumble I hear from outside of my office, I have an idea who is here to see me. What I don't expect is to see a small, shy girl walk through the door. She doesn't look up at me and I watch as Dax, as gentle as can be guide her to the chairs that sit in front of my desk. I can't help but notice the way he guides her is vastly different from the way he did with me, his. I'm so happy that for the first time this week I am handed something that I not only know that I can handle but something I can control.

"Oh, is this Ella?" She looks up at me and smiles.

"Sorry," Dax says, "she's quiet around new people."

"Uncle Dax." She glares at him and I laugh.

"It's okay," I say to her as I get up and walk around my desk, before remembering to put my heels back on, and lean against my desk in front of her. "Ella, I'm shy around new people as well." She laughs and looks at me questioning, "I have had to teach myself over years not to let it show as much," and Dax laughs, "what?" I glare over at him and he puts his hands up as if he has nothing to say. I look back to Ella and hold out my hand, "It's nice to meet you, Ella, I'm Billie, but I'm going to need you to call me Ms. Saxs when in front of people around here." I move my hand to show that I mean the school, she smiles at me.

"Nice to meet you." Her voice is quiet and she takes my hand and shakes it.

KHAN
PART I

"Ella, you can come to talk to me if you need anything." She nods her head. "Also," I say the word quieter and continue in the same voice, "don't let the bitches at this school push you around. I like to think that you understand how to stand up for yourself." She nods her head and I can see Dax looking a little shocked. "Don't start anything" I tell her, "I can't protect you if you start it, but if those girls fuck with you, you finish it. You hear me?" I tell her and I see the shocked expression on Dax's face become even more shocked I'm sure at my use of the word fuck. I give her a hug and I can see Dax's expression turn worried

"El, can you give me a minute to talk too, Ms. Saxs," she nods her head and walks out of the room, closing the door behind her.

"Thank you," he says quietly next to me.

"Sounds like she's had a hard life. I see some of the quiet girls get bullied around and I hate it, but I can't do anything about it unless they come to me and tell me." He nods his head as I run my hand through my hair. "Dax, I need to ask you something?" He looks confused but motions for me to go on. "Did you say something to my husband after you guys left on Friday?" I have my hand outstretched with my palms up when his face suddenly changes as he reaches up and grasps my hand pulling it away from me and closer to him.

KHAN

I thought it was weird when I first walked into her office that she was wearing long sleeves in July. Then I thought I saw a hint of something that looked weird when she was talking to Ella, but when she flipped her wrist like that her sleeve slides down and I saw the purple marks on her wrists and it told me that after she had called me wasn't the end of her being scared. I was going to ask her about that phone call, but then I saw these and now I'm so fucking angry.

"Bil," I hiss out, as I pull her hand to me and slide her sleeve up to her arm. I reach for her other hand and she pulls it away more telling me everything that I need to know... the same marks are on

75

the other arm. "What the fuck" I mutter with my voice growing louder. "Did he fucking do this?" I let my fingers lightly graze over her arm and she winces a little bit. The fact that it's still this sensitive makes me see red. I can only imagine why this all happened. Had she told him that she had called me? Had that on top of the argument at the club sent him over? Is this my fault?

"Isn't violence like a part of your life." She mutters to me still letting me hold her hand with mine. Her comment almost hurts until I look at her and see the smirk on her face. She's trying to make a joke out of it, which pisses me off even more because she is amazing. I don't want to make a joke back because this shit isn't something to joke about so I keep my voice low, my face serious, and look straight to her.

"Only to people who deserve it." I look down at her wrists again and shake my head. "And there's no way that you deserved this."

"How do you know I didn't deserve it?"

I smile at her, "Princess, you could never do anything to deserve that." I raise her wrist up slightly and look at her. I'm sure that my outburst at the club pushed him over the edge to do this. "I'm sorry," I mutter out

"Dax, you didn't do-," before she can finish her sentence and before I can tell her what it is I'm sorry about.

The door to her office swings open as a voice says, "Billie, what the fuck is this shit," her husband yells from the doorway holding up papers that I cannot see from where I sit. I instantly drop her hand. Standing up and I place myself between her and her husband, he's not going to lay another fucking hand on her, especially while I'm here. "Oh, really, I see this shit" he motions to us sitting near each other, "must have something to do with this shit." He shakes the papers in his hand again. I have no idea what those papers are in his hands, but after seeing those bruises on her arm he shouldn't fucking be here. Especially after everyone else has left for the day. He's staring straight at me. "Damn you couldn't wait for the ink on the papers to dry before showing up." He's pointing at me and I feel shocked, putting all the pieces together finally, but I don't let anything show on my face. Papers, me showing up, Bil and I didn't get to finish our conversation but I'm pretty sure she is leaving him. I keep my face stoic as I look at him and he shakes his head. "You've got to be fucking kidding me." But I still don't say a word, I only keep my face in an expressionless stance. He starts to step forward and I shake my head.

"You better not be trying to come at her like that and this isn't the time nor the place to come at me like that," I mutter to him in a slow calm voice as I step towards him and he stops moving and takes a couple of steps backward. I don't stop forcing him out with my much larger frame than his until I make it to the office door. So that he is standing outside of the office. "Now, you need to get the fuck out of here, before I forcefully remove you." Ella sits on the other side of the room, mouth wide open shocked at what just happened. I hate it when she sees this side of me. I don't want her to ever become afraid of me. I watch as he leaves the room and then glance back to Billie, "Are you getting ready to leave?" She nods her head quickly, "Good, get your stuff together, I'll walk you to your car." She nods her head again, eyes filling up with tears. Somehow managing to break my stone, cold heart. Once she packs her bag I hold my hand out for her to hand it to me and she shakes her head.

"I've got it." I feel like I'm at a breaking point, how is it that this is what pushes me over.

"Goddamnit," I mutter to her cutting my eyes and glaring at her, "just let me carry the fucking bag" my voice is quiet but commanding.

"No," she glares right back to me. Matching the intensity, "I don't need you saving me." She pushes past me and walks out of her office into the lobby. Ella laughs at me as Billie walks in front of us and I shut the door to the main office behind us.

"You're going to have your hands full with that one." I hear Ella laugh at my side and I let my head turn down as I laugh.

"Shut it," I mutter to her and she laughs a little bit more.

"I like her." She says at my side and I nod my head telling her that I agree with her. "She would be good for you." I roll my eyes as I look back at her and watch Billie walk out of the door.

"She's married."

"Sure, she is," she nods her head and I motion for her to walk over to the truck sitting in the parking lot. As I walk with Billie to her car she is glaring at me.

"I don't need you trying to save me." She steps into me.

"I know that." I tell her, "Look I'm sorry. I just saw that." I motion down to her arms, "And then he shows up like this." I pause and she looks at me confused.

"What did he mean, you know what he said to you? Did you say something to him?" Her stare is hardened.

And I run my hands down my face "Shit," I say as I turn, taking a couple of steps away and then turn back around and look at her. "All honesty, yeah I fucking said something to him." She stops and her eyes go wide. "Which is why I feel so fucking bad now, I know…" I pause and walk back up to her, and I lower my voice hoping that somehow it can convey the disgust that I feel with myself at this moment, "I know, that it's me that set him off to do that," I point to her wrists, "to you. And I'm sorry." The word sorry barely makes it out of my mouth.

"That's not your fault, but did you tell him that I slept with you?" I laugh and look back over at her.

"No," but I can see how he could make that connection.

"So, then what did you say to him? When were you able to say anything to him?" She asks me… looking serious.

"That's not important." I wave it off.

"Daxton," The use of my full name, which no one has called me since my mother died, makes my walls start to crumble. "What did you say to him?"

"He came up to me at the club and-" she stops me.

"Wait, he was at your club?" She asks me and I groan. This is why I didn't want to get into it. "When?"

"Friday night," I look at her. "He was there with some girl and then accused me of following him. He tried to threaten me and say that no one would believe me because he was a better person than me." Her eyes get big

"Ivy," her words are soft, "god I look like such an idiot."

"Bil, trust me, you look nothing like an idiot," I pause and look at her again, "that's exactly what I made sure that he knew." I can tell that she's connecting some sort of dots.

"Why did he say you wanted to fuck me?" every time she uses those words I can't help but laugh. I think my face grimaces a little bit. "Dax." she glares at me again. How do you tell someone politely that you indeed want to fuck them?

I toss my hands in the air, "I told him that if he fucked it up, I'd be there waiting to make sure he never got you back." The thing with women that I have learned over the years is that I never know how they are going to react to my comments and Billie Saxs is no different. She looks furious and then she gets into her car, starts it, and shocks me more when she peels out of the parking lot. Well, fuck.

I put my hands into my pockets as I walk back over to my truck and Ella laughs, taking one of the headphones out of her ear, and asks. "Is she mad?"

"No, kid, that's how happy people leave an argument." She rolls her eyes at me, placing her headphone back into her ear, and tunes me out again.

CHAPTER SEVEN

...but explosives... I get them... they have a purpose most people don't even have that.

KHAN

"Prez," I hear Ace shout to me as I walk back into the clubhouse, "Dyno needs to see you in purgatory." I nod to him. I'm not particularly a fan of purgatory, which may be why I don't spend more time out there.

"Let him know that I'll head up there tonight." I tell Ace, "I need you to check in on Ella while I'm gone." He nods his head. I can't help but think about the extra amount of work that has been put on the other officers since Oz has left. They insisted that I officially take over the president position we need to find another VP.

"What is it, Prez?" I hear Fury as me.

"We need to get the vacant seat filled soon. Since neither one of you," I point to both of them, "wanted it."

"Fuck that amount of responsibility." Fury mutters.

"Yeah, I got it," I mutter to them.

"Plus," I hear Ace mutter out next to me, "that's a fucking reputation to amount to," he says and I roll my eyes at him.

"Don't try and stroke my ego," I mutter out.

"No, he's right. When's the last time we had a new VP?" Fury asks me looking back.

"Not quite as long since we had a new Prez," I mutter and everyone then sits uncomfortably because as much as I may have run things for Oz over the last few years, the position was still his for the last 18 years.

"You have nothing to worry about," I hear Fury say to me. "Man you know what you're doing. Oz has been grooming you to take over for years now." Now I sit uncomfortably, I hate the term grooming.

"We need to select a new VP this week… So if you two absolutely don't want it, we've got to come up with someone. I'm getting ready to leave to go to purgatory you two put your skulls together and try to get someone who actually wants the thing, and who will actually be fucking decent. We'll talk about it when I get back and then put it up to a vote within everyone else." I know who I am thinking but if they don't agree then I will not offer the suggestion. I could just be playing favorites.

The ride out to purgatory takes a little over 2 hours. It took us 6 months to build it. Oz was very impressed with me when I thought of the idea. Even more, impressed when we had actually completed it. As soon as I get to Joshua Tree, I pull off and grab my phone from my pocket, I turn it off, slipping the SIM card out, and slip the SIM card into my wallet and my phone back into my pocket. We started doing this to make sure it doesn't ping off any towers. I start watching the area around me, making sure that I'm not being followed. It is late at night now, so I turn off my lights. The best part about the desert is that normally there are not many clouds in the sky so you can see in front of you without the lights on. I pull up to the entrance and take one last look around me making sure that no one is here and pull into the side of the mountain with the small opening. The opening is strategically is only as big for our Jeep

Wrangler... with the mirrors folded in, but more importantly smaller than the black SUVs that cops use. Once you get inside of the opening it opens up a little bit more but not much. About 300 feet inside the opening there is a garage door, that sits behind the jeep which Dyno normally uses, I walk over to the soundproof lockbox that is attached to the wall when I open it I see Dyno's sitting in there and wonder why he even has a phone. To see Dyno standing there, "Prez!" His arms are wide stretched as I walk up to him and hug him. "Congrats, glad to hear it finally happen," he says nodding down to my patch on my jacket. I shake my head. Maybe I need to have more people come up here with him. The room that the door opens up too, is a large lab. He has all the chemicals, devices, anything that he needs anything he may need is either here or we quickly find it.

This used to be an old mine... or that's how it started. We reinforced the walls, and carefully, slowly opened up more spaces that we needed. The electricity is fueled from the solar panels that we have randomly placed around the mountainside making sure not to put them too closely together. In case the heat starts getting close to this place, by aerial surveillance, this place still looks like a mountain with nothing around it. We also found a lot of gold while building this... which was more of a bonus.

"Dyno, How are things coming?" I ask him and he nods his head. Probably faster than it should be.

He stands with his goggles on his head wide-crazed eyes and says, "Good, good... I have a new test I'm about to do. I have been waiting for you to come with me." He suggests and I nod my head. As we walk back out of the door that I had just come from. He motions for me to get into the jeep and as carefully as I watch him pull past my bike sitting to its side. We pull out of the mountainside and down into the desert itself. And he drives. I don't ask a word only wondering what this man is taking me to see.

Dyno's position here is to maintain the supply. The club has a pot farm in the state as well. We sell it legally and everything is buy the book, kind of. We account for the majority of it... what we don't account for is for the club's use... which is technically more of a grey area... we count it as waste or bad crop. All of our legit businesses have civilian employees except for at Pistons, which is

more of just a stop for our bikes… the only people allowed to work in there are from the MC. All businesses are technically the property of the LLC that the charter owns. We are each supposed to put in time at each business, I don't spend too much time at the farm though… that shit gives me a headache. But purgatory, out here… this is where no one can find us… this is where technically the illegal activities begin. Our waste from the farm comes here. When we get our shipments everything is stored here… Dyno also makes some explosives and some other things. Dyno's job is to watch over all of our contraband… but I think he's starting to lose it a little. I need to pull him back in. Oz seemed to forget about him most days.

He pulls the jeep over and we get out… he jogs ahead a few feet and he places down the object that he is carrying in his hand… and then he jogs back up to the jeep motioning for me to get back in and jumps in himself. He pulls the jeep back onto the road and begins to drive the road which winds up the mountain. When we get to the top he stops the jeep again and says, "Remember where we just put it."

"Yeah," I mutter grabbing ahold of the bars on the jeep and lift myself up. Dyno is twitchy, well I should say twitchier than normal, as he presses the button in his head and an explosion happens which throws out fireballs to all sides… the fire spreads quickly, but since we are in the desert and there's only dirt and sand it goes out almost just as quick. Also, Dyno is short for Dyn-o-mite. Dyno worked with explosives while he was in the military. He won't tell us which branch, he also won't tell us how long he was in, but by the way that he carries himself and his mannerisms, the only other person I have seen that within is my father. Also, I'm pretty sure he dealt with some shit in the Middle East, his giant scar down his back leads me to believe that.

"Man," Dyno says as he looks back to it and says in almost a depressed tone, "stupid desert,"

"Holy fucking shit, dude!" I shout at him smacking him on his shoulder, jumping up and down using the bar and causing the jeep to bounce as well, and looking over to him. Part of my animated act is to get him to realize how awesome that was and the other part is pure excitement of my own. "Did you make a fucking napalm bomb?" He nods his head, excitedly. I sit down quickly as he speeds back to our mountain. When we get to the opening he flips the car into reverse and like a champ parks it in the tunnel right between my bike and his without even coming close to touching either of them. We both jump out of the jeep and walk back in through the door. "How?"

"Polystyrene." He mutters

"What?"

"Styrofoam," I nod my head again at him.

"Seriously,"

"Yeah, it works best if there isn't any writing on it."

"Do you need more of it?" I ask him thinking about where we could get some from.

"Depends on how many you want me to build." We walk back into the lab and sit down on the couches in the room.

"The way it's made," I pause and think for a second, "is there a way for anyone to decipher that it was made beforehand?"

"Can they tell if it's a bomb?" He asks me and I nod my head.

"Yeah."

"Well, what it's made out of right now, yeah, probably."

"Could you make it in a way which the casing would burn up as well?"

"Yeah" he mutters. "How many would you need?" He asks me and I pause.

"I don't have a plan for them quite yet, but with the leadership transitioning someone is bound to try and test me." He nods his head. "You think you could put together like 6 just in case." He nods his head.

"If you're worried about it not reaching all of the areas, pour some high-proof alcohol or gas … it will go up even faster."

"Okay, so how is everything out here?"

"It's good," he says quietly.

"Dyno, do you need some help out here. I can send some of the guys out to at least give you some company." He laughs and shakes his head.

"They'll fuck up my formula." Dyno is one of those people who are off the grid. He can come back to the clubhouse whenever he wants he just chooses not to.

"You're a weird fuckin' dude, Dyno." He pauses as he looks at me and nods.

"Yeah, I saw some fucked up shit in Iraq," he nods his head slowly, "couldn't really talk to people when I got home. I don't really get them, but explosives… I get them… they have a purpose most people don't even have that." Oh shit, profound. "Want to see how everything is out here." I nod my head and he shows me to the stash of drugs and then to our room of weapons.

CHAPTER EIGHT

...Who does Daxton fucking Wessex think he is...

BILLIE

"Who does Daxton fucking Wessex think he is telling my husband that he will take me from him." I shout to Lucy as she sits across from me at dinner.

"Well, he didn't actually say that, right?" She looks to me, tilting her head as to say that I'm overreacting.

"He pretty much should have. His words caused Brad to react like that." I mutter, not really eating my food, just pushing it around my plate with my fork.

"Bil," she snaps at me rolling her eyes, "Brad reacted like that because Brad's an asshole." She bluntly states for the hundredth time this week.

"Brad has never done anything like that to me before."

"Okay." He states as she picks up her cup and drinks from it. Her tone tells me that she's annoyed with me.

"What, Lucy? If you have something to say, just say it." I mutter back to her.

"Billie," she pauses as if trying to figure out the right words to say, "Brad has been an asshole since the day you met him. The only reason why it's taken him this long to become physical is that he has been gone for 6 months almost every year since the two of you got married. He controls you, even if he isn't violent. He has told you where it's acceptable for you to work. How to dress, how he expects you to act." I start to object and she shakes her head, "I'm not finished. He controls the way you perceive yourself. I've watched you in the gym killing yourself trying to get into the shape that he wants you to be in which let me add is not achievable. He's a fucking asshole and you deserve so much better," She waits to see if I'm going to say anything else and then adds, "someone who knows your worth." I quietly look down at the ground and begin to pick at my fingernails. "Stop doing that." She mutters to me. "I'm not saying these things to make you feel bad. You separated from him. That's the best thing that you can do. I'm telling you this mostly because I have never pretended to like him. I've also never thought that you loved him quite like you thought you did." Many minutes go by before she speaks again, "You were such a spirited person when I met you, the whole time we were growing up. You had all these things that interested you and you surprised everyone by the things that you did. I've watched *that* person and *that* spark fall away, just think about who you want to be and who you want." She then gets up and walks back to her bedroom.

Almost as if he can hear us talking about him my phone beeps.

Brad: I need to talk to you.

Is all it says

Me: No, Brad. I have nothing to say to you.

Monday morning

I'm sitting in my office as my office phone rings, as I answer it I can't help but look at the clock that reads 8:30, on my computer, just to make sure that I didn't miss any scheduled calls.

"Billie Saxs," I say into the receiver but no one says anything. Yet, I can hear breathing on the other end. "Hello?" I say into the receiver and still no response. "Hello, is anyone there?" Once more, nothing in response, "Okay, if anyone is there I can't hear you." I wait for maybe a full minute just so that I'm sure no one is trying to say anything and has accidentally muted the phone. I have done that more times than I care to admit, so I understand. "Okay, I'm hanging up now." I finally mutter out before putting my receiver back on the base.

I mention the phone call to Lucy briefly when we get home and she laughs. "You're too nice. I would have hung up the second no one said anything."

Saturday evening

I'm sitting in Lucy's living room, reading a book, in front of the large bay windows. As I see headlights. They drive down the road and turn around in the cul-de-sac and then drive back to the end of the street again. Weird, I could have sworn last night when I was in this same spot another car did the same thing. In fact, that car seems very similar to this one.

You're jumping to conclusions, someone is probably considering moving into the neighborhood.

I don't mention the car to Lucy.

Sunday night

My cell phone rings I look to my caller ID which reads, **NO CALLER ID**.

Well, I'm not going to answer that.

I think as I click on the side buttons to silence it and send the call to voicemail. A few minutes later the notification that I have a voicemail pops up and I listen to it, but it's just breathing.

That's really weird.

Monday

I have a repeat phone call from last Monday. At the same time as it was last week. 8:30.

"Billie Saxs," I say into the receiver, but again like last week there's no answer, "Hello." No answer again, "Can you hear me? Did you butt dial me?" I ask but still no answer. "Okay, I'm hanging up." I nearly whisper into the receiver, before hanging up the phone.

Thursday

I come home from school and feel weird. I instantly get that strange feeling like someone has been in my room. Nothing has been moved, but everything just feels like something, but I can't put my finger on it.

"Lucy," I say as she walks out of her room, "did you have someone over today?" She shakes her head

"Why?"

"I dunno," I pause as I look around, "it's just in my head." And I walk to the kitchen to get something to eat.

Friday

Lucy and I go out to dinner. We have some drinks.

I drink way more than I ever intended to. So, Lucy drives my drunk butt home.

She's the best, I think as she puts me to sleep.

I swear I woke up in the middle of the night to see someone at the end of my bed just standing staring at me, but when I wake up on Saturday morning I know that I was just dreaming. That whole living in a new house, thing. Even if it isn't technically a new house, I'm just a little uneasy since I have never really lived here.

Sunday

I get the same call from the no caller id and again send it to voicemail. Ending up with the same voicemail as I got last week. Just a voicemail of weird breathing.

Monday

On the first day of school as I am grabbing my bag out of my car, I can't help but notice a very familiar truck pulling into the parking lot. I try not to look over to it to see who it was, but instead, I walk straight ahead. Not breaking to look for even a second. Yet for some reason all I can hear is Lucy's words about figuring out who I wanted, echoing in my head… which seems

crazy since I don't even know Dax. Also, including that whole issue of him being a criminal.

I should have known before it happened that it was going to but somehow it still surprises me when not even ten minutes later there is a knock on my office door.

"Billie," my name comes out of his mouth, rugged. "I had to wait for Ella to walk into the building before I could come in." He chuckles, I can see him look into the lobby of the office and walks in closing the door. "People were coming in…" He trails, "didn't know if you wanted them all to see me in here with my cut on." He reminds me of when I said that to him a few weeks ago before he pauses waiting for me to say anything. "I'm sorry for what I said." He mumbles out walking towards the desk and sitting in the chair. "Ugh," he tosses his head back, "you're really good at this silent treatment, you know," but I still don't look up, "fine, I'll talk." I can see his smirk out of my peripheral, "Ella is doing better." He says almost like he's trying to fill up time trying to wear me down until I say something, anything, "I think finally found someone to replace my old position. It's actually my mentee. Is that the right word mentee? I guess, I should say one of my mentees since apparently the majority of the club I have brought in out of tough spots." I try to hide my smile but I see a smile pick up on his lips so I know that he saw it. "Yeah, known him since he was like 13. He's a good kid. Super young though, which also kind of sucks." I'm curious how much he's going to tell me trying to get a reaction from me. "Actually, I'm sure it's probably similar to your job. When someone new comes into power and people start seeing how much they can get away with." My smile grows before I can pull it back into my stoic stare at my computer. "Especially, depending on their looks, but I guess when I think about it I was around the same age when I took over as VP." He looks off like this is the first time he has realized it. Then he turns to me seriously, probably assuming that I'm going to have to start doing actual work for my job. "Billie, I want to be completely honest with you. I want to tell you exactly what I said to your husband," I stop typing on my keyboard and let my eyes look up to his. "He threatened to punch me in my club, I told him that if he punched the owner in his club that was pretty much an automatic ban for life, or maybe that was just my own rule." I smirk to him, "He said I was a thug trying to go around a fuck every woman I meet." I lifted my eyebrow as to say, *are you?* "I told him that I didn't need to try to fuck women it just happens and at least I wasn't like him running around in my club whispering into some sluts ear while I had a sexually frustrated wife at home," the last part comes out with a grimace because he knows that I will not like it, but I don't let my expression falter.

There is a knock on my office door and the Abby opens it, seeing Dax there she suddenly becomes flustered again and then tells me that my 8:30 is here. I glance at my computer and see that it's 8:25, and I can let him wait for a few more minutes.

"Give us a minute," I nod to her, motioning for her to close the door. When the door shuts I look back at him. He seems surprised for a second and then almost contemplates his last statement because I'm making my meeting wait.

"I should correct myself. I actually said extremely," I raise my eyebrow once again. And he runs a hand over his face. "I then gave him the advice to leave right the fuck now, leaving his girlfriend in the parking lot and going home to you." I nod my head with it tilted to one side as that was good advice and he continues, "I then told him, 'your wife, is not only fucking gorgeous but she is one of the smartest, funniest, and toughest women that I've ever met,' then I promised him that if he fucked it up that I would be there making sure that he never got you back." I stare at him and then glance out the door. He sighs, getting up from the chair and walking to the door.

As his hand turns the door handle to open it I say, quietly and calmly, "And you didn't think to tell me he was there with another woman?" His hand slinks and he looks over his shower back at me.

"Is that what you're really mad about?" He asks, looking back at me shocked, and for the first time I realize that is exactly what I'm mad about, "Would you have believed me if I did?" Then his voice grows quieter, "It couldn't have come from me." As the words come out of his mouth my office phone rings again, I glance at the clock, it's 8:30 again, I answer the phone with a nervous voice and he looks at me with a concerned expression.

I hang it up and say, "no one was there," I try to play it off like this whole thing isn't unnerving.

"Then why do you look concerned?" He asks me.

Shrugging my shoulders, "It's been a stressful couple of months." He stares at me almost as if he's trying to actually determine if I'm telling him the truth before he accepts my answer and slips out of the door.

Tuesday

I get another call at the office on Tuesday only this time it's the breathing on my office phone and I quickly hang it up.

Wednesday

When I get home I have an unnerving feeling like someone is watching me. I push the feeling away as I quickly change and walk back out to the living room, open a bottle of wine and sit back. Only I can't manage to shake the feeling. When Lucy comes home I am relieved as she sits up with me and watches movies.

Thursday

There's a small knock on my door around noon, Abby pops her head in my office and says. "You have a student out here who wants to see you." I nod my head at her and she opens the door. As I watch Ella walk into the office and I instantly stop typing on my computer and turn to look at her.

"Ella," my voice comes out maybe strained, "is there an issue with anyone?"

She purses her lips like she is thinking about something and then says, "Well kind of,"

"Okay, who is it," I say turning to my computer and starting to scroll through the attendance of the school. It's probably Becky Willcox. "It's you." *Um, excuse me?* Maybe she can see the confusion on my face. "Well, it's not really, I don't have a problem with you. It's just. I saw the way my uncle looked at you the other day." I look at her not sure what direction her next words are going to go in, "Underneath all the leather, scars, and tattoos. He's a really good guy." And I smile looking down at my papers.

"I have that feeling about him, but It's complicated." She nods her head.

"It always is, but for what it's worth I've known him my entire life. I know about his reputation but he's a really good guy. When he does care about someone he would stop the world to save them." I don't say anything and she smiles at me again, "Anyway, I just wanted to come and ask you to give him a chance, I've turned his life upside down in the last couple of months and I just want him to be happy. He deserves as much. His life has kind of sucked and well…" she pauses, "I've seen the way that women gravitate towards him, but what I've never seen is him actually care about any of them." Her words make me smile even though I'm pretty sure she just told me that he

cares about me, which should scare me. The way she speaks about him shows me just how much he means to her.

"Did he ask you to come and talk to me?" She laughs at my question.

"He would be pretty pissed if he knew I was here right now. He gives everything for everyone and never expects anything in return." She smiles at me and gets up walking to the door.

"Ella, thank you," I tell her and she smiles at me. Before she leaves.

That evening, I'm sitting on the couch and happen to catch something from out of the window. I swear I see that same car that was driving down the street only this time it is parking in front of the house.

As I'm getting ready for bed I can't help but glance out the window and notice that the car is still sitting here.

Shit, why am I so paranoid all of a sudden? It's probably just at a neighbor's house.

CHAPTER NINE

...You can yell at me all you want to then, okay?

KHAN

Friday

"Prez, we have an issue." I hear as soon as I walk into the clubhouse later that evening. Fuck, I've had a really bad fucking day already. For some reason, I haven't been able to get the conversation with Billie the other day out of my head.

Ace and Fury both kept their positions because neither of them wanted the VP job. I'm not sure why VP is a pretty easy job at least when the Prez is around and actually running things. Instead, I had to figure out who was going to be my VP. I talked with Oz a couple of times, who pretty much told me that I knew what the fuck I was doing and he wasn't going to give me advice on it. The only person who has been around long enough to do the job, who I trust enough, and who is actually interested, is a 27-year-old kid, Ash. The kid is loyal to the core. I mentored him for a long time and in the last few years, he has turned into my *right-hand man* well outside of the other officers.

"What fucking now?" I mutter looking to Ash, I feel kind of bad for snapping at him like this. I get it, it's weird this is the first official week of his new position and I'm jumping down his throat.

"Rising Henchmen," he pauses and looks at me, "they heard that Oz accepted the plea." Fuck me. We were worried that this would happen.

"They're coming into our territory?" I cut my stare down. Fuck, "Call and set up the meeting." I see him become uncomfortable. Fuck me... "Ash, toughen the fuck up." I cut to him and feel bad for him for a second, groaning I look back to him and sigh, "Look, this is the only time I'm going to say anything like this so fucking cherish it. I know this, is all new to you, but you have to toughen the fuck up and make the call. Don't let them sense weakness. They do that... they will eat you alive. I know you can handle this, but I'm not going to hold your fucking hand through this... I have my own shit to deal with." He nods to me and gets up.

"I'll get it done."

"Get everyone in for church later, tell everyone to be ready to go out afterward." And he nods.

Walking up to my house and up to the door I open it, I've got to change and get ready. Get into the mindset.

"El," I stop outside of her door and can hear her sobbing. Ah, fuck... "El," I say loudly as I tap on the door. She opens it quickly without even trying to conceal her crying and she wraps her arms around my waist. "Oh, Ella," I soother her hair down before muttering to her, "shhh, It's okay, I've got you, I'm sorry, El?"

"Uncle Dax, it isn't your fault. You're doing everything that you can possibly do for me and I'm out here acting like I'm ungrateful."

"El, you're not acting ungrateful. This is hard. And no one should have to go through it." I tell her as she continues to cry. I sit down on her bed and pull her close letting her cry into my chest. Once she settles down she moves up and sniffles again. "El, you going to be okay?" She nods her head and as much as I don't want to leave, I know that I'm going to have to, "I have to leave for a little bit, Bullet is going to stay behind. Call him if you need anything at all."

"Yeah, I'll be fine." She tells me and I feel bad. Maybe I should step down and let someone else run things for a while until she is settled. "Uncle Dax, stop. I'm fine. I just needed to be sad for myself for a little bit." Maybe growing up around the MC has hardened her too much. The guys have always been on their best behaviors when she has been around, but the lifestyle, the guys, everything that the-life brings, she still has to deal with day today. The worrying about if what happened to her dad, is going to happen again. I ruffle her hair and get up walking out of the room. I walk into my bedroom and reach into the closet. Taking off my cut and pulling on my Kevlar vest, I pull out one of my black t-shirts from inside of my closet slipping it over my head to conceal my Kevlar, pulling my shoulder holster out of the top of my closet I wrap it around my body. Kneeling down to my safe I press my thumb to the scanner and the safe door pops open. Loading my two Glocks, I then slide them into the holster, making sure to clip them into the place. I load each of the 4 extra magazines and lock them into the holster as well. Taking my pocket knife, popping the blade out, and inspecting it making sure that it doesn't need to be sharpened and when it meets my expectations, closing it, then slipping it into the front band of my pants, so that my belt conceals it. This is my favorite trick. Especially if we have a meeting and have to place all of our weapons. People rarely find it here... even with a metal detector, the beeping they assume is due to my belt. Before I leave the house I stop at Ella's room again.

"El, I'm heading out, you sure you're okay?" She nods her head... looking much better and smiles.

KHAN
PART I

"Uncle Dax, please be safe." She mutters.

"Always my goal," I tell her, honestly as I start to walk down the stairs. The Syndicate is going to have to prove themselves once again because people think we are weak. Setting up a meeting is strictly to be polite because what I should have done is go in there and blow off Tito's fucking head. But I don't really want to start an all-out war. Not unless they start it…

I think back to Billie's words as she said them to Ella a few weeks ago, *don't start it, but if they fuck with you fucking finish it.* Damn, maybe this girl isn't too innocent for me.

I stop a few steps down the stairs and I turn around, "El," she looks back up from her notebook to me, "love you," she smiles.

"Love you too, Uncle Dax." I press my lips into a line and rush down the stairs.

Walking into the clubhouse as Ash comes up to me, "Khan, the meetings set for 11," I nod my head.

"Everyone here?" I ask him.

"Yeah, we are just waiting for you." He mutters and I nod my head. "Khan, you sure you wanna do this?"

"Fuck no, I don't want to, but we have to. They're testing me. I look weak now and if I don't do anything they will never stop until they fucking kill me." Ash nods his head.

"Nah Prez, they're testing me." He looks at me and then looks away almost as if he's ashamed and somehow it's his fault. "Think about it. We all know that you have pretty much been running this shit for years now. They all know you. Me, they don't know shit about me." I contemplate what he is saying.

"Fuck." I mutter and look back at him. "Ash, I was going to have you hang back in one of the SUVs."

"Fuck that," he says to me.

"Yeah I know, you may be on to something there." Fuck I don't really want to go out there with my SSA and my VP. If they take us out then we're all fucked. I'm going to have to move some people around now, "If I have Fury hang back…" I pause and look at him again trying to think of exactly how to phrase what I want to say, "Look kid, I know you're loyal to me…" After all of the things I have seen him do, I don't doubt that. "You're like a kid that I had way too early in life," and he laughs again, "so that's the only reason why I say this… I know this is your first meet as VP so when we get out there. Follow my lead If I give you the sign you fucking shoot to kill, don't fucking hesitate. If you do you'll get us all fucking killed. Now when we go into this room. It's you and me… we have to work together as one. You got that." And he nods his head. We walk into the room and Ash and I walk to the front. I'm standing at the front of the table and someone starts it up.

"What do you have for us, Prez." And the whole room starts cheering.

"All right that's enough," I say in my normal tone and the whole room goes quiet, which surprises me at first, usually it takes more than a couple of words to quiet them down. " We've got some serious shit to attend to. The Henchmen are trying to spread into our territory." Someone yells *fuck that* from the back of the room, "They are testing us because they think that since Oz got locked up we are weak." There's a couple more fuck that's and cheering, in response to the aforementioned *fuck that's,* from around the room, "We have a meeting in an hour and a half at the marina." I pause. "We are going in with three teams." I pause and look around the room… suddenly I feel like I should have talked to Fury about this first. He's going to be pissed that he isn't there with me. "Bullet, I need you to stay behind on this one." He groans trying to argue with my plan. I glare over at him and shake my head. "Bullet, I need you to be here with Ella." I can tell that he is upset about my decision but he doesn't argue with me in front of everyone, he knows better than that. He wants to complain because he's the Road Captain, he should be on the run with me and I need someone to stay with her who I know would be able to take out a handful of men if they decide to come here, "Solo, Viper, and Zodiac stay back with Bullet and guard the clubhouse and Ella. You guys got that?" I ask them all and they nod.

"I need the two other teams to stay a block back in the trucks, in case shit goes down." They all nod, "The north team will be Ace, Tuck, Golem, and Lock," Ace nods to me and then I continue, "Bender, V, Grim, you'll be with Fury at the south end." I can see Fury's frustration as he starts to say something and I move my hand telling him to stop, that we will talk later, "Ash, Lex, and Blaze, will be with me at the marina." I stop and look at all of them and I sigh, "Understand this is them trying to test us. They will probably try and pull some shit. When they do, I need you guys to get to us, immediately. We leave in 15 so be fucking ready to roll. I'm not fucking dying tonight." Everyone cheers and follows my chant of *I'm not fucking dying tonight,* "Bullet." I motion to him and he comes up, as everyone else leaves the room except for Fury who is well, furious with me for making him sit out. "I need you to go and check on Ella, she should be fine but if shit goes down. I need you to get to her, get her safe, and don't leave her fucking side until I get back or you hear I'm dead. You hear me." He nods his head and then leaves the room I say to him to shut the door and he does. I turn to look at Fury, "All right brother, let me have it." There aren't many people that I would let question me at all.

"What the fuck, Prez. I'm your SSA and you're taking Ash with you." He yells his words. "The majority of my fucking job is to make sure that you are protected." I put my finger up.

"That's not exactly your job," I step into him, never letting my voice falter. I'll tell you that I'm a tough motherfucker, but Fury has been able to scare the fuck out of me, I'm just glad that he's on my side of things, "Your job is to protect this club. Which means doing what is necessary for everyone. I can't go out there with my VP and my SSA with me. If shit happens, we can't all go down with the ship, you got me. Normally, I would have you there, you know that, and he would be sitting back," hell the last few meetings that we have had where we were worried about shit going down, it was Fury and I as Oz sat back a block away. "But he has a point. They all know me. They've been dealing with me for years. But Ash, they don't really know. They are testing us mostly because he's the new VP." Fury nods his head understanding why I made the decision. "Hopefully, nothing goes down, but since when does that happen with us?" he nods his head agreeing with me. "And Fury," he looks back to me again, "I need you to have my back on this. I don't need them questioning me as well."

"I know, Khan," he pauses as he looks to the door. "You ready to get this shit done, Prez?"

"As ready as I'll ever be," I respond to him as I place the comms into my ear as he does the same thing. "Fury they will most likely be coming in from the south side, so I need you to let me know when you have eyes on them"

"I know, Prez." That's the thing about Fury, I say that Ash has been my right-hand man because Fury isn't like a hand. He's like my fucking lungs... I don't have to consciously say anything to him he just knows to do what I'm thinking.

We all leave the house in a caravan until the truck that I am in pulls out away from the rest. They already know to go, sit in their spots, and wait. I have to go and get my bike from the shop first. We pull in and I jump out of the truck running to the door and unlocking it, locking the door behind me I rush to the bay which my bike is in and I hit the button to roll up the door as I toss a leg over my bike and right it.

"Wessex" I hear from in front of me and I stop every movement. As I look up I see Billie standing eyes wide. She storms into the bay as I continue to walk my bike out of the door.

Fuck, I don't have time for this right now.

Judging by the look on her face though she is serious so I let my bike lean against its stand and shake my head walking back into the bay and pressing the button to close the button. "How da-" I stop her as I glance at my watch. It's ten-fifteen, with a fifteen-minute drive to the marina I don't have time to have this out with her just yet. I pull her with me into the lobby of the shop as I begin to talk.

"Bil, I'm so sorry, princess, but I don't have time to have this out with you right now." Her shocked expression is all that I can see. And it pains me that she looks sad about me not being able to talk with her. "Believe me. I'm so sorry, I would gladly have you yell and scream at me right now, but I have this meeting set up that I cannot miss or be late too." In fact, I need to get there fifteen early... because that's my reputation. I can smell the alcohol on her breath as I open the front door for her to pass through and lock it behind me. She still hasn't said a word. So I just continue to speak. "I don't know how long I'll be but I can come to see you afterward. You can yell at me all you want to then, okay?" Her head nods and I smile, and I lean over and place a light peck on her cheek.

As she turns to walk away all I can think about is if this goes south and I never get this chance again. I reach out, grabbing her by the arm, and spin her back into me. I wrap my other arm tightly around her back and smash my lips down to her's. I can hear the guys from my SUV at the other side of the parking lot yelling in my ear as they watch it unfold and Fury and Ace confused as fuck trying to figure out what, in fact, is happening. Next thing I know Ash is narrating the entire thing to them, like a goddamn sportscaster. Her mouth opens when she feels my tongue touch her lips, she tastes like cinnamon I can only imagine what she has been drinking tonight, and her arms immediately wrap around my neck. She's forceful in her response as I feel her push her tongue meeting my every move. I reach down letting my hands find the curve of her ass as I easily lift her up and she wraps her legs around my torso in an immediate response. I feel the pull on my shoulders that her legs are just above the guns which rest at my sides as I turn and press her back against the outside wall of the shop. Ash is in my ear telling me to wrap it up because we've got to go as I slow our kiss down until it's just a couple of pecks and her legs unwrap from around me. I place her back down on the ground and look at her, "So, beautiful." I whisper to her looking at her flushed face, her swollen lips, and her heavy breathing. "I've really got to go through." She nods still stunned, before I place one last kiss onto her lips, and turn to walk away.

"Dax," she calls to me as I throw my leg over my bike and I look back over to her. "I'm not at my place anymore, I'm at Lucy."

I smile back to her, "Alright, princess, I'll see you soon."

"Finally," I hear Ash in my ear.

"Can it, fucker." I mutter as my officers start laughing. I drive off to the other side of the parking lot to where the truck sits and lead the way to the marina.

"Hey Fury, do me a favor while we are waiting on them to show. Look up Lucy, Billie's friend, and get me an address." He agrees and within 5 mins tells me he's got it. This is why I keep this fucker around.

When we pull up to the marina there still isn't a sign of them. They park the truck as I park my bike a few feet away and I kick-off of it. "Guys, we should buy a boat." I hear laughter coming from the other end. "Seriously, have an upper hand with these things."

"Clubhouse at sea." Ash says as he walks up to me which makes me laugh, "nothing bitches love more than a fucker with a yacht"

"I'm not sure we have a clubhouse on a yacht kind of money, yet," Ace says, being the most real that he is as well as the treasurer.

"Guys," Fury comes on sounding serious, "incoming" And I turn as I hear the motorcycle turning into the parking lot and watch the guys at the truck shift a little bit.

"You got my back, bro," I say to Ash and he nods his head as we bump fists and wait for them to stop.

The bikes stop in front of us and I wait for Fury to tell me if more men are coming. "That's all of them, just the 4 unless the rest are coming in later or from a different route."

"If you see them come later, Ace follow them in. Fury I want you to hang back. Let Tito think you didn't come unless we really need you."

"Heard, Prez" I hear Fury say, slightly irritated. Tito and X, his VP, get off their bikes and walk up to us. The van follows them in after them and parks next to their bikes. Tito's an older man, in his late fifties and everyone has been wondering when he is going to be retiring. Even if Tito has 20 years on me, he was a prospect 2 years after I came into the MC. He actually started as a prospect in the Midnight Syn with me but jumped ship early on. The only reason he has been the president of the Henchmen for as long as he has is that they keep starting a war with other rivals, we have managed to stay off of their shit list for most of that time though. X is smaller, looks to be a pretty boy, and not one fucking scar on his face, which surprises me. He's young too, but I guess I shouldn't judge too much since I have been the VP of our chapter for the last 8 years and my current VP is pretty young as well.

"If it isn't Khan," I continue to stare stoically at him as they approach.

"Tito,"

"I'm assuming this is your new VP."

"Yeah, I'm sure you have met Ash before." I nod to him standing beside me.

"Looks familiar." He mutters, "Aw, where the Fur-ster," he asks.

"What the fuck did he just call me?" Fury asks into my ear, and I have to fight off a chuckle.

"Had other things to attend to tonight," I tell him and he looks a little hurt.

"More important than me?" He asks and I nod my head.

"Tito we have businesses we have to keep running as well." He nods his head understanding.

"Khan, let's you and I take a walk." Ash steps up with his hand on his gun and I see Lex and Blaze move forward as well, I slightly tilt my head and they all remove their hands from their weapons.

Tito looks a little impressed as Ash says, "Prez, you let me know and I'll shoot him myself." Staring right at Tito not flinching when X steps up to him as if he's going to hit him. Which makes Tito roar with laughter.

"Oh, your Prez is safe with me, for now." And he motions for me to follow him as we walk down the floating dock at the marina. We walk for a few minutes until I stop him.

"Tito, are we taking a romantic moonlit walk." And he laughs. "What did you want to talk about?"

"Kid," he looks at me and I want to rip his fucking tongue out of his mouth, "let me give you some advice on running the MC." I laugh out and look at him.

"Give me advice. Tito, don't ever forget that I gave you your prospect patch, myself. Just because you decided to turn your back on your brothers who were loyal to you because you saw a club that you could move through the ranks quicker... doesn't mean that I forget about all of that" oh yeah, that's why Tito and I don't get along and I can tell that I struck a nerve with that part, "Just because you have twenty years on me doesn't take away from the fact that I have been in this life a little bit longer than you have." I stop and I look at him right in the eyes, stepping in close to him so that only him and I, well and Fury, Ace, and Ash, can hear the words I'm saying. "and while we're at it stay the fuck out of my territory, if not I'll put a fucking bullet in your head."

"Is that a threat?" He looks at me trying me.

"You're fuckin' right, it is. Now, is there something that you want to talk to me about, cause if not I have much better places I could be right now?" My favorite part about this job is scaring the shit out of men who think that they're tough. Emphasis on thinks.

"Alright," he pauses, "there's a place that I'm looking at in Sonston End. It's on the edge of town."

"Tito, what did I just say." I roll my eyes.

"Khan, look we can work out a deal. What if we pay you a percentage for the place?" Aw, shit. I have to get out of this without promising shit.

"Let me talk to the club."

"Bullshit, you're the president now you can make the fucking decisions."

"I know that you were only a part of the Syndicate for a few months, but that's never the way that we have run things. As I said, we'll put it up to a vote." All I can hear is Fury saying *fuck that shit* in my ear, but I'm not sure if he's still upset about the Fur-ster comment. As well as an *already voted it's a fuck him!* from Ace. "I'll put it up to a vote." I turn around and walk back up to the dock knowing that Ash will let me know if he pulls a gun on me or anything because I can see Ash from where I walk. I also want Tito to feel like I'm not fucking scared of him at all. When I get back up to the parking lot I motion for Lex and Blaze to grab the bag out of the truck and bring it over.

"What is this?" Tito asks me as he walks back up. "Think of it as a gift for your understanding." The bag contains a handful of guns, some weed, and a little bit of the party supplies which they usually buy from us. "It's not much, but it's all we could get together on such short notice"

"Prez," I hear come through my ear, and Ash and I both straighten up, "you've got incoming. 6 bikes heading your way." Fury comes through saying.

"Ace, go towards the marina. We're going to sit here. Let us know if we miss someone coming in."

"Tito," I shake my head, looking down. "Why are you trying to fuck us?" I ask him mere seconds before the bikes pull into the parking lot. As Blaze and Lex pull their guns on the 6 bikers pulling into the lot. The black SUV continuing Ace and his group pull in right behind them and all 4 guys jump out guns drawn. I take two steps up to Tito and pull out both of my guns one drawn on Tito and one drawn on X. "Tell your men to get back on their fucking bullshit bikes and run back home. Or both of you will go down at the same time."

"They'll shoot you if you shoot me…"

"It would be so worth it," I smirk back to Tito. Nothing is more terrifying than a man who doesn't give a shit if he lives or dies.

He contemplates the deal at hand. "But come on let's be serious. I would much rather be doing other things tonight than cleaning up 8 bodies. Tell your men to go home." Tito lifts his hand up and the 6 bikers, climb back onto their bikes, leaving just as they came. I lift my head just slightly and watch as the 4 guys get back into the SUV and move out of the marina as well.

"At least we know now what to expect for next time." I hear X say and I laugh.

"If I played all of my cards, you wouldn't be riding back home tonight." X looks shocked. While I'm still facing X, I cock my right arm back and with the pistol still in my hand, I slap Tito across the face. I watch as Tito's face moves with the force of my hit and then his body falls to the ground. X pulls out his gun and points it at me. "I wouldn't do that," I mutter as I point around him. Blaze and Lex are now standing behind him with their guns pointed at X as well as Ash has his drawn in front of him. As Tito lays on the ground I kneel down over him, "Stay out of my fucking territory." I stand back up and hear X yelling at me.

"I'll fucking kill you. I don't need my gun… you fucking pussy. Can't fight with your hands." I motion to the rest of the guys to put their weapons down. As I hear Tito mutter a pathetic groan for him to stop.

"X, want to know how I got my name?" I say to him as I place my gun back into my holster, smirking at him as he raises his fists. "This is a bad idea," I tell him before he charges at me, swinging. I duck his first couple of swings before I let him land one. It's not hard enough to break the skin, or even to bruise. I fail pretty badly at trying not to laugh.

My laughter fuels his anger even more as he charges me again, swinging a couple more times, I duck and dodge those as well. I can see him breathing heavy right before I strike. Let him tire himself out. Run all of his energy out before I attempt anything. All it takes is landing one perfectly placed punch and then I watch X become unsteady on his feet before he falls to the ground.

"Shit Khan, did you have to do that?" Tito snaps at me.

"No, if you would have taught your VP not to run his mouth. It wouldn't have had to happen." I laugh as I nod to Blaze and Lex to come and help load X as well as his bike into the van.

Want to know what's worse than laying someone out. Helping them back up afterward.

CHAPTER TEN

...After that kiss. He's coming.
Maybe in more ways than one.

BILLIE

My head is buzzing when I get back to the car and Lucy sits in the driver's side. "Holy shit," she mutters as I slide in.

"Yeah, holy shit."

"That was the hottest kiss I've ever seen" I nod my head as she puts the car into drive and I watch Dax ride off to the other side of the parking lot and a black truck with dark tinted windows pulls out behind him. I can't help but wonder about what kind of meeting he has at this time of night, but then I remember the whole 1% things and the fact that I'm sure he has guns under his vest and his torso felt harder than normal and I try and push the thoughts out of my head. "Although," she starts talking again as we pull onto the street in the direction of her house, "I can't decide if it was that kiss or just him that has me more turned on." She ponders and I look at her shaking my head.

"Lucy,"

"What?" She asks innocently looking at me. "He is fucking sexy."

When we get home I run into my room, "Luc, watch my phone if he texts, let me know."

"What are you doing?" she asks.

"Shaving." And Lucy looks at me shocked, "You know just in case." I mumble at her which causes her to start laughing.

I turn the shower on and step into it, reaching for my shaving cream, and razor. I shave nearly my entire body.

An hour later, after getting out of the shower, after I have retouched my makeup, and I realize that I never gave the address to Lucy's place to Dax before I left him.

"I never gave him the address." I look at Lucy as she sits in the living room and she laughs. "Should I be concerned that he didn't seem worried about getting it though? Maybe he doesn't really intend on coming over."

"After that kiss. He's coming. Maybe in more ways than one." She looks at me in a sarcastically questioning expression.

"Lucy!" I yell at her hitting her legs as we hear the rumble of a motorcycle coming down the road. "Now, should I be concerned that I didn't need to tell him where you lived?" I ask her and she laughs.

"Probably," she looks at him again, "but a man with that sort of power is kind of sexy. And with that, I'm going to bed." She walks back to her bedroom as I walk to the door and open it.

Watching Dax stand and dismount his bike in one swift movement. When he looks up at me I see the corners of his mouth turn up. "Princess," he calls to me as he walks up to the porch then leans over and kisses me once more. "You ready to hash this all out." I can think of about a dozen other things that I would rather do. But I nod

my head showing him to the room that I'm staying in. When I turn on the lights, I look at him standing there and I look confused as I pick up his hand.

"Dax, is this blood on your hand?" I ask him and he looks down concerned before his eyes go wide when he realizes that it is.

"I'll be right back" he mutters as he walks into the bathroom and I hear the sink turn on. When he comes back he smiles, "Sorry, about that." He sits down and slides closer to me.

"Whose blood was that?" I ask him and he shakes his head. "Dax," I look at him.

"I had a meeting I had to go to." Is all he says. "What did you want to yell at me about earlier?" He asks me and I can't help but smirk and look down.

"Sorry about that, I don't know what came over me. We were driving home and you were getting out of the SUV when we were passing the shop and I told Lucy to pull in. I'm sorry, I held you up." I tell him and he smirks, just a little bit.

"Never be sorry for that." He brings his face close to mine and I have to control my breathing.

"Why did you say that you'd be there waiting to make sure he never got me back?" My words come out in a whisper but I force them out.

"Because," he says as he leans into me before picking me up, sitting me down on the dresser, and leaning into me even more he kisses the crook of my neck and his left arm comes around my body pulling me close to his so that he is now standing between my legs, "I would never," he places the next kiss slightly above the last one, "let you cheat," he mumbles it against my skin and it causes all the nerve ending in my body to be on edge, "but if he fucked up," he places another kiss following the same trail he has been taking, "all bets are off." He mumbles places the last kiss just below my jawline and I tremble underneath him, he pulls back his face and looks at me with the most intense eyes I've ever seen, and says, "Cause I won't stop until I get you."

I try to lighten the mood a little bit, "And what if I don't want you."

"Do you not want me," he asks me, leaning further into me and planting his hands on both sides of my hips, but not kissing nor touching any of my body. "Does your body not react when you see me?" He asks, letting only his breath touch my skin. "Does your pussy not get wet when I'm this close to you?" I want to say no to all of the above statements I really do, but I can't. So instead, I don't say a word. I just sit there. Trying to think of one witty thing to say back to him. As his face is mere inches from mine. "Baby, just tell me you don't want me as much as I want you and I'll leave you alone." I turn my head just enough which is enough for him to take as an answer. His lips are on mine quickly, they are hungry as he presses into me, scooping me off of the dresser and spinning us before laying me onto the bed. He lifts my shirt off of my body, pulling it over my head trailing kisses down my chest, between my breasts, and onto my stomach. But as he trails his kisses back up my body all I can think about is seeing him shirtless. I pull at his shirt and he laughs. "Give me a second." He says as he gets up and removes his jacket, where I see guns in a holster clipped in.

"Dax?" It comes out as a question. And he stops what he is doing and looks at me. I'm sure that my eyes have questions and he sighs as he takes them off. And places them with his cut. He pulls his shirt up over his head and exposes the Kevlar vest which he pulls off and places it with his shirts, lastly, he pulls off the white t-shirt which sits underneath his Kevlar and turns back to look at me.

"Sorry, I should have left them in the truck." He mutters as he struts back over to me and covers me with his body once again. Feeling his skin on mine causes me to not be able to think clearly. I cannot help myself as I reach for his belt and flip it open. Before I can even move his pants, mine are already sliding down my legs. I kick them off and he stands up kicking off his boots and letting his pants fall down to the floor leaving him in only his black boxer briefs with a very promising bulge. He turns around to me and I gasp as I'm sure he can see my eye bulge out slightly. "Like what you see?" He raises his eyebrows and then I look away. I have never seen a man quite like him… at least closeup and in the flesh. Brad was never this fit and… *what am I doing?* How could I have just left my husband and now have a nothing man nearly naked in my bed?

As if he can sense my hesitation he looks at me, "princess, you okay?" He mutters as he comes closer to me and sits down, next to me. "I'm sorry," he mutters looking down, "I was kind of spun up from tonight and pushed it too far. I know that you just split up." He mutters as he slides up to the headboard and motions for me to come to him. He places me into his side and I nuzzle my head into his chest. I can't help but run my fingers within the divots of his muscles he flinches at first and then lets me fall into a pattern of tracing his abs. Until I get to the lower "v" lines as I start to run over them with my fingers he takes a sharp gasp and then smacks my hand away. "Oh princess, you can't keep doing that." And I look up to him with innocent eyes and he laughs, "You keep doing that, that's going to keep happening." He says pointing down to the expanding bulge that continues to grow. "I have no problem sitting here just like this and talking or falling asleep or whatever, but you keep doing that and it's going to drive me insane."

"Where's Ella?" I ask him as he lays drawing small lines on my arms with his fingertips.

"At home."

"By herself?" I ask him and he laughs, slightly.

"Not really. My house is very close to the clubhouse. There are always people at the clubhouse." I nod my head. Wondering how close is close.

"She doesn't stay at the clubhouse?" He laughs loudly and then quickly stops.

"Absolutely not, I'm sorry to laugh like that. I keep forgetting that civilians don't understand." I look at him questioning. What could he possibly mean about understanding?

"Women aren't allowed?" I ask him which causes him to laugh again.

"I mean there are… ol' ladies." I guess he catches my questioning look, "it's a term of endearment. It's what we call women that the guys are in a serious relationship with."

"But only them" and he shakes his head again.

"Not really." His face falls and he leaves it like that.

"Then what?" I can feel him uncomfortably wiggling underneath me now.

"There's Roxy, she takes care of everything around the clubhouse."

"But no one else?" I can't help but ask him.

"Well, there are some girls that hang around." And it all makes sense to me then.

"Oh, so the dancers from the club?"

"Um, well, different from them as well… there's kind of an expectation with the girls who hang around the clubhouse." And I look at him, understanding.

"Oh," I mutter and let the topic die off. "What's the whole story behind the name?" I ask him, to question him. Only he just shakes his head.

"You're not ready for that one just yet." I look up at him cutting my eyes. "Okay, fine. I'm not ready to tell you that one yet."

"Why?"

"Because, I just got you right here and I'm not ready for you to leave yet…" he trails, looking over to me like he is honestly speaking. He stiffens up and looks over at me, instantly changing the subject. "I have no idea what I'm doing with Ella." I hear his tone in his voice and can't help but wonder what he's beating himself up over.

"What do you mean?" He sighs and pulls away from me just a little.

"I'm just worried that I'm not doing something right." And I laugh shaking my head. "What?"

"Dax, the sole fact that you're asking that question means that you are doing better than the majority of parents that I have met."

"How so?" He looks at me questioning.

"A lot of parents that I talk to, especially now, at this school in particular, since a lot of them have money, like more money than one person should, they think that whatever they do is the best.

That their child should never and could ever need anything that they are not already doing. They think that they are the perfect parent. So, when their child asks for something or is showing signs of anything and I tell them. They pretty much tell me I'm fucking stupid and full of shit. Yet you, someone who has only had custody of a child for mere months. Who went from living a completely carefree life to now having to worry about someone else all of the time. Actually asks, listens to her, worries about what you're doing and the impact that it has on her."

"I wouldn't say completely carefree. With the club…" I can't help but hold my hand up stopping him.

"That's a little bit different. Now you have a person who is impacted from nearly every decision that you make whereas before those decisions would only impact you." He nods his head.

"Is that why it's so terrifying?"

"I dunno, the only thing that I can tell you is it's the reason as to why I haven't had kids yet."

"Yeah, me too," He laughs and adds, "yet, that somehow didn't stop me from getting one." And I can't help but laugh harder, "Shit, I shouldn't say that. I love Ella, always have. Half of the time she has taken care of me." I laugh to myself, "Seriously, when my ex-wife and I split and Ella's mom took off. I moved in with them for a few years, you know to help out. Can't tell you how many times I would wake up hungover as hell and she would have laid out water and Advil, or brought breakfast."

"You and Oz are close?" I ask him and he laughs.

"Yeah, he was my mentor."

"How are you handling him getting arrested?" He doesn't answer my question, which is all the answer I need and instead he lets the moment pass. His eyes are closed as I look up at his face and before I can stop myself my mouth starts moving.

"How'd you get this scar?" I ask him as I run my fingertips along the left side of his face, right along his cheekbone. He closes his eyes for a second, leaning into my touch before smiling.

"Oh, you noticed that?" He asks in a way that makes me laugh like most people don't see it. I nod my head as I roll my eyes, "Um," he pauses and then breaths again, "it was just a fight I got into, it was a long time ago."

"You get into a lot of fights?" I can't help the words as they leave my mouth thinking back to the blood on his hand earlier.

"Try not to, only try to get into them when they are justified." He shrugs.

"Was this one justified?" I can't help but ask.

"Absolutely," he pauses and laughs a little, "it actually turned out to be one of the best times I've ever had." I can't help but let my jealousy flare up as I shift uncomfortably, "it's not like that. One day I'll tell you all about it, but it's late and you need sleep." His voice grows quieter as he speaks.

Right before I feel myself fall asleep I feel his breath even out.

CHAPTER ELEVEN

...but the whole time all I could think about was licking the lines to your peen ravine.

BILLIE

When I wake in the morning I hear Dax's phone buzzing in his pocket from the other side of the room. We are still laying in the bed and my head is still on his chest. I nudge him a little bit and his eyes flutter open. "Your phone's ringing," I whisper to him and he nods his head.

"5 more minutes," he whispers back rolling over to face me, wrapping me in his arms, and nuzzling into me. I giggle as whiskers tickle my face and I catch a smile forming on his face... which is followed by a groan as his phone continues to buzz from the other side of the room.

"Go, get it." He moves out of the bed and into the bathroom with his phone in hand, closing the door behind himself.

I get up from the bed, grabbing some clothes, to walk into the kitchen but when I open the door I find Lucy standing much too close to the door. "Luc?" I mutter and she stands up suddenly

"What?" Her eyes are wide.

"Were you trying to…" I say pointing from where she stands to the door that I just came out of.

"What? No." She says as I hear the bathroom door open and Dax walks up to me with his shirt in hand.

"I have to take off," he says coming around the into door way. And looks to Lucy, and smiles, "You must be Lucy," he says sticking his hand out and she stands not saying a word standing and staring at him. I cough out breaking her concentration.

"Oh, yes. It is so good to se-meet you" she says and he chuckles for a second. Then shoves his arms through the holes of his shirt and slides it onto his body. "Noooo," Lucy whispers from the hallway and I hear him laugh under his breath from behind me.

"I'll see you in a little bit," I say to her as I come back inside my room and look at him. "Everything okay?" I ask and he nods,

"Yeah, just the backlash from last night's meeting that I knew would happen." I watch as he presses his feet into his shoes and he slides his cut onto his body.

"I'm sorry about Lucy," I say pointing to the door. Grinning he looks down at the ground for a second.

"It's fine, there's really no point to put forth the effort if I wouldn't be okay with a reaction like that." I look at him and he shrugs. "What?"

"Taking that hasn't been the first time that someone has reacted like that." He grins, shaking his head. I'm not really sure how I would be able to handle that.

"I do recall a whimper from someone in my shop a few weeks ago when I put my shirt back on." He winks at me and I can feel my face flame. He picks up the kevlar and the holsters and we walk to the door. "I'm sorry I have to leave so early, I really wanted to take you to breakfast. I will see you soon." He leans in and places a kiss on my lips and then out the door he goes. I watch as he walks to his bike, leaning against the doorframe. And feel Lucy's presence as he stuffs his kevlar and holster into his saddlebag on the bike.

"Is that a gun holster?" I hear Lucy ask.

"Yeah,"

"Why did he have a-, " she asks without

"I have no idea." And she laughs a little. With one last look back he smirks and starts the bike and pulls off.

I close the door as I turn to look at Lucy. "Holy fuck, I didn't know that real men, like in real life could actually look like that." I laugh a little bit. Last night seemed so normal. We did nothing but talk and cuddle and laugh, but if nothing was wrong and we did nothing wrong then why can't I keep from feeling bad? Why do I feel like a terrible person? I'm trying to fool myself if I try and pretend that I don't know the reason.

That afternoon, I know why I feel so bad. After hours of thinking, the evening is falling and I find myself driving up to Sirens knowing that it's a Saturday night and he most likely will be here. I see the same blue and black bike that was sitting outside of my house this morning sitting in the parking lot and strut inside. I try to keep the imitation out of my mind as I walk inside of a club with half-naked girls trying to talk to the man who I just spent all night with mostly naked on my bed.

I see a very intimidating man looking at me as I walk in. His face looks angry even with the blonde hair that sits on his head and the bright blue eyes... as he standing blocking the entrance in all black and his eyebrows arch when I walk into the door. "Um, excuse me?" My head cocks back as his words register which causes him to smirk, "Are you lost?" He asks me which causes me to smirk.

"Is Khan around?" I ask him. Which causes confusion to form on his face as if to ask me who the fuck I am, "My name's Bil-" he stops me and nods his head waving me to follow him back into the *employees-only* area. The back of the club is a lot nicer than I would have thought that it would be.

I see the small kitchen which looks pristine, I stop kind of amazed by it. To which my escort leans in and says, "Khan's very particular about how things get done. Everything has to be clean. Exceptionally clean or he losing his shit about it... can't really blame him though. In most bars, you don't want to see their kitchen. I used to work in a couple." He shivers which makes me laugh a little bit. "Come on." He nudges me down the hallway. When he stops, I'm still preoccupied with looking at everything around, "Khan, I fou-" because I wasn't paying attention to where we were going but more to the surroundings of the club, I run smack into his back, more specifically my eyebrow hits the bottom of his shoulder blade, that's how tall he is. This causes him to cut off his sentence. He glances behind him and glares at me as I reach up and rub my eyebrow. "I found someone looking for you." I can hear the humor in his voice as the words come out. He moves back and lets me walk into the doorway.

"Billie?" My name comes out in a complete shock, yet excited tone which causes me to smile, "Wha-what are you doing here? Come in." He motions to the chairs in from of his desk. I walk into the room and sit down. The large man closes the door behind me.

"He's intimidating," I mumble causing Dax to start laughing and nods.

"Yeah, he's a pretty fucking big and scary guy... names Fury." I laugh a little. "A secret though he normally isn't as scary as he looks."

"Seems fitting." I get uncomfortable which Dax manages to pick up on immediately and looks at me curiously.

"Come here."

"Huh?"

"Come." He motions for me, with two fingers, and for whatever reason my feet betray me moving me around the desk as he sits me on his desk so I'm looking down at him. "Better. Now, what was it that you came out to a place like this to see me?" His word makes me laugh and I look down again and pick at my nails, "I've seen a lot of women, and when they do that it's never a good sign. So spill."

"Last night," I pause and he seductively, smiles, "Stop you're making what I have to say even worse." He forces his smile to turn into a scowl which makes me laugh again, smacking his chest. "Stop."

"Okay, what is it. You're making me a little nervous."

"I can't do that again... yet... again... yet." I can't decide which word I mean and shake my head after every change of the word until the last *yet*.

"We didn't do anything." He whispers to me, "Dear God, it's worse than I thought."

"What?" I look at him confused.

"Had it been so long since you had sex with him that you forgot," his face lights up with excitement then he adds, "Or did he just convince you that's what sex was?" I'm not sure if it's the playfulness in his voice or what he's saying that makes me laugh more.

"Shut up, I'm serious. I know that technically we didn't do anything," he nods his head to confirm my point, "but the whole time all I could think about was licking the lines to your peen ravine."

His entire head jerks in his confusion as he says, "My what?" I roll my eyes and tug at his shirt raises it up just slightly so that the lines which form the 'v' can show. His laughter erupts louder than I have heard it before. "Sorry," he mummers as he wipes the water which is sliding down from his eyes away. "I've heard it called a lot of things before, but never heard it called that before." Little fits of laughter come out afterward like aftershocks of an earthquake until after minutes he finally calms himself down. "Okay, serious now. Even though that was-," he giggles again, "a crazy hot image of you doing it yet a hilarious name for it. I understand what you mean. When you say not yet..."

"I just feel weird about the whole thing you know, until it's all finalized." His lips purse into a fine line.

"When's that?" He asks

"January. Can't be finalized until 6 months after the papers are served." I pause, to see his reaction which isn't great until I finish the rest of it which is the hardest part for me. "I know that this isn't anything," my words start coming out quicker, "and I know that you... well, you're, you."

"What do you mean by I'm, me?" He asks

"You're Khan-," he stops me.

"First, I wish I didn't but I understand you wanting to wait... it's kind of sweet in a weird way, that is going to be terrible for me. You let me know when you're ready and I'll be here." He smiles at me. I try to say something but he puts his hand up, "Second, I didn't really get the name Khan from that." I look at him questioning and he sighs, "Okay, not only for that reason." He pauses before he looks up to me again, "Fuck it, you'll have 5 months to process this. I got the name because Genghis Khan well he killed a lot of people..." his sentence trails as if telling me that is the end of the story. I wish I could say that I am shocked or that this fact bothers me but it doesn't.

"So, you've killed 40 million people?" I look at him smirking and laughs.

"Of course you would know that number off the top of your head." I laugh not telling him that I have looked up Genghis Khan, since meeting him, "Well, no, but... fuck I shouldn't be telling you this... the first few years I was around." He motions with his hands around insinuating around the club, "I ended up killing a lot of people. A lot of people." He looks to me with a more serious expression the second time he says the words then pauses as if something is sinking in for the first time, "Maybe this time is best... maybe you will find someone who-"

"What are you talking about?" I ask him and he looks away from me. His eyes drop and he looks sad.

"I'm not a good person. I'm actually a really bad person. Not only have I killed before, but I will kill again, it's only a matter of time. And I wouldn't change a single one of them that I have killed."

I pause thinking of the right words to say, "Why did you kill them?" I ask in a quiet voice. He looks up to me, questioning me. Almost as if to question me not being phased by the fact that he's killed people but instead interested in the reasoning.

"Occupational hazard." He lets out a sad laugh, "In my life, many times it's either kill or be killed. Other times, The people just have it coming. Those without any sort of morals." I think he expects this to scare me, but it doesn't… and I can't quite put my finger on why. Maybe he can sense that it doesn't seem to be bothering me. "But we are going to have to get out of here, or I will not be able to resist myself from kissing you again." His words are carefully thought out. Bringing the thought of our kiss last night to me and causes my head to go a little fuzzy and butterflies start in my stomach again, "Stop looking at me like that." His words are deep and rugged they send chills throughout my body.

"Like what?" I ask him pretending to be coy.

"Like you want to rip my clothes off. I'm trying to respect what you want here." He says to me pushing his chair back. He stands and moves around the desk.

I can't help but pout as I toss my head back, leaning back onto his desk, "Ugh," letting my head come around to look at him as he stands as far as he can get away from me in this small office, "but it's so hard." I pout like I hadn't made the rules to this.

"You have no idea." His words are very matter of fact and they come out in a gravely, deep tone and that sets all of my endorphins into overdrive. I laugh at first until I look over and see him, the look in his eyes smolder at me and suddenly I want to repeat his words to him.

I turn my body on his desk letting my legs hang off of the side of the desk instead of behind it. "Stop looking at me like that." I breathlessly say to him.

The corner of his mouth turns up as he stalks over to me, like a lion right before it pounces, he stops standing between my knees and looking down at me. "Like what?" He asks

"Like you want to devour me." My words are even quieter.

"But baby," he leans his head down, his right hand comes up and grasps the back of the neck, and gently brings our faces closer to mine, without his lips touching mine he mutters, "that is exactly what I want to do right now." He pulls back, lets his hand fall from my neck, and takes one big deep breath which causes his entire demeanor to change. Playfully he slaps my hip twice and says, "Now, get that perfect ass off of my desk and let's get out of here before we do something that we both regret." I get up off of the desk, a little sad about his choice of words, but I try to push it down and not say anything.

That's just your self-conscious talking, I tell myself.

He places his hand on the small of my back as we walk down the hall and towards the main room. Fury is looking at us when we make it into the hallway which appears next to the bar. I stop when Dax pulls my arm back and glances down at me as Fury says something into his ear and he nods a couple of times. The music is loud as the girls start dancing on stage and I start to watch them. They are dancing and spinning around on the pole. As they dance all I can think about is how painful it must be to dance on the pole as they do.

Suddenly, I'm pulled from behind, and for reasons that I'm not sure why I am standing behind Dax and Fury as I hear someone shouting.

"Fucking seriously," I hear the voice that I recognize yelling at Dax. "She's my fucking wife. I can talk to her anytime I want to." He shouts again. I put my hand upon Dax's arm. He glances back at me and then steps to the side. I'm surprised when Brad lunges at me trying to grab me.

Fury grabs his arm, twisting it behind his back. "You don't fucking touch her." I can hear him loudly say into his ear. "You want to talk to her. You can do it in front of us." Brad starts to object until Fury twists his arm just slightly and he immediately stops.

"Go home." I hear Dax say to him, "This isn't the time nor the place to do this."

"Fuck you," he yells. The music has now stopped playing, the dancers have stopped dancing, and without surveying the club I know that everyone is watching the scene unfold. "You're only saying that because you're fucking my wife." He shouts at Dax.

Dax starts to say something else, but I place my hand on his arm again. He looks down and sighs, taking a step to the side so I can step up, "Let him go." I say to Fury, who looks at Dax, I see his ever so slight of a head nod and then Fury lets go of his arm. "Brad, I'm not fucking anybody." My use of the work fucking makes all three of them step back, which is the good thing about not swearing much.

"I saw him with you at Lucy's house." *He did what?* "I watched him kiss you before going inside." I sit quietly for a few minutes trying to mentally process what he has just admitted to. "You fucked him. You're a fucking whore." I see Dax growing angry, I press my hand to his side and he stops from saying anything, "Let's face it, anyone who shows up after midnight and doesn't leave until the next morning is a fucking booty call, you're just another one-," I'm not sure if it's fear or anger that courses through me.

"It's you," my words come out. In almost a whisper and I'm not sure if anyone hears them. Before I realize what I'm doing my fist makes contact with his face. Brad loses his balance and stumbles a bit before he falls to the ground. I start to rush him to hit him again as his body hits the ground but suddenly my feet are no longer on the ground. I feel arms around my body pulling me back and I'm screaming at Brad. "YOU'RE FUCKING FOLLOWING ME!" I scream at the top of my lungs. And if I wasn't so mad I would laugh at the shocked look on Fury's face. Dax places me back on the floor, unwinding his arms from around me, but I can still feel him standing behind me, right behind me with his hand still on my back. "You humiliated me. You hurt me. You left me no choice. I never did anything with anyone because no matter how broken we had grown. I still had hope." I'm sure after my uncomfortable confession Dax told the DJ to start playing the music again. To give us a little bit more privacy. I watch Brad pick himself off of the floor and step into me so I can hear him. Fury is right behind him. Dax is still close enough to me that if Brad jumps at me again he will catch him.

"Just admit it to me that you fucked him." He looks at me and then up to Dax.

"You only want me to have slept with someone else to make yourself feel better, I won't lie to you for your own benefit." My words are much calmer as I look at him next, "But Brad, I promise you this. You come after Lucy, you come after anyone that I care about, you jeopardize their safety by any means." I pause stepping into him, "I'll fucking kill you myself." I can see Fury's eyes widen. I stand still and start to turn around when Dax steps up. If you weren't paying very close attention to both of them you wouldn't see Dax look at Fury and you wouldn't see Fury's slight nod to his head. But this slight movement grabs my attention enough to stay and watch what happens.

"Brain," Dax looks at him eyeing him. I'm sure purposefully calling him the wrong name, "this is the second time in a month that you have tried to start shit with me in my club." His words are precise, his mannerisms almost scare me, if I was at the other end of his actions they would. I realize, that this is Khan. He steps in closer to Brad, so close that Brad has to look up to him to look at him, "Don't ever come back here. If you step foot in that door, or any other businesses that I'm associated with," everyone knows when he says *me* he also means the Syndicate. "And if you come after Billie or anything like that ever again. I will take it as a personal attack on myself." Brad's eyes grow larger yet Khan's voice doesn't waver, "I know you're not that stupid, so I'm sure you already know this, but just in case you don't." he smirks at this statement because he's pointing out the obvious, "being the president," Brad's eyes bulge out slightly almost as if he didn't hear about that, "a personal attack on me typically means a personal attack on the entire club. I'll let you figure out the rest." He pats Brad's cheek twice, squeezes his face slightly, turns around, grabs my hand, and pulls me back into the office.

I start to shut the door. "Leave it open." He tells me still standing and looking at me... I frown and I see his shoulder jump up like he laughed a little before he turns to look at me, eyes blazing, "Princess, you shut that door and I won't be able to control myself." He steps into me, his face softens, Khan is gone now, and strokes my arm, "Especially after how hot you just were. I want nothing more than to rip off all your clothes and give you some positive reinforcement for standing up for yourself." I laugh and look away. "And just so we're clear, by positive reinforcement I mean bending you over my desk and giving you the best orgasm of your life." I have to squeeze my thigh together to try and relieve the pressure. I watch him as he walks over to his chair, sitting down and I lean against the side of his desk.

"Billie," my name sounds more like a question and when I look back over to him and see his concerned face he pauses and starts again, "what did you mean by he's following you?" I don't answer him, but I sit quietly. "Billie, please tell me what's going on." He moves his chair a little closer to me and reaches over for my hand.

"I've been getting weird calls at work. No one is on the phone, it's every Monday at 8:30. It started the first week after he got the divorce papers. Then they started coming to my cell phone and even though I don't answer because there's no caller ID there's just breathing on the voicemail. I swear I keep seeing the same car driving past the house. It just drives down the street circles the cul-de-sac and then drives back up. It was stopped outside of the house the other night when I was going to sleep." He looks at me and I swear I see our rage in his eyes, "I keep getting this weird feeling like either someone has been in my room and then other times I feel like I'm being watched, and last week... I dunno it was probably just a dream." I tell him.

"What do you think may have happened?" He urges me to tell him.

"I was drunk, but I woke up in the middle of the night and I could have sworn that someone was standing at the end of my bed. I'm not sure if it was a dream or not though. But now with him saying that he was outside of the house last night. " I hear a noise outside of the office.

"He's out of the building at least." Fury walks into the office and we jump apart. He looks confused as looks from Dax to me. "O-kay,"

"I should go," I mutter and they both look at me.

"Fuck no you're not," Dax shouts at me and I jump a little bit. "After what you just told me there's no fucking way you are leaving, by yourself." I see the look the Fury gives Dax and without even looking over to him Dax starts to explain in a cliff notes version, "He's harassing her, calling her not saying anything. Driving down her street, he may have broken in…"

"We don't know he did any of those things" I cut him off making sure to say what I need to say. I am surprised when the voice which starts talking next is from behind me.

"So, you think that you file for divorce from your husband and it's just a coincidence that all of these things start happening, immediately afterward." Dax nods to Fury to continue to talk almost as if he knows that he has more to say, "And Khan's right. You're not going anywhere by yourself especially after you just laughed at his dick."

"I did what?" I ask him, confused.

"Metaphorically, you laughed at his dick. You hurt his pride, even if you were right, you yelled at him in front of everyone, you threatened him a little bit, and no matter of how fucking hot-," Dax growls at him and he waves him off, "regardless if he," he points to Dax, "tries to kick my ass later for saying this. Punching him in the face was fucking hot, you still, metaphorically, laughed at his dick he's going to come after you for revenge." Dax nods his head.

"That's why I added in the part about if he came after you. You happened to forget yourself when you threatened him." I'm not really sure what to say so I just sit in silence for a moment. Until Dax mutters, "I'll be right back," and he walks out of the office.

"I'm sorry," it comes out as a whisper but Fury clears his throat, "I am. Bringing trouble into your life."

"Meh, we've gone to war for less." He tells me and I don't know what to make of that.

"War?" I ask him he doesn't answer but instead changes the subject.

"Billie?" He comes out as a question and I'm not sure if he wants to ask me something or if he's not sure if that's my name or not. "Why are you here?" He asks me and I look at him shocked. Then he laughs a little, "Khan's a little rough around the edges. The life we have is hard and is tough on relationships. You're a high school principal. You're so sweet and innocent." He smirks to himself as he starts to say the next sentence, "You're like a real-life walking Belle; the original, not the one with Emma Watson, naive but you try to take the world on anyway." I look at him almost appalled.

"Didn't she accept him for who he was, fall in love with him, break the curse, and make him happy?" He sits back. "Just because people look innocent or seem sweet and naive doesn't mean that you know anything about them or what they can take. If I am Belle, I am Emma Watson's Belle, where they made her be a badass princess who could take care of herself." I stand up and walk out of the room.

Fuck him.

CHAPTER TWELVE

...Why is it always a fucking Mustang?

KHAN

Well, tonight has taken a few different turns that I didn't expect.

When Billie was sitting on my desk I thought it was going to be the best night ever. Then she had to say she couldn't do anything until everything was finalized I thought my blue balls would kill me. She kept toying with me, it took everything in me not to push her back onto my desk and fuck her right there. I couldn't. I decided last night when I looked back I saw that she would feel bad about herself. I could never let it happen then. When I finally let myself feast on her... there will be no questioning that she wants it. She won't second guess it. She won't have any reservations.

Then she said that today. As much as it pains me to do it. I will not let it happen. Somehow she means more to me than anyone ever has. I want nothing to make this woman happy. When she started to reference the whole *'you're you'* thing. I wanted to punch myself... she was going to say go ahead and fuck whoever I wanted to. Which honestly makes me fucking want only her so much more.

That means I can't be alone with her.

Maybe I will just not have to see her until January. At least, that's what I was thinking until her husband came in. I'm not sure how she made the connection that he was following her before I did. I wanted to rip his fucking throat out. When Billie punched him in the face, holy shit. Not sure if I have ever wanted to fuck someone more... I had to go jerk off in the bathroom... which is a first for me... especially here. I can usually find someone to fuck, but unless it's Ms. Billie Saxs, I don't want to fuck anyone... anymore.

This woman is going to be the death of me.

Flipping through my contacts I dial Ash, "Hey man, I need you to do me a favor."

"What's up, Prez."

"Church in an hour. I'm taking Billie home now. Are you busy now?" I ask him trying to be somewhat considerate although I don't need to be.

"Nah, Prez. I'm at the clubhouse. Cherry is here but that's all, what you need?"

"Until I get there, can you make some phone calls? Call around reach out to anyone you can think of, ask them if they have sold anything to Billie's husband." I hang up the phone and walk into the office looking at Fury who is still sitting in the same spot looking shocked. "Where's Billie?" He shrugs, "What do you mean, you don't know?" I glare at him... now I'm kicking his ass for calling her fucking hot and losing her.

"I dunno man, she yelled at me about how Belle makes the beast happy and left the room." I pause trying to make sense of that sentence, "You seem to be in a mood right now, I'll explain that later. She kind of yelled at me and then walked out of the room."

"And you just let her leave?" I ask him and he nods his head.

"What was I supposed to do hold her against her will?"

"You could have stood in the doorway and blocked her exit, you literally take up the entire fucking doorway. Were you not in the room when her husband, who is fucked up on something was screaming at her? You said it he's going to come for revenge. So yes, if it comes down to it hold her against her will. Protect her, from herself." He knows that I don't really mean that and that I really mean he should have found her. I turn to move out of the office and stop looking back at him, "Church in an hour."

"What?"

"You were there, you gave me the nod. You agreed with me. We've got to take it up with the club."

"What are you going to do if they don't agree with us?" He asks me and I laugh.

"I'll deal with it myself." I turn and move out of the office as I move into the main room. I scan it quickly but cannot find her "Fuck me," I mutter.

"Okay," I hear as Blossom comes and runs her finger down my chest.

"Not now, seen the girl that punched that guy?" I ask her and she points to the front door. "Fuck."

"Just let me know when you want it." I look at her and she smiles.

"No," it comes out may be surprised that she would keep asking and I rush to the front door. When I open it I see that she is standing and talking to the prospects that I have working the door. "Oh, thank god," I mutter and Lenny, one of the prospects, looks at me with a weird expression. "Why did you leave the office?" I ask her, closing the distance between us and she looks away. "Hey," I step in close to her, "it's okay. I need to go." Then I hear Alfred say behind me, he's the newest one of our prospects and doesn't have a road name yet. We're working on it.

"Hey Prez, we heard that church is in an hour, everyone coming?" He asks me and I look over at him shocked. Lenny gives him a hard glare and tries to tell him not to ask while he was asking the question.

Fuck. Like I don't have enough to deal with tonight. I turn and walk over to Alfred and I stare at him in the eyes, "Do you think with your

position and the amount of time that you have been with us. That it equates you to be a part of church?" I ask him and his eyes quickly dart from side to side. "Have you showed us your loyalty?" I'm not shouting, because usually, I don't need to shout but my voice and words I can visible see it brings fear to the kid. I almost feel bad… almost. "Did we ask you to come?" I'm in this poor kid's face. Again, I *almost* feel bad.

"Well, no."

"Then how did you hear about church?" I ask him and I think he's about to piss his pants. I'm still in this kid's face when Fury walks out.

"Uh, I overheard you on the phone." Fury's at my side, getting ready to lay into the kid, but I wave him off.

"No, this one's all mine," I say without breaking my eye contact with Alfred whose eyes widen almost past their ability. "So, you're listening in on my phone calls now?" The kid shakes his head.

"No, I mean… uhhhh. I just… uhhh." He stutters over his sentence.

"Prospect, the next time that you are wanted or allowed someplace I will personally ask you myself. Just so there's no more confusion." Before I walk back over to Billie I stop at Lenny, granted Lenny is still a prospect, but he's close to getting patched. He's already proved to me everything I need to know. "Lenny, I need you, only you," I glance over to the other one for a second, "to collect the money at the end of the night, drop it, and lock up. We clear?" I ask him and he nods his head. "Don't fuck this up," I tell him and after seeing how I just handled Alfred he just nods his head. "And get your fucking friend in line." I nod my head back over to Alfred.

As I glance over I see Billie is at her car already. "Goddamnit," I mutter and I walk over to her, making sure not to run because I don't want to seem weak in front of my prospects. "Billie," she turns around and I look at her like *what the fuck.*

"I'm going to go home." She tells me and I groan. This woman's going to put me in an early grave. "I shouldn't have come here tonight."

135

"It's not safe there." I ignore her last statement as she shrugs her shoulders. "You may not give a fuck about your well-being, but I sure as shit do," I say leaning into her.

"You can't look after me forever," she tells me. I want to laugh but instead, I just stare back at her thinking *watch me*.

"Why not?" I ask.

"Ugh," she opens her door, so I reach over and shut it. She glares at me, I glare at her right back.

"Lucy's at the house, he knows that if he hurts Lucy it will hurt me more than if he actually hurts me." She says as she opens her door again. And I close it. "Seriously?"

"She can come with us. Problem solved." I exclaim to her throwing my hands out at my sides.

"Where are we going?" She asks stomping her foot… that was adorable.

"My house, then I have to go over to the clubhouse. I have to go to church."

"Church?" She asks.

"It's a meeting with my guys." She nods her head. "Is that a yes?" She shakes her head, opening her door again, causing me to groan as I once again reach over shutting her door. "Goddamnit, Billie, why do you have to be so fucking stubborn?" She opens her door again. I close it. She glares at me. I glare at her.

"Are you going to let me drive?" She opens her door

"No," I look at her like she's crazy. And push her door shut again.

"Then how is Lucy supposed to get there as well?" Door opens.

"She can ride with Fury," I tell her wishing she would just fucking listen. Closes door.

"You haven't even asked him." She tells me reaching for her door handle again.

"I swear to god Billie if you open that fucking door." My mouth barely opens as I say the words staring at her daring her. "It's how things work. I ask him if he'll do something and he agrees."

"Why are you so worried?" She asks me and I shake my head.

"Has Brad seemed different lately? He started having mood swings, anger issues?" I can tell that I'm starting to hit close to home and she slowly nods her head. "I suspect that he's on something. None of my-," I stop myself before changing my statement, "I'm not sure what he's on, but depending on what it is, may make him more dangerous and not give a fuck about anything more than he already didn't. I'm working on figuring out what it is and who is selling it to him, but I really don't want you alone until we know for sure, okay?" I say the last word moving my head down to catch her eyes so she will look at mine. "Will you come with me?" I ask her and she nods her head. "Why don't you call Lucy, see if she's home? Tell her that we are on our way." She nods her head and does just that.

Jesus Christ.

I walk over to Fury shaking my head and he cracks a smile. "I need your help," I tell him sighing.

"I like her." He says nodding over to her and I groan, glaring at him.

"She's gonna be the fucking death of me," I mutter to him and he laughs even harder.

"The door dance was adorable. You should teach a class." I can't help but roll my eyes at him.

"Fuck off." He laughs.

"What do you need, man?" He asks, goofy smirk still on his face, but seriously asking me what I need.

"Her roommate," Fury groans and nods his head understanding what I'm asking him to do. I watch her as she gets off of her phone and grabs her purse out of her car. She hurries over to where I sit on my bike next to Fury.

"Oh shit," she mutters as she grabs her key fob I'm assuming to lock her car.

The next few seconds happen in slow motion. Instead of the car beeping from locking the doors, the car starts "oops," she says as if accidentally pressing the wrong button and starting her car is something she does all of the time. Then all three of our heads turn in the direction of the sound of the explosion.

"I'M GONNA FUCKING KILL HIM!" a voice comes out of my body that I have never heard before. The amount of rage that is coursing through my body due to this man I have never felt in my entire life. I yell so loud that the shocked faces turn from looking at the car engulfed in flames to me. Even the prospects at the door are staring at me, mouths hanging open. "Billie, get on the fucking bike," I tell her and her eyes go wide. Reaching up and smoothing the parts of my hair that I'm sure are haphazardly about my head right now from my outburst, I pick up my phone and I dial the only number that can deal with this right now.

"Jeff, I have a car on fire in my parking lot."

"Damnit Dax, who have you pissed off now?" He asks me and I just shake my head even though he can't see me.

"Car isn't any of my guys." He's silent for a few minutes.

"Whose is it one of the girls?"

"None, that works for me." He pauses again and he's more confused. "Jeff, can you deal with this for me. I need to get her out of here."

"Who did it?" He asks me and I think for a minute. I could just tell Jeff who did it he's most likely on video putting it there. He would go to prison for attempted murder, but that's not good enough. I want to handle this one.

"Jeff, can you get it?"

"Yeah,"

"Thanks, I'll get all of the information you need to you." And I hang up the phone. Fury, is fuming, no pun intended, as well and as I nod to him we both pick our comms out of our pockets and put them in.

As we pull up in front of Lucy's house I stop and Billie has yet to move off of the bike. "Billie," she looks at me, still wide eyes from the explosion, "10 minutes." She nods her head as I walk with her inside. Fury walks inside first to make sure that the coast is clear. We sweep all the living spaces as we go throughout the house. I only wish that I had my Kevlar and more than my one Glock and its one clip. When we clear it we move on to the girls' rooms. Lucy hasn't come out so I knock on the door. "Lucy, you in there?" I ask her and the door flies open.

"Yeah, what's going on? Why do I need to pack?"

"I would ask you to trust me but you don't know me, so do you trust Billie?" I ask her and she nods her head, "Do you want her to be safe?" She nods her head quickly, "Do you want to get caught in crosshairs if someone comes after her," I lower my voice a little and add, "it's fine no one else can hear you." She shakes her head no. "Then hurry we only have the bikes so pack as light as you can, preferably a backpack. We can always come back later and grab more stuff if you need it." She nods her head again. "5 minutes." I say to them as I check out the front windows and I see Fury walk from the back. "See anything."

"Not yet," he tells me.

"Do you think, he thinks she was in the car?" He asks me.

"Not a fuckin' chance." He looks at me asking why, "Unless, he's just an idiot and trying to kill his wife he staked it out and watched." He saw her walk away and probably saw where she was at. "Let's go," I shout to the girls as they both come back from down the hallways with a backpack. I walk out in front and Fury takes the rear. "Lucy you're riding with me." Almost as if Fury can read my mind he agrees when Billie protests.

"No," she runs up to me, instead of listening to the fucking rules, I kiss her. It's a brief kiss but it's what I need after the last hour, after Brad coming in, and after her almost dying. I pull away from her and let my forehead rest against hers. "If we switch the two of you up and he sees it, it might confuse him so we can have a better shot of losing him." I pause, "If he even follows us." I would be shocked if he doesn't.

"Who will he go after?" She asks me and I shrug.

"I have no idea."

"Khan." Fury laughs from behind him. "He fucking hates you, dude."

"I'm not putting Lucy in that sort of danger then." I have a feeling that I'm not going to win this battle, and we really don't have the time. so I groan and just look at her again.

"Whatever, get on the fucking bike." I motion to her and she looks proud for winning.

"Slow and easy brother?" He asks me through the earpiece.

"Yeah, no need in drawing attention to ourselves unless need be," I say to him

"What?" I hear from behind me as I slow down for the light.

"Nothing," I point to my ear, "it's an earpiece."

"Wow," I smirk and shake my head at her.

"Bil, tell me if you see his car."

"Okay,"

I keep a watch on her in the side mirrors on the bike. She keeps a watch out as we roll slowly through traffic.

"Dax," she mutters from behind me. "Black mustang."

"Why is it always a fucking mustang?" Fury and I both end up saying at the same time

"Billie, hide your face. Fury, See if he turns around first." Suddenly wishing that I would have brought along Ella's full-face helmet.

I don't need Fury to tell me he is because the sign is loud. As the squealing of the tires as he speeds around is all the sign I need.

"Billie, hold on." And I speed up as we barrel around traffic trying to speed away from Brad. "At least he most likely won't start shooting until we get out of traffic." Fury laughs

"You think he's that smart?" He asks me and I laugh back, "Cross over breakaway?" He asks to me

"You read my mind, bro."

"You call it," Fury says to me and I nod my head.

"Billie, hang on." Traffic starts to lighten up, which means two things. He may be able to close in on us and he will start shooting if he has a gun. "Fury you see it."

"Yeah, over/under," he says to me. "Over/under? Over/under?"

"Over." More likely to come my way, just have to make sure there's enough room for Fury to sneak in without Brad clipping his bike.

"You got it." We both gun the bikes, pushing them to their limits. We are racing through the streets of downtown Sonston End as the clearing comes up further. There's a light coming up at the intersection of Main and Terminal that I am very clearly not slowing down for, is red, but I can see the sides. I can see that we will be clear to roll through without an issue. "Billie lean with me, okay." I don't look for her nod, but Fury tells Lucy the same thing. We are fine. No cars are coming down the road. I can see in my side-view mirror that Brad is behind me. Not sure if he knows she's on my bike or just assumes. Fury is on our right. We are both pressing our bikes to the limits and at the last second before the intersection of the light Fury flicks his wrist just enough to slow down for a second. Which is just enough for us to shoot above him towards the right and he goes below me to the left. To the left is clear. There isn't anything there. Please god, let him follow us.

"You're right he's turning." Fury calls into my comms but we have already slid down a side street. I slow down as I make the next immediate right and pull up to the stop sign as I see the back end of the black mustang. Looking both ways first I shoot out into the intersection and follow the street. It takes us a few minutes to catch up to Fury and Lucy in a parking lot of a gas station to the side.

"Let's get the fuck out of here," I say into the comms as I roll up to their location and Fury is on my right again. When we turn off onto the dirt road I start to feel the sting in my left arm and I know that there is most likely a graze of a bullet. I try to put the sting out of my mind as I'm winding the bike along the road until we reach the large building which was once an old warehouse. I hit the button for the gate to open. Driving past the old warehouse, which now on the inside actually resembles an old resort, that we restored into a safe haven for the club. We take the short trail back to my house and pull the bikes into their spots.

I wait for her to get off of the bike before I dismount and she continues to just stand there, not moving, barely breathing. I lean my head to the side to try and break her zoned out state as I reach over and unclip her helmet and she looks up at me. "What?" Her lips are slightly parted as she stands shocked.

"Holy fuck." And she leans forward and just wraps her arms around my neck, clinging, hanging on as if her life is still in danger. "I thought we were going to die." Then she leans back and looks up at me again. "Dax, you saved my life." Her look is so intense. "Twice," I fight the urge to lean down and kiss her, losing that battle, that is until Fury's voice starts from beside us.

"Yeah, had he not played the door dance with you, you would be pretty hot right now." I just look over at him trying to control myself from not smacking him, "Oh yeah!" He mutters as he looks up nodding his head as if understanding why I'm pissed with him, "Most people don't almost die more than once. Sorry, I keep forgetting." Billie's eyes grow even wider as I give her a quick kiss on her cheek.

"I'm late to this meeting." I nudge for her to follow me up to the house making sure for the girls to be on my right at all times. I don't need them freaking out more than they already are.

"Where are we?" Lucy asks no one in particular.

"This is Khan's. Well, technically it belongs to the MC. The Prez stays up here. Just makes more sense. But when Oz got arrested and

Khan got custody of Ella before he took over officially as El Presidente, we forced him to move out of the clubhouse and in here so he didn't have to uproot her if he got a new place." I glare at him, "What? Also, there wasn't a question who was going to take over."

I nearly push the girls into the living room and see all the lights are off. Fury's phone starts to ring as I bring the girls upstairs and peek into Ella's room finding that she is asleep. I bring the girls down the hallway to the spare bedroom and nod, "Lucy, you okay staying in here?" She nods her head. "Billie you can sleep in my room." She pulls her head back and looks at me. "I'll stay at the clubhouse tonight. I have a room over there. It's not a big deal."

"I don't want to put you out." She tells me and I smile.

"You're not putting me out. I promise." I smile at her and kiss her cheek again. She nods her head. "Text me if you need anything. Keep the doors locked you should be safe here."

"Should be?"

"The safest place you could be right now." I shrug, pause, and then look at her again. "But if something happens." I pull her to the closet, I can't help myself from hesitating for a moment, just one before I open it and move towards the safe in the corner. I scan in my thumbprint and hear the *clink* of the locking mechanism unlocking, I pull the door open. I take out one of the Glocks and hand it to her. "Ever used one before." She nods her head. "Okay. Remember to text me if you need anything. I'll come back over to check on you."

I come out of the house making sure to lock it back up and nod to Fury as we start to walk over to the clubhouse.

"You know you're bleeding, right?" Fury says in a calm voice as we make our way down the driveway and come up to the path that heads in the direction of the clubhouse.

"Yea, I figured, I was." Matching his calm tone.

"You want me to clean it up?"

"After, we're already late enough." I shake my head.

"Man you really haven't fucked her, yet?" I just move my head to the side and glare at him. "Seriously, last night you were gone-,"

"I'm not talking about this."

"What is going on with you, dude?"

I shrug, "I have no idea. All I know is that when I'm with her everything just seems right. Last night was probably the most memorable night and we kissed, that was it." He cocks his eyebrow at me. "I know."

"Pussy." He mutters at me and I try to stop myself from laughing.

CHAPTER THIRTEEN

...Who he... is definitely, not fucking.

KHAN

"Holy hell, you guys are like an hour late." I hear Ash say to me as we walk into the war room.

"Well, thank god you can't start without me." I throw my hands up, "What have you guys talked about?" I ask, making sure no one else has anything.

"You called the meeting." I nod, furthering my point.

"There was a door-dance," Fury says nonchalantly, trying to give them a reason as to why we are late. I try not to laugh at the confused expressions of everyone else.

"What he means to say, is there was a car that blew up, then we were chased."

"What?" Someone shouts.

"It's all a part of what I called you guys here. I had a feeling it would escalate only it escalated much faster than I anticipated.

Billie is Ella's principal at her new school. Helped me get her in."

"And they're not fucking." Fury says with a mouth full of food, sadly I'm more curious about where he got the apple he is eating than his statement and as if my stomach thinks the same thing, it growls in response.

"She also has a crazy husband, who she is in the process of getting a divorce from. In the last month, he has come into the club twice and purposefully starting shit with me. Last time he tried to threaten me. Turns out he's stalking his soon-to-be ex-wife.-" All of the guys here understand why this is an issue for me. I can also see on the majority of the faces that it's a problem for the majority of them as well.

"Who he... is definitely. not fucking." he says pointing at me and I just glare back to him as if he can hear my internal monologue shout *enough* he tosses his hands up and turns towards the group.

"Anyway, he blew up her car in the Sirens' parking lot. She was trying to get in it to drive away but I persuaded her to let me drive her."

"That's where the door dance came in." Fury mumbles.

"Her car exploded when she accidentally started it from the key fob. Then he chased us down Main Street."

"What you want us to do, Prez?" I pause how do I ask them to do this for me.

"You know we put it up to a vote. You don't have to if you don't want to. If not I will handle it by myself. She's under my protection." I tell them and they all nod.

Bullet stands up towards to back and looks at me, "He threatens you he threatens all of us. If she is under your protection she is

under all of ours." There are mummers of agreement from everyone in the room.

"Yeah, Prez," Fury stands up and I give him a side-eye as he shrugs, "told you I liked her."

"What's the plan?" They ask me.

"I need someone with eyes on him at all times, preferably two at a time. I don't care how you split it up, just send me updates. I also need someone to reach out to everyone we know to try and find what drugs he is on. And I want to run a tox-screen on him to make sure of the drugs he is on."

"How do you want us to do that?" I hear from the back.

"I don't really care, get creative. Ace can you hack into his computer see what he has been up to." He nods his head. I get up and start to walk out of the room, but I pause and turn around looking back to the men sitting in front of me, "One other thing, if he catches anyone, try not to kill him, this one is all mine." I nod to Fury, who gets up out of the chair he's sitting in and walks with me out, he grabs his medical bag and we walk out of the club and back towards the house. Still, I can't really bring myself to call it my house.

I hear a gasp as I pull my shirt off in the kitchen and look over to see Billie and Lucy standing in the doorway. It's not a gasp like Lucy did this morning when I was leaving their house, it's a horrified gasp.

"I'm fine," I mutter to Billie as she just walks to me. And looking at the wound I then look back as I awkwardly look to the backside of my arm and see a small gash. When Fury walks into the room he has his sutures in his hands with him.

Fury walks to the table and sits down. "He'll be fine," he says reassuring Billie. Sitting down the bottle of whiskey he brought with him on the table. He grabs a couple of glasses and pours me and him a drink and motions to the girls. They both nod.

"I just feel bad, this is because of me." She mumbles. She reaches for my chest to touch it. *I'm fine* I mouth the words to her as I reach up and lay my hand over the top of hers.

"You know," Fury starts. "I've caused your boy some stitches as well," she looks over at him questioning. "Yeah, the first night that I met him."

Fury had finished college in 3 years, was accepted into med school at Johns Hopkins, and was three years in when he dropped out, he bought a bike, and he left. He didn't have a destination in mind but ended up in Sturgis, South Dakota. Right in the middle of bike week.

"Ow, motherfucker," I snap as Fury stabs the needle into a tender spot in my arm.

"Stop being a pussy." Lucy and Billie's laughs make me smirk.

"Remember when you used to be nice to me," I ask him causing him to laugh. "No laughing, you'll fuck it up."

"You mean that one fucking time I was nice to you."

"Yeah, that time, what happened to that?"

"I got to know you." He tells, "You should be worshipping me... you know how much worse that scar would be if I didn't stitch it up." He says point up to my face.

"Yeah, you keep reminding me."

"Wait, that's how you got that scar?" Billie asks and I laugh nodding.

"Yeah, saved him from getting his ass jumped and haven't been able to get rid of him since," I say causing Fury to laugh once more as he stabs me and I wince.

"That's not the whole story, and I held my own." He explains, "I was in a weird place my whole family had just died..."

KHAN
PART I

Through the window I see this kid walking around outside of Full Throttle. Poor kid, I can't help but think as I see his brand new all-leather outfit as he clearly stands out in this crowd. We don't expect you to dress a certain way; however, by the way, that he is dressed and since none of his leather is creased... at all... it's pretty apparent that he is a baby biker. My phone rings, groaning I pick it up,

"Khan," her voice comes through the earpiece and I roll my eyes as I nod to Chell for another whiskey.

"Yes," I don't know why she keeps calling, she's the one who decided to leave. All I wanted to do this week is come out here and do nothing, but she has called me every day as if jealous because I didn't ask her to come with me, but she was the one who left. She walked out on me and somehow still expected that I would bring her. I step away from the bar and move closer to the window. She's talking, but I can't hear what she is saying. Instead, I hyper-fixate on the kid outside of the window and the lost look on his face. It isn't a lost look because he feels out of place here, at the rally, the look seems to be more about being lost in life. I see a passing club starts hassling him. Now, I've always had an issue with fights that were very clearly unfair. 6 guys were surrounding him, more like hovering around him. My attention comes back to the phone as she is complaining about something to do with work, "Look," the word is very agitated, "why are you calling me?" I ask her. She says something about she wanted to make sure that I was okay. "Well, I'm not okay." And I hang up the phone and walk out of the door. No better way than to take out frustrations about a soon-to-be ex-wife than on assholes.

I light my cigarette, inhaling the nicotine into my lungs before I start. "Back away," I call to them as I walk out of the bar, standing towards the road but still in the shadows so that they cannot see me. I look down at my hands and open and close my fists a couple of times before I step up to them. I hear the mutters from the men as come out from the shadow and into the streetlights. They see my cut and stop, taking it in as I walk over and step in front of the kid. He's a tall fucking kid. Has a couple of inches on me, but he's still scrawny like he's never seen the inside of a gym.

"Holy fuck," I hear asshole #3 say, "that's Khan." He points to me and I'm not exactly sure how he recognized me. Probably spotted my rockers and maybe as Oz likes to put it the babyface.

"My reputation precedes me." I say as I let my hands come out at my sides, "Come on guys this is a place for people with similar interests, you, me, and the kid here." I move my hand behind me, "We all similar interests. Why pick on someone who you can so easily overpower?" The asshole clan mutters to themselves for a minute as I look over my shoulder, asking quietly, "Can you fight, kid?" He nods his head. Even though I'm not so sure about his skills when the first guy comes towards me. I let him move and close the gap I don't even hesitate until he is almost at me when I jump towards him and put my cigarette out on his chest, even if it will have to burn through his shirt first and then I let my fist connect with his face, I'm always surprised when people blackout from one hit. I see a glint of silver from one of the clan "Fuck, knuckles, kid." He dodges them and I watch as he comes up swiftly and sends his fist into the man's gut, when he looks up I can see his eyes wide open with rage, he may be just as furious as I am, and I don't mean about this fight, but life itself. The man grunts and while he is doubled over the kid roundhouse kids him to the fucking head. "Oomph," the sound comes out of my mouth mostly because of the kick to the head that man just received, and a small part because since I wasn't paying attention I got punched in the gut. Seriously, that's a cheap shot. I look at asshole #3 again as he stands, almost holding his hand, as if it hurts. I want to laugh but I don't want him to see me laugh. Seriously though, I haven't spent every night in the gym since she left, to not have abs that hurts people's hands. Until I start to lunge at him and he runs away.

KHAN
PART I

One of the other assholes catches me with a different set of brass knuckles that I didn't see before. Right under the eye, "Fuck," I shout out as my eyes snap open and the guy in front of me stumbles backward, eyes in shock by just the look on my face. That's right motherfucker you're about to meet Khan. My rage boils up in me and I'm fucking pissed, not just at him but at my fucking self, at my fucking life, at my fucking wife. I'm like Banner and the Hulk. I feel myself hit this fucking guy at least 3 times before I realize that there are cops on us. But I don't give a shit as I start to stalk towards the last of the asshole clan.

"Stop, hands up," one of the 4 officers shouts at us and I hesitate for a second before I hold my hands up.

"He didn't do anything," I nod to the kid, but the cops don't say anything as they cuff him as well.

"Oh yeah," the cop, who sounds like he's really from Minnesota, "then what happened?" He asks me.

"I saw those assholes giving kid, here, a hard time. I could see it escalating and knew that it was very clearly an unfair fight. I don't really stand for that shit. So I came out to help."

"Oh, you expect me to believe that the 1%er," he nods to the patch on my vest, "came out to help defend someone who was helpless." The cop is staring at me clearly not believing me.

"Yeah," I nod my head, "I may be an outlaw, but I'm not an asshole."

We sit at the tables, in cuffs as they cuff all the guys on the ground, as well as the last one standing when I see Chell come out of the bar.

"Khan," her hands are on her hips like she's mad until she sees the blood running down my face. "Oh my god," she shouts a little worried as she rushes over and the officer stops her.

"Ma'am you cannot touch him."

She looks at him with a look that says... motherfucker, you tell me not to, "why not, they didn't do anything. All of those fuckers were hassling this kid-,"

"Um, I have a name" *I hear him say next to me, and I kind of laugh about it. I kick him telling him to shut the fuck up.*

"Khan, saw them hassling him and came out, so they didn't kill him. To help him." *She says.*

"Whatever, I don't even fucking care. I don't want to be here." *And he comes over and takes the cuffs off of our wrists.*

"Thanks, Chell," *I walk up to her and hiss her cheek. She rolls her eyes and smiles.*

"Just stop trying to get yourself killed." *I smile and nod my head.* "Go clean your face up." *I salute her and she laughs. Looking over as they haul the last, starting to wake up, guy off of the ground and into the patty wagon. I laugh as I walk up to the kid lighting another cigarette and look at him. Not a scratch on him, it's kind of impressive.*

"So kid, what's your name?"

"Aubrey" *the audible oh comes out before I can stop it and he looks at me laughing.* "I know,"

"Don't tell anyone here that's your name. Come up with something else."

He laughs and nods his head. "Where are you staying?" *I ask him looking around as if that's going to magically make it appear.*

"Ugh," *he mutters looking around,* "I didn't really plan this trip."

"Oh no, you didn't book anywhere?" *The thing about Sturgis, South Dakota is bike week is the only thing that ever happens* here. It's a tiny town in a state that's claim to fame is Mount Rushmore... although, I personally prefer Crazy Horse. There are three hotels in the town and the next closet town is a handful of miles away. Everyone in the town as well as the surrounding towns leave for the 10 days that bike weeks happens. Something about not wanting to be in the same place as thousands of bikers. They even rent out yard spaces for people to camp out on.

He shakes his head and then says, "I was getting ready to leave cause I can't find anywhere that has any vacancies."

"Do you want to leave?" I ask him. And he shrugs and shakes his head at the same time. I laugh and sling my arm around his shoulder causing him to hunch over since he's just slightly taller than I am. "Where'd you park your bike?" He points in a direction and I nod my head, "Well, it's your lucky day. I have a couch in my room. You can crash on it if you want?" His face picks up maybe a little concerned about what I'm expecting. "Dude, I just helped you fight those assholes. I'm not gonna hurt you. I know the patch," I point to the 1%, "comes off a little scary to some, but the guys are harmless... well unless they have a reason not to be." I laugh, which causes him to laugh, skeptical. I tell him where to meet me at the hotel. When I see him pull into the parking lot I laugh. His bike is very clearly brand new, but he doesn't waver while he rides it and he rolls it to a stop next to me. Oz comes walking out of the hotel and shouts over to me. When he sees my face he comes walking over.

"Where you the fight that I just heard go out."

"Me?" I point to myself, "Never," which actually causes Oz to laugh,

"Who's the kid?" He asks nodding over to Aubrey.

"Dunno, some members from a club out of Texas were hassling him." He nods knowing what I'm going to say next so I skip that part. "Anyway, he's running from something or looking for something. He had no plans on coming here. Just showed up.

Brand new bike, brand new clothes, clearly out of place." Oz laughs. *"He doesn't have a place to stay. I'm gonna let him crash in my room."*

"You sure you want to do that. That's gonna make it hard to get some pussy?" He asks me.

I shrug and respond, "I feel bad for him." That's when Oz looks around and reaches into his pocket handing me a keycard. "What's this?" I ask him

"Since Rod had to bail on us last minute we have an extra room." I look at him surprised. "Find out as much as you can about him. We need some good prospects. If he's looking for something...," he trails, but I understand what he is saying. I nod my head. We watch as he walks up to us standing in the parking lot and then he starts talking.

"Hey man, I really appreciate you letting me crash on your couch. To repay you, I can stitch your face up." I look at him questioning for a second and he sways from one foot to another.

"What do you mean?" I ask him.

"Well," he stammers for a second before clearing his throat, "I just dropped out of my last year of med school. So, I can fix your face. I'm not a plastic surgeon, but I know enough to get the bleeding to stop."

"Oh, fuck yeah," Oz states, and I laugh. "You're going to earn that room." Which causes me to laugh at his confused expression.

"Turns out, apparently we have an extra room. This is Oz, the President of the Sonston End charter of the Midnight Syndicate." I nod at Oz.

"Oh, thank you?" he sticks his hand out, "I'll pay you. How much you want for it?" He asks Oz but Oz just shakes his head.

"You're good, just fix pretty boys face up and we'll be even. What's your name kid?" He asks holding out his hand and Aubrey grabs it shaking it.

"Fury," I nod my head approvingly and Oz laughs.

"Well, Fury, you may wanna bulk up if you stick with that name."

CHAPTER FOURTEEN

...Well, that's really inconvenient timing.

BILLIE

Listening to the boys recount the way that they first met makes me feel stupid that I may have been feeling even a little slight bit jealous when I asked about his scar.

"So, just like that, you came back with them?" I hear Lucy ask Fury and he shrugs.

"I had nothing left for me on the East coast. The guys all seemed decent. And I had gotten enough in insurance money after my parents died that if it turned out to be a horrible idea unless they killed me, I would have been okay."

"Fuck, maybe we need to make sure someone gets hurt more often because your skills are getting fuckin' sloppy" I hear Dax say to Fury and I can't help but laugh.

"Shut up, I'm the only one here who knows how to do this shit," Fury says which makes me laugh again.

"How did you two meet?" Fury nods to Lucy and me.

"Middle school," Lucy quips quickly.

"What? Really?" Dax asks laughing, "You know all about the princess over here?"

"Maybe a princess of delinquents, " she says nonchalantly.

"Lucy!" Her name comes out of my mouth harshly.

"No, no, I need to hear more," Fury says. "What did she do?" He and Dax are both looking from Lucy to myself.

"Lucy," I urge her again but she smirks at me.

"What did she not do?" Lucy laughs as I cover my face with my hands.

"I thought I was past all this." I mutter which causes Dax to laugh, "Plus you were just as bad as an instigator as I was." I sigh as Lucy begins to tell stories about my troubled times with drag racing, "I'm going to bed."

"No, Billie, stay," Fury shouts to me but I shake my head and just walk back up to the bedroom.

I lay down on the bed and I must have drifted off because the next thing I know is I'm being woken up by Dax, "Come on, why don't you get under the covers," he whispers as he pulls down the covers, I undress down to my underwear and slide underneath the covers. He smiles at me and kisses my cheek. "I'll see you in the morning." He whispers into my ear.

"Will you stay with me until I fall asleep?" I ask him, I hear him groan a little bit but then I hear his feet shuffling over until he lays down on the bed. "You're going to stay on top of them?" I can't help but ask him and he nods his head.

"Yes," I slide over to him and lay my head on his chest, curling up into his side.

"Why?" I ask him and I feel him laugh.

"You make the rules." For a second I'm glad it's dark so he can't see me nervously bit the inside of my mouth. "Can I ask you something?"

"You saved my life today, you can pretty much ask me anything." I think I hear him smile.

"Lucy said something about you coming to bed because you don't like it when people tell stories about you from your past." I sigh. I don't really want to get into this.

"Brad, um, he expected me to act a certain way." I feel him stiffen, "He hated those stories because they painted me in a way which he didn't see was acceptable like I am a loose cannon."

"Or they show that you were a normal teenager." He mutters. I can hear Lucy laugh from the kitchen. "Also, they are probably going to fuck tonight." I can feel him point in the direction of the kitchen. I laugh as I smack him, "I'm being serious. I had to come up here because I was feeling like a little bit of a third wheel."

I wake in the morning to find Dax still asleep, still laying on top of the covers, with his left arm bent and his hand underneath his head, with his other arm still around me. I have to force the smile off of my lips as I slide out from under the covers and I grab my book bag on the floor. I debate opening it but decide to just take it into the bathroom which is attached to the bedroom. I turn on the shower letting the water warm up as I undress the remaining clothes from my body, I must have been pretty exhausted last night to strip down to my underwear and let him see me like that again. I slip into the warm water stream. *This feels so much better.* I try and wash all the images of last night from me, but they don't go away.

"How did this escalate so quickly?" I think back to the last 3 weeks… the phone calls, the eerie feeling that I've been getting, last night. Why has so much happened in the last few weeks?

Getting out of the shower I dress before I separate my hair in half and make two Dutch-braids stopping the braid and the nape of my head and letting the rest fall straight. I creep the bathroom door open and see that Dax is still sleeping. Trying to stay quiet as I walk through the bedroom and opening the door. As I step through the doorway, with the door still open, I turn around to see Fury's face behind a partly cracked door where Lucy is staying. He has his shirt in his hands as he debates closing the door again. I mouth to him *I already see you* which causes him to press his lips into a hard line as he gives in and walks out of the bedroom making sure to slip his arms through the holes and bringing it over his head. I can't help but take the moment to appreciate that he does have a nice body as well. Definitely put on a lot of muscle since getting here according to the story that I heard last night. While I'm still standing in the open doorway the door in the middle of the hall opens, the door that belongs to Ella's bedroom. And sleepy Ella emerges from her room, rubbing her eyes, and yawning. She looks at me standing in the doorway to her uncle's room and her eyes widen, then she smiles, and closes her bedroom door behind her, she walks one door down to the door which is between her's and the room which Lucy is staying in, and walks in. Apparently, that is a bathroom and apparently, she doesn't care about what is going on with us. I don't know what to say in response so I just close the door and walk down the stairs. Fury comes down the stairs moments after I do; without looking at him I say, "I'm about to make breakfast, are you staying for some?"

"Fuck yeah, if you're offering." He pauses, "What are you making?"

"I don't know, yet."

"Pancakes are his favorite." He pauses before groaning and rolling his eyes, "I hate so much that I know that fact." His confession actually makes me laugh.

"You guys are close?" I don't know why I ask him... it's obvious, but I let it go.

"Yeah, he saved my life." He pauses and looks around, "Gave me a family again. Honestly, most of the guys here he," Fury points up to his room, "picked us out of bad situations and gave us a home. He'll never take the credit for it. He has a bit of a hero complex... but will never take credit."

I don't know what to say next and let the conversation die down.

"You know, last night." He starts as he glances towards the stairs to make sure no one can hear him, "I've never seen him lose his shit like that." He says the words and I turn around to look at him, "I've known the man for 13 years. He's always been calm and collected. Never once has he freaked out like he did when your car went up."

"What does that mean exactly?" Fury shakes his head like he isn't sure what it means either.

I hear footsteps coming down the stairs, "I smell bacon," she says as she comes into the kitchen and Fury reaches over smacks her on the ass, and then pulls her down onto his lap.

"Gross," Ella mutters as she walks into the kitchen behind her.

"Yeah," looking to Lucy I nod in Fury's direction as I continue to speak, "I caught this one trying to sneak out on you this morning." Lucy looks over at him shocked.

"Oh yeah," Fury asks in a light-hearted response to my statement, "what time did Khan head back over to the clubhouse?" I can see his eyebrow cock up as he questions me.

"I dunno it was probably around 3." He and Lucy both laugh as I hear footsteps walking down the stairs, "Well, that's really inconvenient timing," I mutter under my breath and everyone in the room, including Ella, laughs at me as Dax comes into the room. He glances around the room and then to be the only one not laughing,

"What is going on in here?" Which makes them all laugh harder.

"What time did you make it back to the clubhouse?" Fury asks him and he looks at me as I'm shaking my head, I hold up 3 fingers to scratch my face, then turn around to flip the pancakes on the stove.

"I dunno, late, probably around 3." He pauses realizing that everyone watched him walk down the stairs, "Came back early and took a shower." I can see Fury look from Dax to me and then back to Dax.

Then I hear Fury's words, "You have your own, personal shower at the clubhouse." I fail at holding in my snicker as I see Dax's realization over Fury's words.

"Needed Clothes." He mutters.

"Pretty sure you have that exact outfit you're wearing over there as well." I glance to Fury as now I'm trying not to laugh.

"Then whatever is a good enough reason for you to stop asking me," Ella's smiling now. Then he looks to Fury pointing the finger at him, "I can see why you're still here." I hear Fury whisper something as I feel Dax at my side as he looks over my shoulder, "Oh, pancakes!" I hear the excitement in his voice.

"Told you," Fury says from the table. And Dax smirks.

"Sorry," he whispers at my side, "I should have left last night after you fell asleep. You just looked so peaceful I didn't want to chance of waking you up." He to me, quietly and I can't help but smile.

"Secrets don't make friends." Fury shouts and Lucy starts laughing.

"This isn't going to get old at all," I say back to them and Ella starts laughing again. I lower my voice and look to Dax, "Ella saw me coming out of your room this morning. Didn't seem to care at the moment but…" I trail and he nods his head looking over to Ella. I'm guessing Fury didn't say anything since he saw the glance over to Ella.

"El!" Dax shouts and walks over to the table sitting next to her, "How was your night?"

She nods her head and looks at her uncle.

"We use our words." He groans at her and I can't help but laugh.

"It was okay. Lock drove me over to Ashley's house. I hung out with her for a while and then came home. It was fun. I was tired when I got home so I went to sleep. Woke up to some laughing down here." The four of us stand awkwardly. "Finally got her to come over," she says to her uncle as nodding to me and I laugh to myself. Their conversation sounds like they are talking about me like I'm not here, but as each one looks to me as they speak it's more like they don't care if I hear.

"Not exactly, she's kind of in danger." I sit the plates of food down on the table.

"Kind of?" She asks him, looks at me, and then his eyes go large when he looks at the pancakes as he grabs 3 from the plate. "Are you okay?" I nod my head.

Dax's next words are nonchalantly but the words in any other situation would be shocking, "Her car got blown up." My mouth hangs open almost shocked that he would just tell her like that.

I expect her to ask me an onslaught of questions, but she doesn't instead her face turns hard as she looks at the two men who sit at the table and says, "You two, got her car blown up," I can't help the laughter as it comes out and the two men look at me.

"I'm sorry," I look at Ella, "no, my soon-to-be ex kind of blew it up. After he yelled at him." I say pointing to Dax, who shrugs.

"She's leaving out the part when she punched him in the face." Fury adds from the side as he shovels in a heaping of eggs.

"WHAT!" Lucy exclaims and looks to me, "How did you not tell me that part? I have been fighting the urge to do that to him for years."

"Yeah, right in front of everyone it was awesome." Fury adds.

Lucy groans and looks at me, "I wish I could have seen it… ugh, I always miss the good stuff."

He laughs looking at her and says, "I'll find it on the security cameras and show you."

"That," Lucy says pointing to me, "Is the Billie that I know."

"Anyway," Dax says smirking looking at Ella, "they," he nods over to Lucy and me, "Maybe staying with us for a while, you okay with that?"

"Yeah," she says grabbing a piece of bacon off of his plate and eats it.

Dax turns to look at Lucy and I say, "We'll go by the house tonight and grab whatever you need."

"Can't we go get it?" I ask him not wanting to tell him to grab certain things from the house.

"Absolutely not," Fury says to me and then looks to Lucy glaring at her. "We have a covert way about things. If he's staking out the house we'll be able to get in and get out without him knowing."

CHAPTER FIFTEEN

...Suddenly wish you didn't work out so much?

KHAN

Fury steers the car out of the compound and drives down the dirt road. "You two looked cozy this morning," I tell him as he pulls onto the main road and he laughs out.

"She's fun," he responds, "don't worry, I'm not going to fuck this up for you." I roll my eyes at his comment as he laughs. "You get a nice repayment for *saving her life*?" He asks me as he says the last three words his voice becomes more high-pitched as if mimicking Billie's.

"Fuck off, I'm not having this conversation with you," I tell him which causes him to shake his head.

"Seriously, bro? Still?" He looks over at me until I glare back. Then he grunts and says, "You got the list they gave you?"

"Yeah,"

"How bad is it?" He asks me and I laugh.

"I mean," I shrug my shoulders. "You fucked her, you get to get her shit together." He groans again.

"Same as usual?" He asks me and I nod.

Fury drops me off a block from Lucy's house. I crouch down as I run through a backyard and then stop at the fence which leads to the next house. I check over the wooden panels to make sure I don't get attacked by a dog and then in one swift motion I lift myself up and over the fence. Crouching down again, hugging the backside of the fence as I run towards the next side. Stop, check to make sure, hop the fence. Rinse and repeat until I make it into Lucy's backyard. I pause as I stand within the fence of the neighbor's house.

"Fury," I quietly whisper.

"Yeah, you're good." I hop the last fence and crouch, run to the backdoor. "How's it looking there?" He asks.

"Oh, you know, trying to make sure I'm not walking into a trap." I hear him laugh through the earpiece. "Just tell me if you see fucking movement," I mutter to him.

"Nothing, yet."

"You talk to Bullet?" Who is on the duty of watching Brad, which is the whole reason why we came out when we did? He's been watching the house for most of the day and left shortly before we got here.

"You gotta be fucking kidding me," I mutter looking at the window that is in the bathroom which Lucy told me was unlocked.

"What?" He asks.

"This window, the one in the fucking bathroom, it's gonna suck to squeeze through." I hear him laughing. "It's one of those small windows, probably 24 by 16." He starts laughing even harder.

"Suddenly wish that you don't work out so much."

"Shut the fuck up," I mutter to him. Grabbing a chair on the patio and sliding it over to the window. I flip the window open and I lift myself up pushing my torso through the opening. I can feel the metal scratching at my stomach as I try and suck in what I can. When all that's left are my legs I move my hands to hold onto the outside of the window and I slowly lower myself. "I'm in," I reach up and lock the bathroom window behind me.

"See that wasn't so hard was it." I'm stepping out of the bathroom and walking into Lucy's room. "If it's that easy to get in it, she really shouldn't keep it unlocked." Fury mutters.

"Catching feelings for the girl?" He bites out a *fuck you*. I clear Lucy's room making sure to check all of her windows that they are at least locked and move into the hallway. My eyes have adjusted to the darkness of the house and I push the cracked door of Billie's room open. Her clothes are scattered everywhere and I see the closet door is open. I peer in to make sure that it is empty. I do a quick visual check to make sure that no one is in here and move into the bathroom, it looks about the same as the bedroom, ransacked. I'm assuming he was looking for some sort of clue as to where she had gone. Or where I lived. I slide the shower curtain back and check it. Check all the windows. The last thing I need is someone coming in behind me in one of them.

"You good, Prez."

"So far," I whisper just so he can hear me. I take a deep breath walking down the hallway inspecting the front door. Making sure it's not wired up to anything, since he did blow her car up. Then moving into the living room. No one; dining room, clear; kitchen, Clear. "Looks clear," I mutter to Fury after I check the back doors making sure that they are not rigged up as well. I unlock the back door as I check the glimmer of something out of the corner of my eye. "Awe, fuck" I snap, whispering.

"What?"

"Change of plans, get Bullet on the phone now. Get inside through the front and pack her shit." Fury patches the phone call through the comms.

"You still have eyes on him?" I ask the kid and he says he does. "Okay, don't let him out of your sights."

"Prez, what is it?" Fury whispers as he walks in through the front door.

"Motion sensor..." I nod back to the kitchen, "maybe it didn't pick anything up but I doubt it."

"You think it's the girls?" He asks me.

"Don't you think they would have told us about it?" I clap back as we walk down the hallway. I hand him the list, "I think I'm good. You go and get all of Lucy's shit. He was clearly here and looking for where she went, Billie's shit is ransacked." I whisper to him as I point him to Lucy's room. I go back into Billie's room grabbing duffle bags out of the closet which she told me were there and I being shoveling everything off of the floor into the room.

"Prez," I hear Bullet say. "We got movement."

"Fuck," I mutter, "how far are you out?"

"20 mins."

"Fury we have got to be gone in 15"

"Got it." He bounces back as I'm working my way from the bedroom into the bathroom.

"Bullet, update."

"15 mins out," *fuck*.

"Okay, Fury almost done?" I mutter as I stuff all of the toiletries into the bag. Along with her make-up, her hairdryer, her straightener.

"Yeah," he pauses, "Khan, you think when it says all of my toiletries, written all in all caps it means everything."

"Yeah, that's how I took it."

"Like even her tampons?" I groan, looking up to myself in the mirror.

"Seriously?" I ask him.

"14 mins out," Bullet mutters.

"Yeah, it's kinda gross." He responds.

"Stop being a pussy." I gripe at him as I hear Bullet laugh,

"Bro, you don't care about those."

"No, because I'm a fucking grown-up." I clap back to him and can hear Bullet chuckle through the comms continuing.

"10 minutes out," Bullet mutters, through chuckles

"It's just I don't want to think about them."

"Weren't you going to school to be a doctor?"

"Yeah, a lifetime ago, and I dropped out, remember." He says sarcastically.

"Fury were you inside of her last night?"

"Ugh, yeah, and?" he mumbles.

"Okay, so that's the only place those go... so pretty much you are the same."

"7 mins," Bullet is now laughing.

"Fury, get the fucking tampons, and let's get out of here," I tell him slinging one duffle bag across my body and bringing the other two in tow. We make our way out of the house and to the SUV tossing the bags into the back seat.

"5 mins," Bullet says. "We're turning into the neighborhood."

"Lucy wanted to get her car." Fury looks at me and I shake my head.

"He blew up Billie's car. There's no telling what is on that one." He nods his head, agreeing.

"Get in the fucking truck" he shouts to me. I move around the truck as we hear Bullet tell us 3 mins and jump into the passenger seat.

The truck is already on and moving before I can even get my door shut. We see the black mustang come skidding around the corner, we pass him, and come to a stop at the sign. We both watch him in the rear-view mirror as he whips into Lucy's driveway. Bull is sitting just past the stop sign, so he doesn't realize he's being followed.

"Bullet, we're out," I say as Fury turns the truck to leave the street.

"Good to know. I'll stay on him and let you know when he leaves." And he hangs up the phone.

"Could you have cut it any closer?" Fury asks me and I shake my head.

"Really dude, if I didn't have to convince you to grab the fucking tampons. You're thirty-fucking-six years old." The phone is ringing as we pull onto Main Street and Fury presses the accept button on the steering wheel.

"Prez, he's fucking pissed. I could see him through the windows as he was watching something. Looked to be a recording of you guys packing shit. Did anyone grab a laptop, looks like he's tracking something?" He asks us and I look to Fury who slowly nods his head.

"Are you fucking kidding me?" I shout at him and he cowers a little.

"Fuck, pull the fuck over, now," I shout at Fury, as I pick up my phone and quickly dial Ace, placing it on the center console on speaker. Fury pulls the truck off onto a side street. The phone rings quick, Ace knows that we have gone out and is waiting just in case.

"Yeah."

"Walk me through how to see if a tracker is put on a laptop." Ace groans.

"Prez, he's walking back to his car."

"Fuck," Ace groans. "Mac?"

"Yeah,"

"Okay, click the finder."

"Got it."

"Click on the Mac HD under location"

"Yup"

"Press control Shit and the period key and then look at the grayed out folders. Read off the ones that don't look like they belong."

"LoJack"

"Yeah, trash the folder."

"Fuck it wants the operator password."

"We're almost to Main Street," Bullet says through the phone.

"Lucy password for the computer." I hear Ace shout back to her.

"pillsberrydoughboy. All one-word lowercase." I hear and look at the phone where the voice is coming from. Fury starts laughing even in the serious situation, looking at him as I punch in her password all I can think about is maybe this relationship is going to be more than he's bargaining for.

"Turning now," Bullet says and I type the password in, and the folder deletes.

"Fucking go, Fury. Ace, tell Lucy that if that didn't work I'm chucking the laptop" I say as the tires almost squeal off of the side street and we turn the corner then I hear Ace convey it to her and she groans but agrees. We start to move in the opposite direction of the clubhouse making sure that he can't track us any longer.

"He's pulling onto the side street, he's getting out of the car. He looks fucking pissed." He's quiet for a few minutes and I can hear Brad cussing through the phone before Bullet adds, "Yeah you guys are good. I'll stay on him for a little while," he pauses as we can hear his squealing tires from the mustang. "He's turning right."

"Good." And Fury ends the call.

"Really," I look at him, "you fucking know better."

"I didn't think that he would have tracked Lucy's computer."

"Fury, he's an asshole, not fucking stupid." We drive back to the clubhouse in silence. I'm so angry with him at this moment and at the same time, I'm glad that we had someone tailing him.

When we make it back to the house I walk in, carrying the bags, and drop them down in front of Billie she smiles and I see Ace looking at me, his expression is less than excited. "Fuck me, what now?" and he nods for me to follow him outside which makes me nod to Fury to follow us as well. "What is it?"

"This guy is a fucking asshole."

"Yeah, already figured as much out." I pause, "Before I forget will you look over the laptop and make sure it's good."

He nods his head and then starts talking, "Looks like he's been looking at his life insurance policy on Billie"

"He has one on her?" Fury asks.

"Yeah, it's with the military. The spouse has a 100 thousand dollar life insurance policy" I tell him.

"Yeah, that's not all of it, looks like he took an additional policy out on her the day his ship left to go to sea," He pauses. "It's 500 thousand."

"Fuck me, he's been planning on killing her for some time now." And Ace sighs.

"Yeah, looks that way."

"Khan, this isn't good." I shake my head, agreeing with him. "She's planning on going to work in the morning." I nod my head.

"We were already going to have to take her." Fury nods his head. "Are you over Lucy yet or you good taking her to work?"

"I can do that." He smiles and I roll my eyes.

"Khan, there's one more thing." *Fuck,* "It looks like he's on heroin." *Fuck... but I can work with that.* "And it looks like it's been reported through his chain of command. He's getting kicked out for it." That is information that I need and actually appreciate hearing.

"How long until he gets kicked out?" I ask him.

"A few months," I nod my head, "Why?"

"If he's planning on killing her, he's going to want to do it before he gets booted. That way he gets both policies." I nod thanking him for digging everything up and walk back into the house and hand him Lucy's computer, then I tell the girls the plan for the morning

"You can't do that," Billie tells me.

"Can't do what." *Do you know who I am?*

"Take me and Ella." She says. I start to open my mouth to speak and she puts her hand up as if asking me to let her finish. "What I mean is, you can't take both of us, together. First, if he's watching he can't see Ella get out of the same car as you or me." *Shit, how did I not think about that?* "And second, if the kids see her come to school with me they will give her a living hell." *Another valid point.*

"I'll get Ash to take Ella."

BILLIE

"Billie, there are a couple other things that you should know," Dax says to me as I walk into the bedroom to go to sleep. I stop and look at him.

"Besides the fact that my husband tried to blow my car up, track me here, and is an asshole." He slowly nods his head, trying not to smile at my statement. I take a deep breath and say, "What is it?"

"It looks like he's on heroin." I can feel how wide my eyes go and he stops. "It's not good. It does explain his behavior changes.

Apparently, his command is already aware of it." He shrugs, I'm sure there's a piece that he's not telling me. "I've dealt with people on it before and this can make him pretty dangerous. Look, we have a safe house in the desert."

"I'm not going to hide out any more than I already am," I tell him staring at him. "He blew up my life and then he literally blew my car up. I'm not letting him take anything else away from me." He nods at me and I get up and walk into the bathroom.

"There's one more thing." And I stop, turning around I look at him.

"Of course there is," my use of sarcasm makes one of the corners of his mouth twitch.

"He took out a life insurance policy on you. That with the only the military has." I nod my head as I cut him off.

"Yeah," I say to him and he tilts his head to the side.

"You know about that?" He asks me and I can't help but laugh.

"Yeah, we got them when we first got married. The one that the military provides. I mean, it's a good chunk of money but it will run out quickly." His face grows from confused to utter shock. I'm sure it's about the fact that how could someone be so greedy, "What? We were planning on having kids. It just didn't work out," he opens his mouth and I stop to let him start talking, but he closes his mouth.

He opens it again, "You have another policy?"

"Yeah, you just said that."

"No, I said he took one out." He stops, rolls his eyes, and nods his head understanding where he went wrong. "Fuck, I should have said he *just* took one out." He makes sure to emphasize the word just.

"Wait, what?" I stop staring at him. "He just took one out? When did he take out the second one?"

"The day he went out to sea." His voice goes quiet.

"How much?" My words are whispers. He looks away, "Dax, how much?"

"500 thousand," my mouth goes dry.

"He's been planning on killing me since he left?" I pause and stare at him, "He has already made a plan, spent 6 months perfecting it." I'm pacing back and forth processing everything that is going on.

"Billie," he says scooting in close to me, but I stop him.

"Dax, he's never going to stop. He is apparently an addict. If his command knows about it, then he's getting kicked out," Dax nods his head. "He stands to make over a million dollars if I'm dead." The last words are a strained whisper.

"I'm not going to let anything happen to you." And I laugh.

"What are you going to be my bodyguard 24/7?" I stop and look at him. "Seriously, you can't be my bodyguard 24/7."

"If I have to, I will." And I laugh. "But I do have someone watching him at all times. So, I know where he is." He pauses and I look over to him wondering just how much power he has and what kind of things that he is capable of making happen. "Do you mind if we have the same sleeping arrangements as last night?" I nod my head as I walk back into the bathroom, brush my teeth, take my contacts out, and I walk to bed. I slip in underneath the covers and feel as Dax takes off his boots, and strips off his clothes. He crawls onto the bed with his boxer briefs on and I laugh.

"You're going to get cold," I tell him

"I'll be fine." He says.

"Just get under the blankets." I laugh as a child-like excitement comes from him. I sit in a quiet trance-like state for a moment before he breaks it.

"What you thinking about?" the darkness of the room conceals his face.

"How stupid I am," I whisper back

"About what?"

"About the fact that my husband was planning on killing me this whole time. I should have slept with you that first day I met you." He laughs, it's a full-body laugh that shakes the entire bed.

"Which day do you consider to be the first day?" I can hear the smile on his face.

"When you came in for Ella's meeting at school and I never got those types of feelings for people."

"Yeah, I thought about fucking you on your desk."

"Dax," I say playfully, smacking him

"Seriously, I can't tell you the last person who stood up to me when I got mad." He tells me. "It was so fucking hot. I wanted to pull you over the desk and lay you across it." I'm suddenly thankful for the cloak of darkness because if not, he would be able to see my bright red cheeks. "But it's better you didn't because you would have hated yourself for it. That's not who you are." He pauses again as he brings his arm around my body and pulls me into him, "Although, when all of this is done, we're revisiting that desk idea."

His words cause me to laugh a little bit as he leans down and kisses my forehead. It's such a gentle gesture that I melt into him, "Good night, Billie." I'm a little surprised that he doesn't try anything with me or even kiss me more than on the forehead.

CHAPTER SIXTEEN

...you have no idea how hard that was for me to stop.

BILLIE

"It's time to get up," I hear Dax whisper into my ear, as he rolls over and wraps his free arm around me.

"Did you sleep?" I ask him. I can feel him laugh, one of those laughs where only air comes out of your nose.

"A little," he whispers, leaning in and kissing my forehead, "couldn't sleep." He looks down at me as my face wrinkles.

"Why not?" I can't but ask him as if I didn't already know the answer.

"I usually don't sleep much." He confesses.

"You did the other night." He laughs.

"Yeah, I had also just been shot. And drank a whole lot to numb that." I look away from him and he holds me tighter. "Hey, it's not your fault." He looks at me forcing me to look at him.

"It kind of is." He shakes his head.

"Get ready." He smiles down at me pressing a kiss to my forehead again.

KHAN

I watch her as she walks across the room and into the bathroom. I only let the groan come out as I hear the shower come on. I lay in the bed, staring at the ceiling, watching the ceiling fan spin above me, wondering how it is I managed to get myself into this situation. Maybe, I'll never learn.

The ringing of my phone breaks my self-loathing before it can get any worse. Reaching over I can see that it's Jeff calling.

Fuck, I didn't go to see him yesterday.

"Jeff, I'll come by this afternoon," I say into the receiver

"Fuck, Dax. I cleaned up the scene. You were supposed to come by yesterday. Couldn't fucking call?" He snips out at me.

"I had some other shit to deal with," I mutter to him.

"Fuck Dax, really. You had shit to do." He yells at me, "I need something better than that. Meet me at the diner at 8."

"Jeff, I can't. Make it 8:30."

"Fucking 8 Dax, or I'll put your fucking name in the report."

"Jeff," the word comes out of my mouth in a fucking angry growl. Deep down I know he wouldn't, but I can't chance that and I also know that if he's threatening it then he is really pissed about the whole thing.

"Dax," he laughs in response, "meet me at 8. If you're fucking late…"

"Yeah, I got it." I snap into the phone and end the call.

I call Ace first, "Send me Billie's info for her car." Hanging up and then call Fury. I can hear his phone ringing from the other room. And I roll my eyes.

"Prez." He mutters.

"Get up. I need you to leave early and take Billie to the school."

"I thought you-," I cut him off.

"Yeah, well, Jeff is in a mood."

"Got it," he mutters as I hear him tell Lucy to get up and get ready. I get out of the bed and pull on my sweatpants. Walking out of the room and knock on Ella's door.

"El, you awake?" there's no response so I open the door and peek in. "Ella," the words are louder than the first. I see movement as she rolls over, "Ella, you gotta get up. Ash will be here soon to take you to school."

"You're not going to take me." Ugh, I forgot to talk to her about it.

"Not for a little while." I look at her and walk in, sitting down on her bed. "Billie's ex is dangerous. He knows who I am, he's pretty pissed at me right now."

"Cause she's staying with us." She asks me not to say specifically that she's been staying in my room. I think she's implying that Billie cheated on him.

"It's not like that." I look at her, "Even if he thinks that it is." She tilts her head to the side in a confused look.

"Uncle Dax," She gives me those sweet big brown puppy dog eyes and I shake my head. For years, Ella was the only one who used my real name, well her and Jeff, but Jeff knew me before I was *Khan*. Until Billie came along, she was the only one I allowed to use my real name. "Don't lie." I laugh and look at her.

"I would never lie to you, kid. It's not like that. She never cheated on him. Even with me tempting her too." She laughs, looking a little impressed, and nods her head.

"Oh, someone who resisted the infamous Khan." I shake my head.

"You know too much about me." I say laughing and pointing to her as she laughs, "He showed up at the club one night with some girl, then accused me of following him and then of me sleeping with her. I kind of called him out for him being a scum bag. Anyway, my words made him go home and hurt her." Her eyes widen. "She left him but that hasn't made him stop harassing her. And I have very good reason to believe that he's going to try and kill her." She's sitting up now. "Since he hates me, and wants to get at her. He cannot see you with me. You understand?" She nods her head.

"Can't he find out that you're my guardian?" She asks me and I shrug.

"That would take some digging since you're a minor." She nods her head. Then I smile at her, "Plus, I'm pretty sure he only knows me by my road name."

"I understand." She nods.

"Now get ready for school." This is such a weird role that I've taken on. "Lucy's going to have to get a shower in a minute. Hurry up." When I walk out of Ella's room I can hear moaning coming from Lucy's. I knock on the door hard, one time, and say, "Ella's awake." And keep walking back towards my bedroom. When I open the door I can hear that the water has stopped and knock on the door. I hear her mutter some words but open the door anyway. She's standing with a towel wrapped around herself.

She looks gorgeous.

I can't help myself as I walk up behind her and wrap my arms around her nuzzling my face into the crook of her neck before lifting rest my head on her shoulder and looking at her through the mirror as I talk to her. "Jeff called me this morning, I have to meet him at 8. I tried to push it but he wasn't having it. Fury's going to drop you off before he drops off Lucy. They are already awake." She smiles at me.

"I'm guessing that means that he stayed the night again?" She laughs I just nod my head.

"I'm going to jump in the shower," I tell her watching her as she nods her head.

I slide my sweat pants off and turn the shower back on. I strip off my boxers as I keep my back turned to her and step into the shower, shutting the glass door behind me. I can't help but glance to see her standing in the mirror watching me. Mouth slightly agape. I step into the stream of water.

I would be lying if I said I didn't do that little show just to fuck with her.

BILLIE

I thought I could feel his erection pressing into my back while he was hugging me. So, when he started to strip off his boxers I can't look away. He keeps his back to me as I take in his very muscular ass, but I still can't bring my eyes up from his body. For some reason, I needed to see him. When he closes the glass door to the shower and turned towards the water I nearly drop my towel and jump in with him. If only I had the time.

I'm not sure if I am more shocked that he just nonchalantly undresses and gets into the shower or of the impressive cock that is on full display.

I force myself to turn to walk out of the bathroom. Stopping as my hand touches the door handle.

Fuck it.

I drop my towel and walk back towards the shower. I open the door and slide in as Dax is washing the shampoo out of his hair. He looks so perfect. I want to run my fingers down where the water runs down his body, but instead, I reach up, clasp my hand around the back of his neck. His eyes pop open as he lets them gaze down my body and his lips crash down to mine. I feel his hands roam down my body and then clasp my ass as he lifts me up and I wrap my legs around his torso. My back presses into the shower wall as his head

falls and kisses down my neck. A moan escapes my lips and returns his mouth to mine.

I can feel the tip of his cock pressing into me as his hips move with the rhythm of our kiss. His hand coming up and his thumb and finger rolling my nipple causing a gasp.

Just as quick as my decision was to come in, he breaks the kiss, unwraps my legs, and places me back down on the ground. Almost as if my reaction to him touching me was what broke the trance. I watch as a long sigh escapes his mouth and he shakes his head. I'm humiliated as I scurry out of the bathroom, grabbing my towel. Walking into the bedroom and pick up the clothing that I had left out on the dresser the night before. I slide on the black dress slacks and then the sleeveless button-down followed by the black blazer. I walk to the duffle bag that Dax threw all my shoes into and pick out my black pointy-toe heels. I am almost done putting on some quick makeup when I hear the water stop, and he emerges from the bathroom. Watching him in the mirror as he walks over to his closet. I see him look at me once, I quickly look away, and he turns to face the closet. He grabs a pair of jeans and a black t-shirt out of the closet and tosses them onto the bed. I hear him sigh as he walks over to me, he reaches for his drawer, I move out of the way as he reaches in, grabs out a pair of boxers. I look away from him. He quietly gets dressed then looks back at me.

"Billie," he mutters and walks behind me.

"What?" The word is a whisper.

"Not like this," He says the words as they are barely above a whisper.

"Like what?" I ask him.

"This, while you're still married. I mean," he rubs a hand over his face, but he doesn't look back to me, "sure, I have fucked married women before. But," he pauses and turns to me, walking closer, "none of them thought twice about being married and I didn't care about them. If I'm being completely honest I didn't care about how it made them feel either." He pauses again, "But you," he takes a breath as a knock comes on the door as Fury tells me they're getting ready to leave. "We'll be right there." Dax calls out to him without breaking eye contact with me, "You're different. I don't want you to do anything that you may regret later." He sighs and pulls me close to him wrapping his arms around me, "You have no idea how hard that was for me to stop."

"I think I may have an idea," I say smirking as he glares at me.

"You're an asshole, you know?" And I start laughing. He grabs my hand and walks with me out of the bedroom and into the living room. Ella comes in shortly after we walk into the living room as she looks at everyone standing.

I hear someone walk into the house and when I look over I see a younger guy walk in. He's roughly the same height as Dax with bleached hair and bright eyes. He's not nearly as muscular as Dax or Fury are yet somehow he's just as intimidating as the other two, he reminds me of Angelface from Fight Club, but with the look in his eyes after he got beat to hell and back. I can see the tattoos where the end of the sleeve sits all the way down his arms and I can't help but wonder how far up that they go, but there's something about his eyes. His eyes tell me that he has seen some shit and then he smiles and his face changes drastically.

"Ash," I hear Dax say. As he nods. "Wait 15 mins after we leave before you leave, you know, just in case." He nods his head again and then Ash looks at me.

"This must be Billie," he mutters as he looks at me, "I can see why Khan is so-," Dax cuts him off when he kicks his leg from behind him and says something about minding his fucking business. But his action only makes Ash laugh while shaking his head.

The four of us move outside as Fury unlocks the truck as it sits in the driveway and Lucy and I get in.

"Fury," Dax calls to him, talking for a moment when I see Lucy look at me from the front seat.

"See you two are getting close," I mutter to her, nodding out to Fury.

"Just fun," she smiles and looks away, "you slept with him yet?" I'm shocked as I look at her, "What? Fury and I have a bet going on." My mouth drops open and she laughs. "So have you."

"No." the word almost sounds pained.

"No!" she shouts so loud that both men turn and look at the truck. She waves it off and looks back at me. "What do you mean no, you've spent the last three nights in bed together?"

"I kind of told him that I wanted to wait until the divorce is finalized."

"What, why?" She asks me and I shrug.

"Just, I don't want Brad to be able to use anything over me." She nods her head.

"I can understand that. How does he," he nods her head in the direction of Dax, "feel about that?"

"At this point, he's the one enforcing it."

"What?" Fury asks as he looks to Lucy, who is turned around in her seat looking at me, mouth hanging completely open.

"Nothing," I say as I glare at Lucy telling her not to say anything.

"O-kay," Fury says backing out of the driveway. He waits for Dax to come out on his bike and follows him out to the dirt road.

"Why is he doing all of this for me? I barely know him." And Fury laughs, "What?"

"Nobody really gets it," he shrugs. "He watches out for people that he either deems worthy or thinks is in an unfair battle," he pauses again looking up to the mirror, "protecting people will probably be what kills him."

KHAN

I pull up to the diner on the outside of town, nodding my head at Jeff as I walk past where he sits and to the door. I walk in and towards the table, sliding into the booth, and look up to Jeff.

"What the fuck is going on, Dax?" I hear him even though the words are whispers they are stern. The waitress comes over, greeting me by name, and brings me my usual cup of coffee.

"Thanks, Sandy," I tell her. She smiles at me because she always does and then she walks away. I turn my attention back to Jeff, "What do you mean?"

"I mean, I have a car on fire Saturday night and Sunday I have some guy coming into the station asking questions about it." And he leans in, "Now, what the fuck is going on."

"Did he give a name?"

Jeff shakes his head, "Nah, that's why we didn't give him any information. He kept saying it was his car. Wanted to know if his wife was inside."

"Fuck,"

"Dax, what the fuck is going on." I've known Jeff for a long fucking time. We have an understanding, some things he doesn't ask, and some things I don't offer up. He also understands that some things following by the book don't help.

"Jeff, it's best if you don't know. I've sent you the information for the car." I tell him

"Dax, I need more information than that... I can't make this disappear unless I know what I'm making disappear." I groan as look around.

"The woman's whose car it is..." I pause again trying to get the words out.

"You're fucking her?" Jeff says point-blank.

"No, well... no, it's complicated... look she needs help. Crazy as hell husband that she served divorce papers to," I lower my voice and look at Jeff, "after she severed him papers he started calling her not

saying anything, breathing on the phone, stalking her, sitting outside of her house, breaking into her house." Jeff's eyes look around quickly and look at me, "He's shown up at the club a couple of times, has yelled at me."

"She works for you?" He asks and I shake my head no.

"She's a principal at a fucking high school." Jeff smirks I'm sure at the thought of me and a principal, "He was at Sirens right before her car blew up. She yelled at him, punched him in the face." He looks down now, "Anyway, we did a little digging, he took out another life insurance policy on her before he went out to sea."

"Goddamnit Dax, he's military?"

"Yeah, he's getting booted out though. Jeff, he stands to make over a million if she dies." Jeff's eyes grow large. He's seen men trying to kill off their wives for far less than that. "He's a bad fucking guy."

"She needs to get a restraining order." He whispers to me.

"Fuck, good those do. I remember what happens." He knows how I feel about them, "He's smart Jeff. Rigged up her house with motion sensors and cameras. Put a tracker on their computers." He looks around.

"What are you going to do?" He asks me and I shake my head.

"Not sure yet, I'm watching out for her, though."

"Dax, you know there are some things that I can't get you out of." I nod my head.

"Jeff, if I don't do anything, it'll happen again."

"I know, you know that my hands are tied though. I have to have some sort of evidence that it's him. It can't be circumstantial." I nod my head.

"I know, that's the difference with us."

"Damnit Khan," opposed to everyone else in my life, Jeff only uses my road name when he's pissed off at me.

I lower my voice and look at him, "Jeff do you think I'm wrong?" He doesn't say anything, "Do you think that if she got a restraining order, and I did nothing, that she will live?" I ask him and he doesn't answer, "Goddamn, fucking answer me." His eyes widen and he looks up at me.

"Sadly, statistically probably not," he won't look me in the eyes.

"Okay, Jeff all I ask is that if you find the body. You don't press too much into it." I look hard at him.

"What do you mean?" My words confuse him. I hear the door close and when I look up I just shake my head.

"Is that the fucker that came in yesterday?" I nod to the counter where Brad sits. Jeff turns his head glancing at the counter and nods his head. "That's her husband, Brad." Jeff stiffens in his seat and looks back up at me.

"Why is he here?"

"Why do you think?" I ask him.

"Right, because you're not sleeping with his wife?"

"Yeah, and I kind of told him that if he fucked his marriage up I would-," I pause as Brad approaches the table.

"Khan!" He exclaims and I nod my head.

"Bobby," I say poking the bear with what I know isn't his name. At that time my phone buzzes in my pocket. I bring the phone out of my pocket and check my text.

"That my wife?" He sneers at me. I don't answer him and he doesn't look at Jeff. Funny since he spoke with him yesterday at the precinct. His anger is centered on me. Sandy calls to him that his food is up as he walks back over to the counter I'm surprised to see the food in to-go containers but I am thankful that he is leaving.

"Was it his wife?" He asks me and I smirk nodding my head.

"She was just letting me know she made it to work okay." He looks at me concerned.

"Holy, shit." Jeff says the words as if all the pieces have finally fallen into place, "You're in love with this girl." He doesn't say it as a question but as a statement.

"What, no, I haven't known her for long enough. That's what you told me when I got married"

Jeff actually laughs, "No, what I said is you haven't known her very long AND you're not in love with her." I can't argue with him on that point. "But you were never in love with her." I look at him started to protest when he starts again, "Dax, you never loved her. You thought that you were falling behind in life. Your parents were already married and had you by the age that you were at the time. Your marriage was a good idea for you. She made you feel good about yourself. That's it. When she left it hurt your pride more than anything else." He pauses again, looking at me, "But when you talk about this girl. Your whole demeanor changes. And you really mean you haven't slept with her?"

"No, I think it may be what kills me." He laughs so hard that it startles Sandy at the other end of the restaurant.

"Why not?"

I shrug, "She was still with Fuckstick, when I met her, he's been messing with her head over the course of their marriage, and she isn't ready yet."

"You're okay with this?" I shrug my shoulders.

"I don't want her to feel bad about it afterward for any reason," he roars with a laugh.

"Holy shit," he pauses, "but are you still… you know?" He asks

"Fucking other women?" He nods, "No." his mouth falls open so far that I see food fall out, "This girl is killing me." He laughs and then grows serious again.

"Fuck, you really are in love." I just roll my eyes in response to him. "What's he on?" Jeff asks.

"Heroin." Jeff's eyes grow larger and he nods his head.

"Makes more sense now. " he pauses as he looks at me. "Dax, if you get in over your head… hand it over to us." I nod my head and then his voice lowers as he looks at me and leans across the table so that only he and I can hear, "Whatever you do, don't let it trace back to you."

"Jeff, how long have you known me?"

"Way too fucking long." He mumbles and I actually laugh.

"Have I ever let it trace back to me." I grab a 50 out of my wallet, tossing it onto the table, and start to walk out.

"It's on me." He mutters as I begin to walk.

"You bought enough of my meals."

I say back to him, turning around and throwing my hands up as I continue to walk out the door. He smirks at me as I walk out of the door.

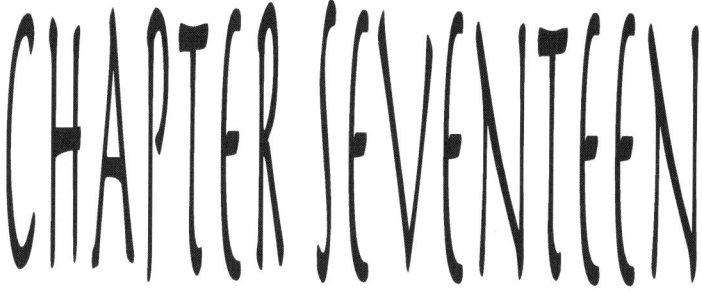

CHAPTER SEVENTEEN

...It's like a game of house, but skipping all the good years.

BILLIE

It's Monday morning so the same 8:30 phone call comes through. Only this time it isn't dead air. Instead, it's Brad's voice, "I ran into your boyfriend this morning. I was surprised to see that he wasn't watching you more closely when his lackey dropped you off at work, but then I saw him at the diner and that he had a more important meeting to attend to. I get it. I've been married to you for long enough to understand that you're only good for a good fuck."

"Brad, what would you know about me being a good fuck? You have barely fucked me in years." I should antagonize him. I should just hang up, but I don't… I can't help it.

"SHUT UP YOU FUCKING SLUT!" He screams it into the phone and I hang up.

A few hours later I walk out into the lobby of the office as I find Abby and smile at her.

"Ms. Saxs," I always hated that she called me that, but Brad insisted on it.

"Please, call me Billie," I tell her. She looks hesitant at first until she sighs slightly and looks back at me.

"Billie," I smile at her in acknowledgment.

"Thank you. I wanted to talk to you about something." I pause, I can't help but hesitate, "If Brad comes here don't let him back."

"Is everything okay?" She asks and I nod my head.

"Yeah, we are separated and he hasn't taken it very well." She looks concerned… maybe for my well-being. "I'm fine, it's just that he's been calling me every Monday at the same time… sometimes other times."

"Have you thought about getting a restraining order?" She asks me.

"I haven't, but maybe. Thanks for the suggestion." She nods. I'm not sure how well restraining orders actually work. I've heard people getting them but still getting harassed.

"Billie, I don't mean to be intrusive to your personal life, but I have to ask does this have anything to do with that man that keeps showing up for you? Wessex?" Her face flushes when she speaks about him.

I smile and I look down, "to do with what? divorcing Brad," I let a laugh slip out, "no."

"but…"

"He has made it known that he's interested." It's the easiest way that I can explain it. She nods her head more in an understanding that I don't want to talk about it anymore.

Around 4 that afternoon, I receive a text from an unknown number.

Unknown: It's Fury, I'm outside. I gather my things and walk out the door.

"Hey, kid," he bows to me and opens the door.

"You're like 5 years older than me?" I can't help it and he laughs as he nods his head. He gets in the truck and pulls off from the sidewalk of the school.

"You hungry?" He asks me, "I'm starving. Lucy finishes up work in an hour. Let's drive out and grab something." Pulling out my phone I look at the screen.

"He had a meeting with Jeff this morning, and then something came up that he had to go take care of in the desert. He will be back later tonight."

"I wasn't-," I try to defend myself but he cuts me off.

"Sure you weren't." He nods his head

"Who's Jeff?" I ask him, remembering him calling Jeff when my car exploded. I say remembering like it was so long ago. Although it was only 3 days ago it feels like a lifetime has passed since.

"He's the police captain of the precinct that the businesses and clubhouse are in."

"What is he like on your books?" I say phrases that I have no idea what they mean and he starts laughing.

"Not exactly, at least... I don't think so. I dunno, ever since I've been here he's just been someone we can rely on. He and Khan go way back, have a really weird relationship. He calls him Dax." I look at him kind of surprised, since Ella and I seem to be the only ones who call him that. Fury nods almost like he can read my thoughts and is agreeing with them.

"What do you mean?"

"I dunno, I've never really asked. Khan doesn't really like to open up about himself especially before he joined the MC so I don't push. If he offers up the details I'll listen but that doesn't happen too often.

All I can tell you is that when Khan joined it came with Jeff as an ally... eventually."

"What do you mean eventually?"

"Awe, shit, I think I've already said too much." He says, pulling the car into the parking lot and getting out.

"Come on, please" I grin like a little kid. He nods in the direction of the coffee shop and we walk in. We order coffee and some baked goods and go to a table sitting down.

"All I know is the rumor. Khan was really young, younger than most when they join. He was 15." I nod my head already knowing this part of the story. "Anyway, the rumor is that Jeff showed up at the clubhouse one night and forcefully removed Khan from the house. They made a truce that night that the Syndicate would kind of clean up their act and he would try to see that his precinct wouldn't crack down on us so much. The club also tried to help him along in getting promoted to captain as much as possible." I'm sure he sees the shocked expression on my face and he sips his coffee and continues,

"What?" He shrugs "That's the rumor, at least," he pauses as he takes a sip of coffee and a bite of his muffin, "but Oz was the last one here that was around during that time. So, there's really no one besides Khan can really talk about the story."

"But you know more about it don't you?" I ask him and he laughs, nodding.

"Of course, but that's not my story to tell." I guess from my facial expression he can see that I am not impressed, "Plus, Khan may trust you, but I'm not sure yet."

"You're fucking my best friend and we're living in his house." He shrugs

"Still don't know you well enough. Sorry, I like you and all, but I'm still not sure how you will react to this life and I'm more concerned about my friend and my club than anything else." Then he started laughing. "But after the stories that Lucy told me about you from

high school and college. I'm a little bit more convinced." I groan and he starts laughing even harder. "See, you hate those stories."

"I don't hate them, I just hate it when she does shit I ask her not to." He laughs again and then nudges me that it's time to go.

As we get into the truck he looks over at me and laughs again, "Which story did that make you think of?"

"I just can't believe you drag race."

"Correction, I used to drag race. Brad said that it was degrading for a woman to race a car."

"I'm sorry to be so blunt, but from what I've seen of him and what I've heard about him he sounds like a dick, why were you with him for so long?" He asks as he cranks the car and guides it out of the parking lot.

"I dunno," I mutter and he looks at me.

"Humor me." He says maneuvering the car back to the road, "Try to explain."

I look out the window as he starts to drive in the direction of Lucy's work. I think about everything over the last 10 years and I think about this whole time I have been afraid to say what I really feel. We are at a stop like a couple of blocks away before I speak again, "I was young. I was 20. It seemed like a good idea. I didn't have the best environment growing up, was afraid of being alone. So, I married him. Turned out being married to him I would be more alone than if I was actually alone. He would seclude me from people when he was home but he would go out all the time. I honestly don't really think I even cared that he did or maybe he had me so brainwashed that I didn't even realize what I was doing." I lean my head against the window as I watch the road pass up by.

KHAN

I enjoy driving out to the desert most of the time, but I hate doing it during the day. I usually go at night but when Dyno called me today, it sounded like it was urgent and I wanted to be back tonight to spend time with Billie, the fuck is this girl doing to me.

"Hey Dyno, what's up?" I walk into the lab and talk to him.

"I finished those bombs you wanted. Need any more yet?"

"Not yet, things took a kind of interesting turn."

"How so," he asks and I laugh as I talk with him. It's weird being out here with Dyno because not a lot of the club comes. It's really mostly me. So, I feel like I can talk to him about things.

"You know weird shit. I have a woman currently living in my house."

"You're fucking with me right?"

"Nope, her-," I stop mid-sentence and look around, "can you make chloroform?"

"Yeah, that shits easy, you can make chloroform. Or a very close substitute." His eyebrows furrow as he pauses and then asks, "Are you using it for this girl that's living with you?"

"What no? What do I need to make it?"

"Isopropyl alcohol and bleach."

"Iso-what?" He laughs.

"Rubbing alcohol."

"That's it?" I ask him and he laughs, nodding his head.

"Also, do we have any heroin here?"

"What?" His word comes out as a curious exclaim, "Are you doing-,"

"Fuck no. You know I don't touch that shit. Just do we have any?" I ask him as he thinks. When our charter of The Syndicate started to progress from a complete outlaw club there was an unspoken rule that was made with our charter. The only drugs we would "fence"

would only be *party drugs*. We didn't want shit that people regularly became addicted to so we decided to try MDMA, mushrooms, and sometimes acid. Peyote on the rare occasion, although that shit goes quick. The guys at our parent chapter were hesitant at first but when they saw the money that was made from it, they were shocked. After some time of searching his brain, Dyno looks at me nodding, "Yeah, there's some back there."

"Also, why do we have heroin?" Dyno sighs a little and then says.

"You don't want to know." I take him at his word and keep moving through the fallout shelter. "Khan, the reason why I called you out here is I'm pretty sure that I figured out a way to make the MDMA purer."

"What?" I ask him and he nods his head.

"I think, I have perfected the technique," he pauses wondering how much I want to know, "it's all about filtering. You want to separate the layers and then filter them. When you crystalize it, it's a more pure substance.."

"Dyno, I have no idea what you are saying, but you are a fucking genius." He shrugs his shoulders.

"Khan, I've been thinking about what you suggested and I think I could use some help around the lab." I nod my head.

When I get back to my house it's late and I'm tired so I just go home instead of stopping by the clubhouse. Walking inside, the whole house is dark, grabbing some water out of the fridge I head upstairs. Knocking on Ella's door I peek inside to tell her that I'm home, but she's already asleep. Walking towards the bedroom door I can see that the light is still on and I smile. How have I known this girl for two months and she's already infested my life? Opening the door I walk in to see her sitting up, leaning against the headboard, reading a book.

"I was just about to text you and make sure that you were coming here." She smiles, looking down shyly. I sit on the end of the bed and take my shoes off, then let my body flop onto the bed. "You okay?" She asks.

"Yeah, just had a weird day," I tell her as I let myself roll up to where she sits and lay my head on her lap. It's weird how comfortable this is, how comfortable that all of this intimacy that I have never really done before is with her. Even if we haven't slept together I still have shared more intimate moments with her than I have any other woman in my life. She sits down the book then she runs her fingers through my hair.

"What was weird about it?"

"I met with Jeff. Got everything with the fire sorted. Ran into your husband-," she cuts me off.

"Yeah, I heard about that."

"How?" Now I'm intrigued.

"Um, he called me again today."

"What!" My voice comes out louder than I meant for it too. "You should have called me. Or Fury."

"I was fine. I was at school. He couldn't have just gotten in." I nod my head knowing that she is somewhat protected at school. She pauses and then looks at me, "Who's Jeff? I'm sorry if I'm being nosy and you can tell me to stop but..." I stop her word vomit from embarrassment as I look up to her, smiling.

"It's okay. For whatever reason, I don't mind telling you things." I pause trying to put the words together since it has been so long since I have told anyone about how I met Jeff. The last person I told the whole story to was Oz, 20 years ago. Even then when I recanted the story to him I hadn't quite dealt with it nor did I let myself feel anything. "I'll make a deal with you." She nods her head. "I tell you this story and you tell me why you were living with Lucy in high school."

"She told you about that."

"It was a sentence she said in a story." And she nods her head.

She's still running her fingers through my hair and I take a deep breath. "Jeff was one of the officers that reported to the house when my mother died. First on the scene," I can feel her nod her head, and I take a deep breath again, "or really maybe I should say it like it was when she was murdered." I can hear a slight inhale of her breath when I say the word, "My dad was deployed, I was 10 and I came home from school to find her." As I say it I close my eyes and I can see the scene like it just happened like it was 10 years old me again opening the slightly ajar door to see the blood river which branches off into bloodstreams as it trickles in from the kitchen the only thing keeping me from spiraling into the entire scenario is her fingers stroking my hair. "While I'm talking please don't stop doing that," I whisper to her and for the first time since talking with Oz that night, I try and open up about it. Only this time, I try and completely open up to her because for whatever reason I feel like I can.

"There was a man in our neighborhood who was in love with her. But the admiration turned to stalking pretty quickly. She told my father but he just told her that she was overreacting and that she should appreciate that people still found her attractive. Which was ridiculous because she was 29. When he left for deployment it started getting worse. I remember going with her to the police station while she filled out the paperwork for a restraining order." Her fingers keep me here as I think about that day sitting in the chair next to her in the station, "She told them about the phone calls, the drive-bys, the letters he would send her. This went on for a few weeks after he was served with the restraining order and she would call the cops and they would tell her that since he never signed the letters and that no one would speak on the phone there was no way to prove it was him. She bought a gun. A month before my father was due to come home is when I found her. I called 911, they asked me if she was breathing, to check for a pulse. Even being so young I knew she was dead when I saw her, no one can lose that much blood and live. Jeff was the first officer on the scene and found me sitting outside of the house, nearly covered in blood, and sat with me. He actually let me stay with him and his wife, Mary, until they got the Red Cross message to my dad and he got back stateside. Jeff was a rookie cop, at the time. Just started on the force, maybe 21. He kept up with me for a while. When my dad died, I hadn't seen Jeff in probably a year, or so, but he showed up at the funeral and sat with me through it. Even though my uncle had custody of me. Jeff was kind of more of a father figure than him or really my dad ever was." She's still quiet as she still runs her fingers through my hair.

"I heard there was a rumor that he dragged you out of here when you first joined the club."

"Yeah, that happened." I'm also going to kill Fury. "He was really concerned. I mean here is the 15-year-old kid who's orphaned all of a sudden hanging around with these outlaw bikers and they were a lot rougher back then. Jeff came in one night when I was here. I had a girl sitting on my lap, he pulled her off of me and pulled me out of the clubhouse. I told him I hated him that night and I wish he would have never come that day when she died because had it been anyone else they wouldn't have still given a shit about me. Oz heard me say it and then sat down with Jeff and talked to him. They came up with an understanding that if the club *toned down* their illegal activity then the cops would *tone down* their pursuit in us. They made a plan to do so Oz would help him however he needed to make captain and take over the precinct. Now, it's your turn."

"My story is boring, comparatively," I roll my eyes, but at the same time that she thinks so. I would never wish someone having to live through that shit. "I never knew my father. And my mother was a character."

"Was?"

"I guess I should say is, although she's pretty much out of my life… haven't heard from her in years…" I nod my head understanding. "She had some mental issues and never dealt with them. She would come and go whenever she felt like it. Beginning of middle school Lucy and I became friends. After a year or so of knowing her is when her parents realized that my mother was leaving me home for weeks on end, alone and they unofficially adopted me. It was an unspoken rule between all of us that whenever my mother went on her *vacations* that I come and stayed with them."

"Benders?" I can't help but ask.

"Similar, my mother's addiction was men. She had to have one loving her at all times, it's the only way that she felt like he had any

worth. She would meet a man, follow him to LA, Seattle, one time she went to Maine. Lucy's parents took me in and gave me everything. Literally everything, they bought me clothes, all my school supplies, they gave Lucy and me a car when we were 16, paid my insurance, my college tuition, they always treated me like I was their daughter. They always wanted another kid but Lucy's mom almost died in labor with her so they decided that it wasn't worth the risk."

"They still around?" I ask her and she nods.

"Yeah, they live up outside of Bakersfield." I slide to the side of the bed and undress. I can feel her eyes on me as I slip my shirt off and then my jeans. I pull back the covers and crawl into bed.

"That's good that you have them," I whisper to her and I wrap her up in my arms, pulling her into me.

"Yeah," her voice is sad though.

"What is it?"

"I'm so grateful that they are a part of my life, but it doesn't take that pain of my mother not wanting to be around away. I almost wish that she would have left when I was a baby. Put me up for adoption hell even leave me at the fire station." I try not to laugh at her comment about the fire station, "It's almost like the fact that she was around for longer-,"

"Made it worse that she left when she did?"

"Yeah, like I wasn't enough for her." She sighs which causes me to pull her tighter into my chest.

"I want you to know," I start leaning up onto my elbow and looking down at her, "doing that this morning." I point towards the bathroom talking about the shower and she blushes, "took every ounce of willpower in my body. You keep tempting me and I dunno how many more times I'll be able to do that…"

"What if I don't want you to do that?" She asks me shyly and I shake my head. "No, listen. This is weird. It's like a game of house but skipping all the good years." I laugh. "I feel comfortable and safe with you. It just seems to all make sense when I'm in your world, when for so long of my life hasn't."

I shake my head as I look at her, "No, you said."

"I know what the fuck I said." I look at her stunned with her use of the word *fuck*.

"Princess, I don't want to push you into anything and you're right this is kind of weird, but I don't want you to be anywhere else. And anytime it feels like it's too much can go over to the clubhouse…"

"Please don't." She whispers, I just shake my head knowing that I'm not finished.

"…I can go but if I do I will just worry all night that something is wrong. Even though it is safe. Let's figure out how we're going to handle the situation with your husband and then we'll worry about this." I say the last point while moving my finger between her and me.

Leaning over I place a small kiss on her lips before she grabs a hold of me and presses her lips harder to mine. Which fuels my ache for her as I let her deepen the kiss. I feel her tongue skirt on my lips so I let them open and let her in feeling her tongue pressing against mine as her hips turn, grinding up against mine.

Fuck…

I know that there is no way she can't feel my growing need for her pressing back into her pelvis and when she lifts her leg up laying on top of mine I nearly lose it. I can feel how wet her pussy is through the small pair of shorts she is wearing as well as my boxers as she pressing them into my cock. I know I should break our kiss. I should cool it down, but my willpower and my cock are on the same team at the moment. The little moans coming from deep in her throat causes my dick to twitch, craving to be buried deep inside of her.

"Princess," I groan at her pulling back as I feel her fingers slipping underneath the waistband of my boxers.

"What?" Even with the lights off, I can hear the innocent tone she tries to play. Groaning I roll over, standing up from the bed, "Where are you going?" She asks confused.

"To take a cold shower," I mumble as I walk across the room, "and I'm locking the door." I actually hear a small giggle come out of her mouth before I shut it and turn the shower on.

This woman is trying to fucking kill me.

BILLIE

There's a strange feeling of normalcy that comes from living at Dax's. It for whatever reason just feels right.

During the daylight hours, we play *house*: getting up, getting dressed, eating breakfast, lunch, and dinner, it all just kind of comes together.

At night as we lay in bed, somehow comfortably wrapped in one another and we talk, we laugh, we kiss… Dax always makes sure to break it off before it gets too heated. If he let things escalate further I wouldn't stop them. It's almost like he sees me. He seems inside of me to the person that I really am and he accepts me for it all.

This is something I never had while I was with Brad. I was always on alert when it came to him. I was always hiding who I really was. It's why it worked with him being gone. At first, I could hide who I was while he was here and then let those parts of me out when he was gone. At some point though, I stopped letting that side of me out.

I guess that's how emotional abuse works. It's a slow battle that takes years but for some reason those who like this game get off on the length of time it takes.

CHAPTER EIGHTEEN

...Don't kill your biggest buyer

KHAN

"Tito is coming to the drop tonight," Ash tells me as he sits down next to me in the office.

I can't help but groan thinking about our last interaction. "Did he still sound pissed?"

"Nah, although I do think he wants to talk to you about the house again." I roll my eyes and look over at him as he stands at my desk. It's been a month since we met with Tito last. A month for him to get over me pistol-whipping him. A month for him to get over outsmarting him. Tito has always had a problem with me. Even before he was the president of the Henchmen, hell even before he was with the Henchmen. He had a mid-life crisis bought a motorcycle and decided that he didn't want to work the solid 9 to 5 anymore. He blames me for the reason why he left our club and went to the Henchmen, but I remember him talking about the turf wars that the Henchmen kept having and how their officer positions can't changing. It seemed like they had a new officer every month and we had started to transition away from certain aspects of illegal activity. He blames me for it, which is kind of my fault, but it's also the reason as to why in the 20 years that I have been a part of this club only a few of us have gone to jail and Oz has been the only one who seems to be doing a long stint. Next thing I knew Tito was gone. Renounced us. We have a weird understanding with the Henchmen, that I have always respected. We sell our drugs to them, for them to sell, and they stay the fuck out of our territory.

"Oh, and Marissa came by Sirens last night looking for you." I stop, looking at him not really sure who he is talking about.

"Who?"

"Whiskey." He laughs, shaking his head.

"Oh, why? Is she trying to get her job back?"

"No idea, Prez, she just came by and said that she needed to talk to you and only you. Wouldn't tell me why."

"Okay," I make a mental note that she is looking for me but I'll probably just wait until she pops back up, "let's fucking make a trip to purgatory."

"Wait, I'm coming with you?" He asks causing me to laugh, nodding my head.

"Yes, you're fucking coming with me. I'm not driving the jeep out there by myself." I pause when I look at him, "When's the last time you were out there?" And he looks around. All the guys feel like Dyno's fucking weird and don't get me wrong. He is. He's a weird fuckin' dude, but he's good, nonetheless. "Shit, we've got to start getting everyone to go out there more often," I pause thinking about the guys that are in the other room. I think about yelling out but I know that if I do no one will be able to hear me with the music playing. "Go get V," I tell Ash. It's still weird to me to give out orders. Although everyone is right I have been doing it for years. The only difference now is that I'm doing it from a different desk, it was easier to just move desks than it was to move all of Oz's folders over to mine. I hear the music turn down in the other room, some shuffling, a door open and then close, then Ash shows up with V at the door a few minutes later, V has pants in hand.

"Jesus Christ, V, put your fuckin' pants on." I snap to him as he slips them on his legs. Then he walks into the room, standing at my desk. Ash walks into the room and sits down in his chair. "How long have you been here?" I ask him, knowing for myself, but wanting him to tell me. I want to make sure that he's keeping track.

Without any sort of hesitation, he looks at me, "Got patched last year. Was a prospect for the normal year and a half."

"Have you ever been out to purgatory?" He nods his head.

"Once,"

"What'd you think of it?" I ask him.

"The lab was really nice. Dyno's cool," He tells me. He's one of the only ones who got along with Dyno, mostly because V is also a little weird and a lot nerdy.

"How would you feel about going out there a couple days out of the week?" His face lights up.

"Really?"

"Yeah, Dyno needs some help in the lab. He's gotten some formula he's working on. I thought with your background that you could help out." He nods his head and I can see the wheels turning in it. V stands for volatile… fucking chemistry nerd.

"Am I being banished out there?" He asks me and I can't help but laugh.

"No," I try and I pull myself together, "we haven't had anyone who likes it out there. Dyno does a great job, but he needs help and he needs to be around people more often." He nods his head. "I keep telling him that he doesn't have to stay there all the time, but he losses track of time while he's working and forgets to come back." I pause having to lay down the rules for him, I stand up as I walk around my desk and come face to face with him. "Two things about going up there. Never put it in your phone or GPS," He nods, "and don't ever take anyone there without approval from us first." He nods his head. He already knows all of these rules since it's the same rules that apply to the clubhouse, but I have to make sure that he knows that it also applies to purgatory. "Be ready to go in an hour. You will follow us on your bike. That way you can come back when you need to." He nods his head and walks back out of the room.

"You're going to let him up there with Dyno."

"Yeah, Dyno asked for some help."

When we make it to Joshua Tree we pull off I watch V in the side mirrors as he turns his phone off, takes out the SIM card, and puts them away again. "Ow, fucking paperclip," Ash mutters from beside me and I just shake my head as he stares at his finger, a small droplet of blood forms on the tip of it.

I grab the top bar of the jeep and pull myself off of the seat and slide out, "Make sure you pay attention." He nods his head. This is where it gets tricky for anyone who doesn't come up here regularly. We turn off onto the dirt road which takes us up the mountain. When we reach the entrance I pull forward, letting V go in front of us into the entrance, I reach over grabbing the headrest and lifting myself slightly off of the seat as I back up into the entrance. This is the whole reason why we ride up here without the doors and the whole reason why it doesn't have any running boards on it. It's so close that both sides of the jeep are mere inches away from the walls. It only lasts for a couple of seconds until the entrance expands and we hop out of the car.

"Jesus, you done that before?" Ash laughs.

"Once or twice." I nudge V off of his bike as the three of us walk over and place our phones in the lockbox.

"So, why do we have to lock up our phones? If we turn them off and take out the SIM cards?" V asks and I just look over to Ash, asking him if he wants to take this one.

"There's a possibility that the software can listen to you while it's off. Don't want to take any chances so while you're doing anything here, the phone stays locked the fuck up." Ash explains to him and V nods his head, understanding.

I shut the lockbox and turn the key so it stays closed and then presses the code into the pad, the door opens. Dyno stands at the door and I can see the bags under his eyes and completely disheveled, "Jesus, Dyno when's the last time you fuckin' slept?"

"Huh?" he looks at me barely aware that we are in the room with him.

"Sleep, when's the last time you went to sleep?" He thinks about it.

"What's today?" He asks me and I shake my head.

"Wednesday," and his eyes widen.

"3 days,"

"Jesus Christ," I mutter as shake my head and look back at him, "you've gotta start coming back up to the clubhouse."

"I like it out here." He tells me and I just shake my head,

"Dyno, come out here Monday thru Thursday. Friday thru Sunday come back up to the clubhouse." He looks at me, the only way I know how to describe it is pouting, I swear it like

having 15 kids. "We'll readdress it in a few weeks." He nods his head, still pouting.

"Wha-what am I going to do there?" He looks sad.

"Drink, party," Ash says at my side, "fuck some chicks or you can find some chick to play house with like Khan here." I cut my eyes at him without moving my head. Dyno's eyes widen as he looks at me.

"You…" Dyno points at me.

"It's not like that."

"It's like that. Exactly like that, he's not even fucking her."

"Fury has a big fucking mouth." They all laugh at me. "Okay, we're going to load up the jeep. You two come back tomorrow."

"He's staying?" He looks at me confused and I nod my head.

"V is going to start coming up here with you."

"Um, we, um can't leave it empty that long."

"It'll be fine. Between the secure doors and the security cameras we can keep an eye on it." I tell him and he starts to object. "Dyno, enough." My words are loud and I hear them echo off of the walls around us. Dyno looks at me wide-eyed. Ash and V just stand slightly uncomfortable. It's the closest thing that I get to yelling. Except for when Billie's car blew up. I haven't lost my shit like that in well over a decade. I try to remain calm and collected. "This is secure. No one knows it's here. There's a keypad to enter. We have a security system all around it… it's secure. No one really needs to be here."

After we're done loading up the jeep and replace the false bottom and clip it into place.

"At least with the tabs we don't have to carry it around in a giant van anymore," Ash mutters to me as I shut the door.

"I'll be right back," I tell him as I walk up to Dyno who is closing up the vault, and make sure that V isn't around. "Dyno, sorry about earlier, man. I just worry about you up here all by yourself. You are putting a lot of stress on yourself and you've kind of got that mad scientist thing going on." He looks at me and nods.

"It's cool. I am really tired. I know you're looking out for me. I'm just not sure I even know how to interact with people anymore." I laugh

"That's why I gotta get you outta here." He nods agreeing with me. "Look out for V. He's a good kid. Chemistry major should be able to help you out with some shit." I walk out of the lab closing the door.

"Shit almost forgot my phone," I say to myself and walk back to the lockbox. Grabbing it out and jumping into the truck and leave.

"What times the meet?" I ask Ash as we pull onto the main road.

"11."

Pulling up to Pistons at 10, I see the two trucks sitting outside. I press the button in the jeep as the door to the bay lifts and I drive the jeep into the bay. Like a NASCAR pit-crew, the guys get to work. And within 5 mins everything is locked back into place.

"Same as last time. Don't be fucking surprised if he has some shit planned," I start as I glance around the room of men. "Same teams as last time. Except for Fury, you're with me, Ash you're on the South end." Everyone nods. "Blaze drive the jeep down there. Don't do a fucking thing until I tell you to."

"Got it, Prez," Blaze looks at me, I turn and walk towards my bike. Watching the groups of men get into the black SUVs and begin to drive in the direction of the marina.

"Why are you wearing those fucking ugly ass gloves," Fury asks me which makes me laugh.

"So, when I pistol whip fucking Tito, Billie doesn't ask why I have blood on my hands." He starts laughing. As he nods his head. "She good at home?"

"Yeah, told her you had shit going on today." He pauses and asks, "You going to finally fuck her tonight?"

"Jesus Christ Fury, fuck." He laughs, "Why are you all over my dick about this? You would think you're the one not getting laid." I tell him which makes him laugh harder. I put in my comms as does Fury. "Ash, Ace you guys there." I hear a yes in unison and I nod as Fury and I ride out to the marina.

"Bro, all I'm saying is that she's been living in your house for a month and you haven't fucked her."

"Fury, you have a fucking death wish?" Ace's comment makes me smile under my helmet at least someone seems to have my back.

"Fuck off, Ace. You're just trying to get him to wait three days, so you win the pool."

"The fucking, what?" I force my voice to sound more angry than humorous, as I actually feel about the situation.

"Goddamnit, Fury, you weren't supposed to say anything." Ash quips in, "I was with him all fucking day and was able to keep it a secret."

"Fuck you guys," Fury claps back, "I don't give a shit anymore, I'm already out." Fury, I, and the jeep turn right onto the road to the marina.

"Ash I need you to keep a lookout of the rest of the Henchmen. Although Ace, stay on guard they will probably come from the north this time. You know how they work..." I pause, "Now that is out of the way I need to know more information about this pool." I can only imagine if we were all sitting around in the clubhouse that they would look back and forth from one another uncomfortably. A full minute passes, "Well?"

"Fury started it." Every day I swear it's like I have a bunch of fucking kids.

"The fuck," I hear Fury, "you just gonna throw me under the bus like that, Ash?" I'm laughing my ass off as I come to a stop on the bike and sling my leg over the bike taking my helmet off.

"Bro, you have a big fucking mouth," I say at him as he takes off his helmet.

"It's just fun and games." We walk up to the water and look out over it. Tito should be here in 15 minutes. He's probably going to be early though because he's always trying to beat me here.

"So, how long did you have?" I ask looking at Fury. He just looks down at the boats in the water.

"Weren't we talking about getting a yacht last time?" I'm trying not to laugh at his attempt of changing the subject.

"Pussy." Ash mutters through the comms, "Khan, he had 3 days."

"What the fuck," I say as a smack him in the chest and he starts laughing.

"Bro, I haven't seen you go longer than like 24 hours since I met you, 13 fucking years ago and you already had gone like a month." I hate it when he makes a valid point. "And let me just point out the fact that I would have been fucking right if someone wouldn't have suddenly found morals." I glare at him,

"Oh yeah, Billie told Lucy about the whole shower thing and Lucy told me."

"What shower thing?" I hear both of the guys on the comms ask.

"Nothing-," I groan "I'm not sure how much I really like the fact that you're still sleeping with Billie's friend." I pause as I look at him and then ask. "You seem to be keeping her around a lot longer than normal." Trying to get the heat off of me this time.

Fury laughs loudly and then starts talking again, "Khan here, got mauled in the shower," I'm gonna kill him, "she jumped on him in the shower and he shut that shit down."

There's silence on the comms for a full minute before I finally say, looking straight to Fury, "You know, I fucking hate you, right?" I see the smile on his face as the sound of bikes come in through the entrance. The reason why I pick the marina is because unless you come in through the water, there's only one entrance, so we can't be blindsided.

Tito pulls up to where Fury and I stand and we make sure to compartmentalize our conversation that we were just having and put on serious faces. Fury's a scary fucking looking guy but is also one of the goofiest motherfuckers that I know. Tito takes his helmet off and can see a slight yellow/green tint on the right side of his face where I had struck him with the gun in my hand last time. That could mean one of two things; he could either know not to fuck with me this time or he's going to try and retaliate. Fury walks up to him and Fury says it for me. "We going to have the same fucking problem this time?" It's like I think it and it comes out of his mouth.

"Fury, I missed you last time," Tito mutters to him and Fury stands his ground. "What you get sick last time?"

"I don't get sick. Didn't answer my fucking question." He stares back at him.

"No," he pauses and looks to me chuckling, "you know I had to test you Khan. I mean I have been the president over here for a lot longer," *don't kill your biggest buyer.* "Khan," he says moving over to me, he sees that Fury moves his hand to his gun, "calm down, Fury, we're just going to talk," he has to sling his arm up to get it around my shoulders and he moves me down the floating dock just like last time, "Have you guys thought any more about our little deal that we talked about last time." Yeah, the brothel, I nod to Blaze and Lex to start unloading the jeep.

"Tito, that's not something that the guys and I want in our territory. Something happens and it's coming back on us," which is exactly why he wants it there. "I'm sure you can find a similar deal within your own territory."

"You mean that your precious daddy Jeff doesn't want it in his territory," I chuckle as look back at him.

"No," but that is a very large secondary reason, "as you know we do have an agreement with him that would be very detrimental for us if we broke it," although if done right, and I brought it to him, he would probably be okay with it, but that's what Tito was hoping for, "we're just still not okay with selling women," I tell him and shrug my shoulders. "Maybe, the next Prez will be, but I'm not."

"Yeah, I heard you got soft."

I hear both Ace and Ash in my ear, "Fuckin' what!"

"What do you mean, Tito?" I ask him.

"I mean, I have this kid coming around my club asking all kinds of questions about you and your club." *Fuck.*

"What kind of *kid*?" I ask stressing the word kid.

"I dunno, probably a few years younger than you are. Asking all kinds of questions. Saying that you're shacking up and fucking

his wife." I think Tito can see the anger building in my eyes. Or maybe he can see the muscle on my jaw twitching.

"And what did you tell him," I ask him through clenched teeth.

"Bender, fucking get Bullet on the phone right the fuck now," I hear Ash say through the comms. Instantly I know that making this kid my VP was the best decision. "Billie's fucking husband is asking Tito questions about us. We need to get an update on Billie."

"Didn't tell him too much, you know I could make sure he doesn't find out too much. But it will cost you." My expression doesn't change. It will cost me approximately a brothel in my fucking territory.

"FUCK THAT GUY" I hear Ace and Ash say... I can guarantee that Fury is also thinking it but he's standing silently with X as the guys exchange money for drugs.

"Tito, just tell me what the fuck you told him." I'm glaring at him now.

"He was looking for you, so I told him where he could normally find you." I can see my nostrils flare as he says that words.

I can hear Ash as he shouts to Bender to tell Bullet to go check on her now... "right fucking now... call back as soon as he gets there."

Tito steps into me and laughs, "That's for pistol-whipping me you fucking asshole." Ace is losing his fucking mind through the comms. And he starts to walk up to the rest of the group. I follow behind him calmly as we walk back up. The guys shut the van doors and leave. X and Tito both get on their bikes.

As I walk up to him my words start, "Tito," my words are quiet but deadly, and all I can think of right now is how I forgot to turn my fucking phone back on after leaving the desert. My words start out quiet, so low that I know X won't even be able to hear them. "If he hurts her in any way... You'll wish the only thing I did was pistol-whip you." I don't break eye contact until he has driven out of the marina.

"Ash, heard anything yet?"

"No, prez... sorry." *FUCK!*

I motion to Blaze and Lex to go ahead and head back to the clubhouse. Then I pull the phone out from my pocket, slip the SIM card back inside, and turn it on. Seeing I have a new voicemail. It's from Billie and she left it an hour and a half ago, but the most worrisome part is that it's a four-minute voice mail.

"Hey," her voice is quiet and she giggles, the only time I've heard her giggle like that since she's been at the house is when she's tipsy. I smile and then her words start coming out fast and jumbled "I know you've been busy all day, but I just wanted to call you. I'm lying down getting ready to go to sleep and it's just a little weird to do it without you here." She giggles again, "Lucy convinced me that it was a good idea to split a bottle of wine with her tonight, and I just got to thinking. I don't believe in fate and all that bullshit but it's just funny how you come into my life before all of this happens and then my life completely shatters. I dunno maybe I'm falling in love with you, oh fuck I shouldn't have said that..." she pauses,

And at the exact same time, I hear Ash come back over the comm saying, "Khan, Bullet says Billie's not there but Ella and Lucy are. He says that there some blood on the floor in your bedroom"

But I'm still listening to the voicemail, "What the fuck is that... are you home?" Then she gasps and it sounds like something is rubbing against the microphone.

"Yeah, I'm listening to it now... she was leaving me a voicemail." Fury looks at me, eyes wide. Walking over to me, "Ash, head over and see if you spot a black mustang Leaving the compound. Ace, go as well… split up see if you can find him. It happened over an hour ago they're probably gone, but who knows. And take your fucking comms out." My hands are shaking with rage now, Fury takes the phone from out of my hands, pressing the speaker button, and continues to play the message.

She screams and there's a loud hollow noise and then a thud as she fell to the ground. "Get the fuck up," you can hear Brad's drug-fueled voice as he whisper-yells at her, he knows that Lucy is in the house as well, that if Lucy hears him she will fight him until he leaves, "or I'll make everyone else come with us."

"No, puh-please don't, they have nothing to do with this." She whispers between sobs, that tear out my heart

"Get the fuck up," he tells her, "unless you want me to shoot you."

"No, please don't." My eyes burn and I'm not sure what this sensation is, "Then fucking get up and walk down those stairs without saying a fucking word."

"Oh-okay, I will." She whimpers.

"Shut the fuck up. Or I'll knock you out and wait for your fucking boyfriend to get home and fucking shoot him in that face you like so much. See how tough he is with a fucking bullet in the brain." He laughs.

"Please don't." She whimpers. "Brad, my head really hurts." She says and I can hear the front door shut. And her whimper "Brad, I'm feeling a little woozy."

"Shut up," he mutters,

"I'm sorry. My feet…" She mutters and he laughs as another loud thud comes through the phone.

"Fuck, Billie, stop being ridiculous. Get up." You can hear as he pushes against her. Fury looks up at me and then his face becomes shocked and quickly looks back down to the phone. "Guess I'm gonna have to fucking carry you back to the car." Then a grunt, he's muttering to himself, and then you hear a thud as I can only imagine he throws her into the trunk. Lastly, there's a faint sound of the car starting.

"Dax," her voice whispers and my mouth falls open, "before this cuts off I faked passing out. I'm leaving the phone in the car so you can track him." Then the message cuts out. I find myself wanting her to say it one more time. Wanting to be able to say it back.

"Khan," Fury says to me and I look up, but my vision is a little blurry, I'm not sure if it's from rage or what, "she's okay right now. She is so fuckin' smart. She's going to figure out a way, okay. You just have to find a way to get her, she's going to stay alive until you get there." I just stare at him dumbfounded, "Pull yourself together," it's only then that I realize that tears are what are causing the stinging in my eyes and my blurry vision. I wipe my face and take a deep breath.

"Give me the fucking phone." Fury hands the phone back over. "Pick up, pick up, puck up," I mutter pacing from my bike to 6 feet away and then back to my bike.

"Yo, kiddo."

"Jeff, I need your help." I've never said those words to him. I've said I needed a favor but I have never said *'I need your help.'*

"Yea-yeah, what is it." The shock in his voice doesn't get past me.

"He took her." Jeff whispers *oh fuck* to himself, "I need you to track her phone."

"Dax, how do you know-," I cut him off.

"She was leaving me a voicemail when it happened. She told me after he put her in the trunk that she was hiding it."

"Okay, Dax. Don't go in there alone."

"I won't."

"Let us come with you."

"No, fucking way Jeff, this fucking piece of shit broke into my fucking house." My emotions are turning from sadness to pissed, the fuck, off and the motherfucker known as Brad is about to meet fucking Khan. "Attacked my fucking girl, threw her in the back of a trunk. This motherfucker is mine." And then Tito is next.

"Daxton,"

"Jeff no, I'm not going in alone." I look to Fury and he nods his head. "If you don't want anything to do with it. I'll fucking find him my way." I'll burn this whole motherfuckin' city to the ground. And he knows it. "Jeff, I'm not letting it happen again."

"Dax, just let us-,"

"What if it was Mary? What would you fucking do?"

"I'd break down the fucking door and shoot him right between the eyes." He sighs, "What's the number." I rattle it off to him, "I'll send you the coordinates." They are back to us within minutes. Looks like the car has stopped in the run-down side of town, but luckily for us, we're not too far. I punch in the coordinates into my GPS and Fury follows me out of the marina. At least I came prepared as I think to the contents of my saddlebag.

CHAPTER NINETEEN

...Give him hell baby, I'm coming for you.

BILLIE

I had to play unconscious when the car finally stopped moving and Brad came back to the back of the car. I'm going to burn this fucking car to the ground... if I ever make it out of here. "Son of a bitch," he mutters as he lifts me up and flips me over his shoulder. I wanted to cringe when Brad touched me, but I knew I had to pretend to be out of it. I hope that Dax gets my message. I had hidden my phone underneath the flooring in the trunk. Where the spare tire goes hopefully that will be enough.

He flings me down on the bed but with such force that my head flings back and hits the wall so hard that my conscienceless actually becomes a little questionable. I can feel him check my pockets he frisks me as I feel something cold and hard touch my wrist and then I hear the noise of the handcuffs closing. *He's a fucking asshole he knows that this is my biggest fear.* He continues to frisk me as he lets his hand linger over my breasts and then he maneuvers to my legs as he starts running his hand up my thigh to my pussy my eyes flip open.

"What the fuck." I shout at him and try to punch him only to have my hand yanked back by the handcuff. He laughs, but I punch him with my left instead.

"You fucking cunt," He shouts the words at me. And I feel a blade pierce my flesh on my arm. I don't wince instead I look him straight in the eye as I feel the blood drip down my arm. "You think you're fucking tough." He whispers to me, pressing the blade into my arm even further, but even though I feel every second of the sharp blade slicing through my muscle I don't so much as flinch. "You think that because you're fucking some big bad biker that makes you tough," he laughs out. "You're the same pathetic, worthless, unlovable cunt that I tricked into marry me 10 years ago."

"What do you mean tricked?" I ask him and he laughs. Maybe if I just keep him talking Dax will get home see that I'm not there and come and find me.

"This was the plan all along." He smiles at me, "Marry you for 10 years and then kill you for the insurance money. Well, I was going to wait for 15, but kinda shot that plan in the foot." He shrugs.

"Because of your heroin addiction?" I ask him and he just looks at me smiling. His smile causes a sense of dread to course through my body.

"Yeah, anyway, No one will question it. I also wore you down over the years. I manipulated you out of the strong independent person you were to someone who needed to be taken care of."

"Well, you fucked up a little. You just took out a new insurance policy on me." And he smiles.

"Yeah, I'll probably be questioned about that, but all I have to say is after the miscarriage I was worried that you would have some sort of lingering health issues and if something was to happen to you while I was out to sea it would be much easier to get everything straightened out." He smiles and stands up.

"Trust me, all of this," I motion around me to the area which we are currently in, which looks like a run-down motel room that hasn't been taken care of in some time and then over to my wrist which confines me to the bed still, "makes me feel so much better."

"Better about what?" He asks me. I smirk at him, and for a second I think I see that he's afraid of what I'm going to say next. "Better about what?" He screams into my face. My face falls dead serious now. As I look at him.

"It makes me feel better about the fact that I've wanted to fuck Khan since the moment I met him right there on my desk, in my office. There's just so much passion between us." His face nearly turns completely red, "Oh, and his cock… it's just so much bi-," this time everything actually does go black.

KHAN

"What's the plan?" I hear Fury ask me through my comms as we ride through the city… splitting lanes, which I usually hate doing, but these fucking cars are in my way.

"Kill that mother fucker." Fury laughs. "Let's get there first, case the place, and then we can figure it out."

"Got it." He pauses for a little bit, "Is it weird for you?" He asks me and I try to figure out what he's talking about.

"Going to save her?" I ask him and he laughs.

"Fuck no, you have a fucking hero complex… you'd save Tito if he was kidnapped. Is it weird with her? Whatever you guys are? Is it weird for you?" He's actually talking about feelings. It's weird especially when we're pushing 100 down the freeway.

"I don't even think about it when it's happening, but yeah, I guess, it's kind of weird. I've never given a shit about a woman. She told me she loved me." I mutter out the last words and I sigh, "And all I could think is if I'm not able to say it back. Not run the fuck away but run to her and save her life so I can take her home and just be with her."

"But you haven't even fucked her yet?" And I laugh.

"Bro, it's fuckin' weird. She said it was like playing house without the good years." And Fury starts laughing.

"I've known that you fuckin' care about her, but I didn't think it was- until back there." I know he means at the marina, listening to the phone call, he saw the tears in my eyes, "It's just like all of this is so fast, I dunno. I guess I can't really talk." He mumbles out the last part.

"Whoa, what?" I yell the words "we're here." I tell him as I can barely see the motel. "He or they are going to be expecting us." I can see him nod his helmet as I glance down the street. I can hear wheels on concrete as a car pulls up next to me and I whip my Glock out of its holster. "Fuck Jeff. What are you doing here?"

"I scouted it. There are 4 guys outside. There's a building across the street that we can get onto the roof."

"Jeff, I can't let you go in there. You'll lose everything." I tell him and he laughs.

"At this point, all they can do is force me to retire." He shrugs, "Come on." He moves his car out of the street and down a side street. He parks and Fury and I push our bikes into a parking garage that isn't used anymore. Reaching into my bag I pull out what my plan consists of then move over to the other men. We all walk carefully down the street without saying anything until he motions to a building. The three of us all have weapons drawn as we walk up the stairwell. My phone buzzes and I look to the screen seeing that it's Ash,

"We found her. Well, kind of. Yeah, go ahead and head down here. No, don't bring everyone." Then I hang up. We watch from across the street at the motel in front of us and can see 4 guys with assault rifles standing in doorways, attempting to be concealed. I stand looking at the scene when I look over at Fury.

He nods, "Call him."

I dial Ash right back and as he picks up the phone I mutter, "Bring, Grim."

"Grim?" Jeff asks me and I nod.

"The Grim Reaper." Fury answers him, "Sniper." Jeff looks at us shocked.

"What made you change your mind?" I ask him not really sure what part he changed his mind about.

"You're right. If Mary was in trouble I would be right there. He'll most likely kill her before we can get to her, but if you guys go in..." he trails and looks at me, "But Dax, I had to come out because if anything happened to you. I could never forgive myself. Mary would never forgive me."

"Thanks." I pause, "For everything." He smiles at me.

"Who's all coming?" Fury asks as we still watch I see Brad come out of a room. We all see it and take note. Room 108. At the same time, 4 more guys come out of other rooms and I groan.

"Ace, Ash, and Grim." Fury nods.

"What's the plan?" Jeff asks us and I press my lips into a firm line.

"What are you thinking?" I ask him and he just shakes his head.

"Like I said if your guys go in. Then we go by your plan, not mine. Your guys, your brothers. They trust you. So you are in charge."

Then my fears are expressed before I even realize it is the reason why I am afraid. "But what if my plan gets her-,"

"It won't be," Fury says.

"Dax, in the time that I have known you, you have never made a bad decision." Jeff takes a brief pause and shrugs his shoulders just slightly, "Except for getting married." Fury lets out one chuckle. "Every decision you have made has been well thought out. And has always been the best possible decision for the situation. You are a born leader. And if you weren't you wouldn't fucking deserve her."

I can't help but smile a little bit, "You ran a background check didn't you."

"Of course I did."

"I'm gonna need to see that after this." He nods.

"She's just your kind of woman." I smile.

"You're," I say pointing to him. "not going to like the plan."

"This asshole, try me," The door behind us opens and all three of us point weapons at the unknown presence.

"Jesus Christ, it's just us." I hear Ash say as the three of them walk out of the door.

"You were supposed to fucking text me." He looks around and then at the bag he's carrying and I reach into it.

"I still don't understand the bleach."

"Shut it. I'm getting to it." I snap at them

"What the fuck is he doing here," Ash says looking at Jeff, "I thought he-,"

"Shut the fuck up. He's here helping." Ash rolls his eyes at me. Glaring up to him as he takes a step back. "Grim, you stay up here with your gun. You have our backs. If shit gets hairy. Take 'em out." He nods his head as he twists the silencer on the gun's barrel. I can't help but see one of the "guards" walk into 108 and I grow furious. Why is he in there alone while she is being held against her will?

"Dax," Jeff grabs my arm and I see the faces of Ash, Ace, and Grim all shocked that he just used my real name.

"You 4 deal with the guards outside. Mix bleach and rubbing alcohol and it makes chloroform. Knock them out... I'm going in." They nod. "Do not take them all out or let them know that you are there until Brad comes back into the room. That motherfucker is mine. He's fucking dead."

"How are you going to do it?" Jeff asks me and I pull out my bag that was on my bike. I open the rolled-up cloth to reveal a syringe, a spoon, a lighter, and a bag of heroin cut with Fentanyl than he is used to. Jeff nods his head. "I'm not going to lie, that's kind of impressive."

"Don't fire your weapons unless you absolutely have to. Chloroform everyone and put them somewhere... I don't fucking care where... lock them in the fucking closets, I don't care." They all nod their heads.

I see the man who just walked in, walks back out, and motion to Brad who is down the sidewalk. He walks back into the room and I lean my whole body quickly to the side until I can see Billie, sitting on the bed, "I can see her yelling at them," Grim says which actually makes me smile, "Oof, she just kicked one in the face."

Give him hell, princess, I'm coming for you.

BILLIE

When I come to again, a strange man is sitting very close to me.

"Can I help you?" I glare at him and he huffs, getting up, and walks out of the room. My arm is throbbing now, but I can't let the pain show. Instead, I swallow the pain and work on breathing exercises. Brad walks back into the room again. The strange man comes back

up to me, maybe trying to makes me stop from screaming and I kick my foot up connecting with his face.

I groan as I look at Brad and scream. "Why don't you just kill me already?" I dare him and he smiles, does this weird body twitch, and looks at me like he is a child with a secret.

"Yes, yes, yes," he mumbles, "Why don't I just kill you? Yes, I was so excited about this question." His words are so fast that I'm sure he's high, "I knew it would come up. I can't just kill you. It has to be an accident." He says accident like it's an exciting word.

"So, feed me alcohol until I pass out, put me behind a steering wheel, and let me drive into the water or a wall."

"Nah, that takes away the fun." I look at him wondering how blind I have been all my life.

"What fun? Of torturing me? You didn't get enough of that in the last 10 fucking years."

"Oh, look at you with the potty mouth. That boyfriend is a bad influence on you." He says flopping on the bed with his head resting on one hand. Then he stops suddenly and stands up, "But no I don't want to torture you anymore, now your boyfriend... he's a different story?"

"Why do you hate him so much?" I ask him, "You don't love me you've already said that."

"You're right I don't love you. But you still belong to me. He feels like he can have whatever he wants whenever he wants. And that's not okay."

"Really that's it?" I ask him and he stops.

"Pretty much, fuck with a man's property." He pauses and looks back to me, "I've seen him over the years walking around this town like he fucking owns the place. Women whispering about him and falling at his feet."

"So, you're jealous of him. You're jealous that women find him more attractive, that he has power and you're just a peon who will never amount to anything." He lunges at me and I feel his hands wrap around my throat. I try and pull them off with my one free hand, but I can't... every time I try he screams in my face, tightening his grip. I can't breathe even though I'm gasping, no air is filling my lungs.

My vision is going blurry and then it's black once again.

KHAN

We moved around the buildings surrounding the motel until we are coming up from behind them. Billie is in the room on the corner and I watch as Brad leaves. I check to make sure that all the guards are focusing on something else, most of them not focusing on anything really and I pull the handle slipping into the room. Fury shouts into my ear, that he has one down. Who is locked in the closet of the first room.

"Tell me when he's walking back," I tell him and they all agree. I see her eyelids move under her eyelids as I speak to the guys as I turn back to her, "Billie," I pause, "it's me."

I can see that she's handcuffed to the bed and there's a pool of blood under her arm from the wound to her bicep. There's a bruise that's already forming on her cheekbone and around her eye. And I can see the red marks around her neck. *I'm going to fucking kill him.* "Princess, wake up, please," I say as I move her head gently trying to check to see if there are any other marks on her. "Billie," my words are strained, "I love you, too. Please wake up." Her eyes flutter open, just like in all the stupid romantic comedies.

"I knew you'd come." Even with her voice struggling to make any sound, I smile, I lean in and kiss her once, at least she's alive. "He's trying to torture you." Her voice is strained which I am guessing has something to do with the marks around her neck.

"Shh, don't speak. How long has he been leaving." She shrugs. "How do you not know?" I whisper to her and she closes her eyes. "He's been knocking you out?" and she nods her head. "Has the one guard been coming in a lot?" She shakes her head no. "Okay, when Brad heads this way the guys are going to let me know." I say, pointing to my ear, "if that guard comes in I want you to be awake so he gets Brad to come back in."

"What are you going to do?" Her words break in and out as she asks me.

"I'm gonna kill him," I tell her looking her in the eyes, no hesitation in my voice...

"Go-good.' She squeaks out in her horse voice.

"Brads on his way back." Fury mutters

"How many are left out there?"

"4."

"Good, get them down."

"Got it, Prez."

I move into the closet as I hear the door open, leaving the closet cracked so I will be able to slip back out without being heard.

"I'm really disappointed, Bil." He walks around the bed and stands next to it, "I really thought he would come out, trying to play the hero, and try to save you. Turns out you have the habit of picking the villains. That passion that you speak of is all bullshit and it was just in your head. I guess you were just another fucking whore to him." He turns towards the end of the bed and sits down on the second bed in the room. Perfectly placing himself for me to come out without him seeing me.

"Prez, they're all down."

"What you were so talkative earlier now you don't have anything to say?" He pauses, "Say something." His voice raises many octaves as he shouts and as I slide out of the closet and make my way to standing right behind him, chloroform rag ready to go, "Fucking say something." He screams at her.

"I prefer anti-hero," I mutter as his body becomes rigid and I place the rag over his mouth holding him in place until he stops moving.

Carrying a limp body is never as easy as I remember it. I rummage through his pocket and find the key for the handcuffs going and unlocking the cuff on her wrist. I pull out the bag and unroll it. She points to questioning. "Heroin, strong enough to… " I let my sentence trail off for a second. "Will look like an overdose." She nods her head. I look to her again and cup her face in my hands she presses her face harder into my left hand. "I'm so fucking glad you're alive," my words are barely audible, her head nods once more. I force myself to get it together. "Fury will be in here in a second he'll take you back to-," she puts her hand up in a protest and shakes her head. "No? No, what?" I ask her and wish she could talk normally.

"Not," her voice cracks and the word surpasses her, but she brings her hand up to pat her chest, "leaving."

"Billie, you shouldn't… I mean you don't have to be here." She nods at me staring at me, daring me to tell her to go home. "Okay," I hesitate, rubbing my hands down my face. I don't fucking like it. I don't think she should be here. But after what she has gone through with him I don't think I can force her to leave. "Do you want me to wait for him to wake up, or do it now?"

"Wait." She pauses as if trying to take time to figure out the words. "Me." She points to herself. Fury comes into the room and tosses me some items to tie him down with and helps me.

"Hey, kid," She rolls her eyes, but smiles, "ready to go" he smiles at her. She just stares at him shaking her head. Not sure if he took out his comms, if he just wasn't listening, or if he's just trying to convince her to leave because he knows I don't want her to be here for this.

"She wants to do it, and she wants to wait until he's awake." I toss my hands in the air looking at him.

"Billie, are you sure?" Fury asks her, she nods her head, staring right at Brad sitting in the chair… She takes a deep breath and she forces the words out.

She takes a deep breath, "He cheated, he lied, he broke me." She whispers and my heart breaks for her. She's looking right at me now, "I'm so glad that you pissed him off that night because if not I

never would have left and he would have killed me then." She pauses and shakes her head. "I'm doing it." And I nod my head.

"Okay Princess, Fury get the syringe ready."

"What the fuck, why me?" He asks which actually makes me laugh.

"You're the med school guy. I don't know what the fuck I'm doing." He laughs with me as he heats up the heroin on the spoon and sucks it into the syringe.

"You sure this is, enough?" Fury asks me and I nod my head.

"It's cut with fentanyl." His eyes grow wide. "Prez," Fury says to me and then nods to the sink that sits outside of the bathroom. Walking over to it he whispers to me, "You're going to let her do that?"

"What choice do I have?" I ask him, "I mean wouldn't you want to do it, if you were her?" I ask him and he just presses his lips into a firm line and nods his head.

"You think she's going to be able to handle it?" He whispers, looking concerned to Billie as she sits glaring at Brad.

"I think she may be stronger than we realize. She's pretty fucking pissed off right now and she's been through a fucking lot in the last couple of months." I pause and look back to Fury, "It's not my decision to make. No matter how much I worry about it fucking her up." He nods his head. "How much damage?" I ask him.

He shrugs his shoulders, "I can only tell so much without further testing." He tells me.

The three of us sit on the bed in front of where the chair, which contains Brad, sits when he wakes up. He looks at us and then surveys his predicament. "The tables have turned," I mutter out to him as he thrashes around in the chair.

"I wouldn't do that," Fury says holding his gun on him. And his eyes grow wide. We have him tied to the chair with a piece of piping tube tied on his arm to make the veins bulge. I even marked the spot that she should prick... even though he has track marks all over his arms.

"What are you going to do?" He asks which actually makes me laugh.

"Just what you enjoy doing," I tell him and I smile. "But I'm not going to do anything." I nod to Billie sitting next to me as she holds the syringe between her gloved fingers. His eyes somehow get wider.

"What is it?"

"I guess," I start, "someone sold you some shit that was cut and forgot to tell you, what a shame." He looks at Billie and starts breathing heavily.

"Billie, please don't... you know you loved me."

"I thought I did," her voice is strained and she winces when she speaks but she needs to say this. She gets off of the bed and takes a few steps to him, "You made my life hell and made me think that I was the problem. Who the fuck do you think you are." She sticks him with the needle and he winces a bit, "Don't be a fucking pussy. You do this shit to yourself all the time." Fury laughs.

Cutting my eyes over to Fury, his laughter dies down a little before he says, "What? She makes me laugh."

"Hey Brad, I'll take good care of her." I mean for it to come out like I'm an asshole but it doesn't, it comes out genuine... because I mean it. I will take care of her. But his eyes fill with rage as he cut them to me. Billie pushes the plunger down and sits, watching... I try to move her as he seizes, but she shakes her head.

"I have to know." When the small trickle of foam comes out of his mouth she finally looks away. She takes the straps off of him and puts them back in their place.

"Jeff," I call into the comms and he comes walking in.

"I mean, he just overdosed." My words are lighthearted and he shakes his head.

"You guys get out of here. Billie, you need to go to the hospital. So, you need to stay."

"No," she mumbles.

"What?" All three of us look at her.

CHAPTER TWENTY

...I refuse to be a fucking victim anymore.

BILLIE

"No," I force my vocal cords to work. I push through my pain as much as they protest, I make them, "If I go to the hospital then for the rest of my life I will be seen as his victim." I swallow hoping that my saliva will moisten them just enough to make the pain subside slightly, "And goddamnit I refuse to be a fucking victim anymore." Jeff and Dax both look at each other and look away. Almost as if they are not sure how to respond to what I just said.

"Bil-," Fury nods his head as he walks up to me grabbing me by the shoulders, gently moving me to face him. "Billie," his voice is concerned and his actions take me by surprise as he pulls me in for a hug,

"I'm pretty sure that you have some degree of laryngeal trauma. It's what is causing your hoarse voice." I wish I could respond but my throat is begging me not to speak so I nod my head, "It could be minor, or it could be really, really bad." He pauses again holding me a little tighter, his eyes are concerned as he looks at me and I smile for a second. To tell him that I understand. "And Lucy will kick my ass if anything happens to you." His comment is meant to ease the tension that has formed in the room.

I start to hear muffled yelling from other rooms. "Everyone is starting to come around." Jeff says as he looks around us, "We have to figure out what we are doing. I have to call this in," he's not talking to me or even looking at me but for some reason, I nod my head.

"Where is everyone else?" Dax asks Jeff.

"I told them all to leave." Dax nods his head in response, his way of saying it was a good choice.

"Go ahead and call it in." He pauses and looks at Jeff. "Call it in, I'll either be out of here or going with you... either way." He nods as we hear Jeff call into his phone he needs backup and the address. "Fury, get out of here."

"Prez," Fury starts to argue.

"Go," the amount of command in his voice shocks me. I watch as Fury's head drops, he turns and looks at me, gives me a reassuring pat on my good arm, and heads out the door. "Billie," Dax whispers to me as he steps, kneeling down in front of me so that he is nearly at my eye level. "You need to go to the hospital." I wince as he reaches up and touches my neck to remind me why I need to go. "You can stay here with Jeff and have them take you or I'll take you up there."

"Dax," Jeff speaks from our sides. "If you do that, they won't ask any questions first they will arrest you for domestic violence." I can't let him do that.

"It won't be the first time I've been arrested for shit I didn't do." He smirks at me. What has he been arrested for before? "Just let me know what you want to do." He mumbles the words out and looks at me. I nod my head I look to Jeff and then down at the ground, sitting down on the bed behind me. "You want to stay" I nod my head. He pauses and looks over to Jeff. "Will she have to recount the story?" He asks Jeff.

"I'll tell them all that she shouldn't talk, but that I already got the story. I'll keep the story out of the media." Dax nods his head.

Dax looks back at me and sighs. "Are you sure?" He asks me and I nod my head.

"Dax, you have got to get going," Jeff says.

"No, I'm staying with her." He says standing up and looking at Jeff.

"Kid, if you stay. They are going to try to pin all of this," he raises his hand pointing at Dax, "on you. I can't protect you from all of this."

"That's fine." He mutters, he starts to speak again and I force myself to place my hand on his arm and he turns, facing me.

"Go." The word doesn't have any sound but I try and force them anyway, "I'll be fine."

"You sure?" I nod my head, "I love you." He smiles down at me as I try to speak, he just shakes his head. "I know," he kisses me softly as if he's afraid that he's going to break me, and then he looks back to Jeff.

"I've got her," and he nods with one last look back at me. I can tell that he doesn't want to leave he hates himself for doing so. I nod my head once more and he opens the door. It only takes a few minutes before I can hear his bike start in the distance.

"Let's get out of this room," Jeff tells me and I follow him outside, sitting down on the cement stairs, "I'm putting in my report that I got here, you were still handcuffed to the bed, unconscious. Brad was already dead." I nod my head, "I got a tip that there was questionable activity in the abandoned motel, that's why I came out here. I'll say that I don't know how those guys ended up in the closets," he pauses and points to me, "you say the same thing. I'm leaving Dax's name and anything to do with The Syndicate out of the report." I nod my head knowing that is for the best.

Then he laughs and I look to him questioning the laugh, "I've known that kid for a long time. I-," I see the pain on his face as he thinks about the scene he walked into when he found Dax, I place my hand on his arm, "He told you," I nod my head. "Holy shit," he mutters as he looks away, "I don't think he's told anyone that story," he pauses again and I can hear the sirens growing closer,

"I've never seen him act the way he does with you, with anyone else." He finally tells me, I look up to him with a questioning looking. The flashing lights of the cop cars are lighting up Jeff's face as he talks.

"But-," my voice cracks and he shakes his head.

"Don't talk," he shakes his head, "but he was married?" I nod. "He never really loved her. He was afraid that he was falling behind in life. He's by no means perfect," I hear the officer call to Jeff, as he walks over and Jeff straightens up.

Everything next happens in a blur. The paramedics show up and pull me into the truck. They check me out and just like Fury had said says something about a laryngeal trauma. The officer who interrupted Jeff comes up to me asking if there's anyone I should call. The paramedics tell her I shouldn't be talking so she hands me her notebook and I write down Dax's number. She looks at the name and then back to Jeff. I watch as the gurney containing Brad's body, which is encased in the black body bag, rolls out of the room and I swallow. When I decided to be the one who did it, I saw the concerned look on everyone's faces. Worried that it would break me. That I would fall to pieces but I'm not fragile. At least, the real me isn't fragile. Maybe the Stepford Wife that Brad made me believe I was maybe, but she's gone now.

The doors shut to the ambulance and the next thing I know we're moving.

"You're really lucky that Captain Dietz found you when he did." Paramedic 1 says to me and I nod my head. "You're arm has been bleeding for a while. I'm surprised that you're still awake." And like him acknowledging it makes it real, my eyes grow heavy.

KHAN

I'm sitting on my bike in front of Pistons. Fury and I don't talk. I'm staring over to the street as the sun starts to peek out from over the mountains.

"What's taking so long?" Fury asks as he shifts from one side to another.

"Call Lucy, have her get some clothes from there for Billie to change into when she leaves, get her from the house, I'm sure that she will want to be at the hospital" I pause having to take a second to remember all of my responsibilities, "Have someone take Ella to school," I tell him and he nods. "Hold up," I mutter as my phone starts ringing.

"Mr. Wessex?" I hear the woman ask me through the phone.

"Speaking…" I try to say in a calm voice.

"We had an incident with Ms. Saxs this morning, she wanted to call you and let you know that she's heading to West Valley Hospital." I know everything that happened and my mouth still goes dry. Something about them saying those words.

"Is she okay?" I ask, this time not knowing the real answer to my question.

"She is with the paramedics now." She pauses, "I believe that she's lost a lot of blood though." Yeah, I could see that as well. "We can tell you more when you get here."

"Oh-okay, Thank you," the last two words are quieter than I anticipated. I hang up the phone as I look to Fury, "West Valley." My back tire squeals as I peel out of the parking lot and head in the direction of the hospital.

"Saxs, she should have arrived not long ago," I don't mean to shout as I approach the nurses' station. The nurse doesn't look up at me but says,

"It's going to be a minute." I groan as I lean against the wall behind me to stabilize myself. "Sir?" the nurse calls to me questioning, "Are you okay?"

"I'm fine, I just need to know where she is." I'm not sure if the mixture of the emotion that coursing over me and my size, if it's my

overall appearance, or if she knows who I am that leads to her shocked expression. "The doctors are evaluating her, it's going to be a little while. They will come and talk to you when they are done." I try to say thank you, but the words don't come out as instead I just mouth the words to her. She gives me a weak smile as I stand in the waiting room.

I can't fucking just wait around in here I think as I walk out to the parking lot, I sit down on a bench and stare at the sky as the colors change further from daybreak into daylight. I feel the weight, of the bench, shifts which causes me to look over to a man sitting down next to me. *I just want to be alone.*

I smell the aroma before I even open my eyes to look in his direction. "You think I can bum one of those?" I ask him and he nods then he starts talking, "I'm waiting on my wife, she's having testing. Nothing serious, You?" He flicks the cigarette pack open and I pull one from the pack.

"My girl," I pause, " she was in an accident," I tell him. He mumbles an awkward *I'm sorry*, gets up, and walks back into the hospital. I hate the sound of pity in his voice. I've heard it from nearly every fucking person since I was 10.

Placing the cigarette between my lips, I let my head fall back again as I roll it between my lips. It somehow manages to settle my nerves some even without lighting it, as I close my eyes. The cigarette is snatched from between my lips as I look up to Fury staring over me.

"Really, you quit 6 years ago," I'm sure my face falls down in a frown.

"I wasn't smoking it."

"Were you going to?" He asks me.

I can't help but smirk as I say, "I don't have a lighter on me," I see Lucy standing to his side, her eyes are red she walks up and hugs me and I embrace her. Her grip on me tightens as a sob escapes her lips. "Shh," I mutter to her, Fury's face falls in an expression that I don't recognize, as he looks at her. I'm trying to figure out if it's sadness for her, maybe for Billie, mixed with a little bit of hostility towards me for hugging her. "Let's go inside," I say as I release her and nod to the door. Fury steps up and pulls Lucy into his side, as they walk behind me inside the building.

I sit down in the waiting room as the duo sits down across from me. I can't keep my feet still as Fury starts talking, "Closest to the day without it passing."

"What?" I ask him when I bring my attention to him.

"The pool, if the day passes you're out." Lucy starts.

"You know about it?" I ask, pointing to her as Fury starts laughing.

"Whose idea do you think it was?" Her head nods quickly as Fury adds, causing me to laugh even harder. "Yeah, everyone's in on it, even Rox… Chell."

"You guys are unbelievable." I quip at them and she laughs.

"Who's left in it?" I ask them and they look at each other.

"Ash, V, Dyno, and" Fury pauses as he looks over, "Lucy."

"You bet on. Wait, Dyno's in on it." Suddenly it makes so much more sense why all of the guys keep being very talkative about my sex life. Lucy laughs as she looks away and Fury just looks to her, "There's more isn't there." I ask him. Fury looks to me, slowly nodding his head, and cutting his eyes as he looks over to Lucy like she's the keeper of all secrets.

"Tell him," Fury urges Lucy as she begins to laugh a little bit harder. "Tell him, what you *just* fucking told me."

"Well," she laughs biting her lip trying to calm herself, "It's a little rigged." She quietly says as she pulls at her shirt.

"What do you mean rigged?" I ask her sitting forward in my chair. Her bottom lip shakes as she tries to control her laugh.

"Billie may or may not be in on it."

"What?" My question is mixed with the laughter that comes out of my mouth.

"Yeah, I told her that Fury and I had a bet. She instigated the whole thing, convinced me to make it bigger. Like, get Fury to get everyone involved. And then she and I will split the money."

"These two assholes," Fury motions to Lucy as she sits next to him and I laugh.

I hear the doors slide open and are surprised as I see the entire club walk into the waiting room. I'm also sure that the hospital staff is as well. Since their waiting room just filled up with bikers flying their colors.

"What are you guys doing here?" I ask them and they all look at me.

"If one of us has shit going on, we all have shit going on. You taught us that." I hear Ash tell me and I nod to him. "Plus, we like her, we want to make sure that she's okay," I smirk to them as I feel a little relieved that they are here with me. I can see the nurse who seemed concerned about me earlier look over to us, the group of bikers all around me, she's concerned about the growing number of *outlaws*, in her waiting room.

"Did Jeff give you the background check?" Fury asks me and I laugh, shaking my head.

"On Billie?" Lucy asks

"Yeah,"

"Oh, I can tell you pretty much all of that." I can't help but cock my eyebrow and look at her. "I'm telling you, she was so much more fun until Brad warped her mind. I mean don't get me wrong, I love her no matter what..."

Ash looks at her and says, "What do you mean, fun?"

"She just wasn't as cautious. So worried about what he thought. It's why I kind of like the idea of the two of you together." She shrugs and then goes on talking, "She was arrested twice for drag racing," *what*, "we were detained at the Mexican border once," *fucking what?* "Let me tell you my parents were not happy about coming to get us that time." Everyone kind of chuckles, "The background check only says what we got caught doing. It doesn't tell about the time that we were almost arrested for indecent exposure. And then one time-,"

"More on that story," Fury turns to her. We all look at her and she laughs.

"It's really not that good of a story." But now all heads are on her as she talks. "Really wish we could wait until Billie was here to help tell it." All of the guys continue to shake their heads no, so she keeps talking.

"Storytime," Fury says to her as he turns in his seat, placing his elbow on his knee, supporting his head, and looks at her. "What type of indecent exposure?" He asks her which makes me laugh.

"Saxs." The doctor asks as Lucy and I stand up and walk over to her. She's a younger woman and I can't help but be cautious about how young she looks and her taking care of Billie, but then again Bil doesn't look her age either. "She lost a lot of blood for the wound to her arm, but we have given her some blood, stitched it up, it's fine. And we have done an MRI and endoscopy. She has small stress fractures on her larynx."

"What does that mean, Doc?" I ask her and I guess from my nervousness of the question she smiles.

"She's gonna be fine. We're going to keep her here for 24 hours just for observations but we're pretty confident as of now that she's going to be just okay. She can't lift anything heavy until her arm fully heals and vocal rest for 7 days. We will want to see her again in a week just to make sure that her larynx is fully healed before we give her the all-clear to come off of vocal rest." I nod my head back at her, "We're moving her back to her room now. When she situated we'll have a nurse come and let you know you can visit her"

"Thank you," I tell her.

Lucy hugs me, "She's going to be okay." Her eyes are watering up.

"Can we see her yet?" Fury asks me.

"Soon," I mumble to him and sit back down.

"What?" Lucy exclaims as we all sit and stare at her trying to get her to finish her said story. "No way." She states holding up her hands. "Plus, how is it I say we were detained at the border and you want to hear about the public indecency?"

"Well yeah," Ash looks at her with a serious face. "Naked chicks always trumps anything else."

Fury glares at him for a second until he looks at him, "What?" He's staring at Ash telling him that it's his fucking woman that he's talking about being naked.

"Fine," she grunts, rolling her eyes. "We were at Burning Man when we were 18. Dropped a little bit of acid." half of the group looks highly uncomfortable the other half of the group looks confused as she says a little bit.

"What is a little bit of acid?" Fury asks.

"Shut it," she looks at him smiling. "The story isn't even that good. We were there, took some acid, and somehow came across a pool. Felt the need to go swimming, we didn't have swimsuits, so we jumped in naked. Anyway, cops showed up apparently we were in someone's pool. We had to jump the fence and run."

"On acid..." Fury makes sure that he's following the story. Lucy just nods her head.

"Why do I feel like you're leaving parts out of the story?" I hear Fury ask Lucy.

"Saxs. Two at a time can go back."

"Khan, come on," Lucy says to me, standing up, she leans over in front of Fury and whispers into his ear. If I wasn't sitting directly next to Fury at the time I wouldn't have been able to hear her. "You know how some people experience a lack of inhibitions?" She pauses, without giving him enough time to answer, she has now piqued my interest wanting to hear the rest of the story, "Well we agreed to never talk about the rest of the story." My imagination instantly jumps to only one scenario. I try to control my expression as I know that I am sitting eyes wide in a very uncomfortable situation. "Come on, Khan." She mutters to me.

I nod my head more times than need be while holding up my index finger, "I'll be there in a minute." My voice actually squeaks as I try and speak.

"Seriously, the shit that I know you two have done and seen." She looks at us, rolls her eyes, and walks down the hallway.

"Dude," Fury says under his breath looking at me, "they have totally..."

"Agh," I shout covering my ears.

"What?" He looks at me confused.

"Bro, I haven't had sex in like 3 months. You can't put that image in my head right now." I say which causes him to laugh. I try thinking about anything to calm my dick from pressing any further into my zipper. Dead puppies. Old people. The normal things. I take a deep breath and then stand up, trying to adjust myself as I know the rest of the guys look at me like I have lost my mind. "Do not say a fucking word," I tell Fury again which makes him laugh even harder. I flip him off as I walk through the double doors. Trying to refocus as I walk down the hallway in the direction of her room.

When I walk into her room I see Lucy standing over top of her and I hear a growl come out of my mouth as the sounds leave me Billie's eyes flutter open. "Good morning," I smile, moving over to her bedside and sitting down. "They tell you that you're on vocal rest?" She nods. "I'm so glad you're safe and okay," I say, leaning over, I kiss her hand. Lucy comes over and sits down on the other side of her. I can't look at both of them in the same space. Because I haven't had enough time to process.

Apparently, Billie instantly notices how uncomfortable that I am and that I'm not looking at Lucy. This causes her to turn her head and look at Lucy. "Oh, that?" I turn my body more so that Lucy cannot be seen out of my peripheral. "Burning Man may or may not have come up." I see the glare that Billie gives her which causes me to laugh. "I mean I didn't tell them what exactly happened-,"

I cut Lucy off, "Unless the next words are it's not nearly what I made it out to be and that nothing actually happened. Can we drop it? I'm not sure if my dick can hear any more, of that story." Looking at

Billie I hold up three fingers, mouthing the words three months and then pointing at her so that they understand that the throbbing coming from my dick is too intense. Billie's eyes widen, so does Lucy's, as well as a different doctor from before, while he is walking into the room. "Fuck," I mumble under my breath. Of course, it's Dan. He looks at me confused for a second, then to my hand which is holding Billie's as she lays in the bed which causes a more confused look to form on his face.

Knowing someone your entire life gives you almost an unspoken language. Even after not speaking to him for over a decade all I have to do is cut my eyes at him, which he knows is my way of telling him, *listen here motherfucker, you don't even think about it. SHE'S MINE.* He nods his head telling me that he understands. Then tilting his head to the side he looks at me trying to tell me *as long as she is okay with that.*

Fuck him.

CHAPTER TWENTY-ONE

...Don't miss this time.

KHAN

""I know." I say as I pull over onto the side of the road, "Let me hold your phone." I tell her and she sends me a questioning stare. I get it, believe me, I do. "Do you trust me?" I ask her and she sends me a look that is trying to say that she's not sure, "Just give me the damn phone." I tell her. The grin on her face causes me to shake my head. I pop out the SIM card of her phone and tell her to put it somewhere she's not going to lose it. I watch as she slips it into the watch pocket of her jeans. *That's going to be a pain in the ass to get out later.* I shrug as I put mine into my wallet and then flick the light off, "Don't worry. I do this all of the time. It will be fine." I tell her before I lift the bike up and pull back out onto the road.

Pulling off of the road as I steer us up the mountain to purgatory. She clutches me tighter the higher up the mountain that we go. When I flip the bike around and slowly start to back us into the mountain she's looking back to see where we are going as well. Her eyes are wide as she sees the tunnel widen and then the jeep sitting. She looks back at me and I smirk.

Turning the bike off I look at her. "I know." I whisper back to her, "Dyno is coming out and we're heading to our test spot." I tell her as I place both of our phones into the lockbox and press the code on the keypad to open the door.

Dyno comes hectically around the corner. I'm sure because he heard the door open. "Shit, sorry Prez, I lost track of time... I'll be a few minutes." Nodding to him I look to Billie to come into the door.

"Come on in," I mumble to her as we walk inside and we sit down in the chairs that are as soon as you walk into the lab. I'm not really sure how I can tell what she is thinking since she can't talk, but I can. "It's an old mine shaft," I tell her. She smiles I'm assuming because I can apparently read her mind. "We reinforced it, created a lab. We store some stuff up there." She just nods her head, not asking me any follow-up questions.

When Dyno comes back Billie and I stand and get into the Jeep with him. I was expecting some kind of hesitation when I told Billie we were heading out to the desert... but she didn't. Apparently, she really does trust me.

The night is growing later as we drive to our test spot. Billie sits in the backseat as I glance back to her to see her looking around somehow in awe. I understand her excitement the desert at night does have a sort of appeal to it.

As we approach the spot you can the outline of what we are approaching and I can tell Billie is trying to see what exactly it is as she moves forward in her seat. She's trying to focus on the object.

When she can make out the Mustang outline she smacks me on the shoulder. One of the biggest downfalls of her not being able to talk is I end up getting hit a lot more.

"Yeah, Jeff called and wanted to see if you wanted it. I remembered you said you wanted to set it on fire, so we went and picked it up." I pause looking back at her, "I mean you can keep it if you want to." She quickly shakes her head, no. "You can blow it up if you want to?" She nods her head even faster. "Okay."

Nodding to Dyno as he stops the Jeep and looks at her. "I've put a propane tank in the trunk…" he pauses. This is why this dude is awesome. It goes back to the thing he said about understanding explosives and how they have a purpose. "We'll pour some gas on it. And then light it, then we have to put some distance between the car and us. Because it's going to explode, and it's going to be loud. It may draw some attention, but probably not. I've blown up a lot of shit out here before…" he trails as we pull up right next to the mustang. Getting out of the Jeep I reach over helping Billie out and picking up the gas tank off of the ground handing it to her. I don't want to take away any part of this for her. Leaning against the jeep I watch as she pours the liquid onto the seats of the car.

Once she's done she looks back to me, but honestly, I have no fucking clue what I'm doing either so I look back to Dyno. Who shrugs, nodding his head. Holding out the generic zippo to her she looks back at me. Smiling she takes it from my hand, opens it, steps up into the jeep, up in the backseat, she flicks the flint wheel and watches the small flame ignite. She tosses the zippo at the car.

The smallest *clink* happens when the lighter hits the side of the driver's side door and hits the ground and the way the lighter hits the ground the top flicks closed and the flame goes out.

You've got to be fucking kidding me. I watch Billie mouth to herself as I laugh again, take the few paces to pick it up, and hand it back to her, laughing.

"Don't miss this time," I whisper to her which causes Dyno to let a laugh escape his mouth.

Once more she opens the lighter, flicks the flint wheel, and tosses it into the car. This time it actually makes it through the window and we are already moving away from the car as the seats catch on fire.

BILLIE

Watching Brad's car light up in flames gives me a sense of relief that I didn't know I would get. As Dyno moves us away from the explosion I turn around in the jeep and watch the flames until we turn to make our way up a different mountain and we stop once we reach the top of it.

The car is on fire for a few minutes before it is fully engulfed in flames, which in itself is comforting.

The explosion when the propane catches fire fully satisfies my sense of revenge. I know it doesn't make sense because I killed him, but the amount of relief that it gives me to hear that fucking car which he was so in love explode gives me a different sort of satisfaction. It's my insult to injury.

"Let's get out of here. Just in case." Dyno looks in the rearview mirror at me as he maneuvers us back to, as what Dax called it, purgatory. I can appreciate the name since it's all the way out here in the desert and you wouldn't even know it was here.

That night, when Dax drops me off back at Lucy's house he walks me to the door. I want to be a smart ass to him, but the fact that I'm on vocal rest makes that difficult. So instead of making a joke about how underneath the ruggedness of his exterior there's a gentleman there I just give him a facial expression that is supposed to read as in awe.

"Shut it." He mutters to me as I turn and look at him at the front door. Then I follow it up with an expression that I mean to say *but I didn't say a thing*. "Yeah, I know, but you forget that I can read you like a book." He smiles at me as he leans down and kisses me gently, once.

Pulling him into my body on the front porch of the house, he leans in pressing me into the wall. His tongue slipping past my lips and into my mouth as we frantically devour one another. His hands slipping down my side until he rests it low on my hip.

He pulls away from me just as quickly as I pulled him into my body. "Billie," he growls as he cuts his eyes to me. "You're trying to kill me. We cannot do that yet. You're on vocal rest."

I'm on vocal rest doesn't mean I can't sleep with you... is what my expression is trying to pass off instead of using words.

Shaking his head he leans his head down, pressing his body flush with mine, and whispers into my ear, "Princess, when I fuck you I'm going to have you screaming my name so loud. Which means that you cannot be on vocal rest." My mouth hangs agape, I'm not sure if it's because of his words or the length of his erection poking into my stomach that is causing my shocked expression.

With that, he turns quickly and struts back to his bike before he takes off down the street.

*...Just go and fuck someone else
since you don't want to fuck me...*

BILLIE

"Everything looks good. You can come off of vocal rest. And come back in about a month to get the stitches out of your arm." I nod to him. "You're very lucky." I hear my doctor ask me.

"Yeah, super lucky," I mumble feeling weird to be able to actually talk for the first time in a week.

"Ms. Saxs, I don't mean to overstep here but I couldn't help but notice that when you were in here those bikers were hanging out is the one your boyfriend?" He asks me and I send him a confused look. Mostly because I don't really know how to answer that question. I don't know what we are. I know that I'm in love with him and he loves me but it's complicated.

So instead I answer his question a different way, "You know him?"

"Everyone in this town knows who he is. It's just he has a reputation." I bring my eyebrows together and look at him, "He's dangerous." His words come out quiet and I stare at him.

"You're right, doc." I mutter to him and then laugh as my next words come out, "You did overstep. He may be dangerous to you and he may be dangerous to anyone else in this town, but he did kind of save my life."

"Okay, but was it his fault that your life was in danger in the first place."

"No," I laugh as the word comes out, "it was my fault." I stand as I start to storm out of the room. His words stop me before I make my way all the way to the door.

"I'm sorry," he seems sincere. So I turn and look at him, "I just wanted to make sure you knew. I've known of him for a long time and maybe a little jealous." Wondering why he's jealous, "If things don't work out you can come and find me." He scribbles something down on a piece of paper and hands it to me.

I roll my eyes as I see his cell phone number scribbled out on the back of his business card.

KHAN

I'm waiting for Billie as she pulls into her driveway in my Land Rover that I have told her to drive until she gets her car situation figured out. She smiles at me. I stalk up to her and wrap my arms around her body. I kiss her. Instantly regretting it though I know what I need to do. What I came here to do, but looking at her standing there smiling at me. It sets my whole body on edge.

She walks to the back of the SUV and opens the door to grab the bags from the grocery store.

"I got them," I tell her and reach in to grab them. I wish I could be could to her, but for some reason, I can't.

"Come on," she tells me while walking into the house.

"You shouldn't be talking," I tell her even though her voice sounds better and she no longer looks like she's in pain.

"The doctor told me that I could if it wasn't painful. And it's fine now." She stops, looking at me, and then adds, "Lucy is staying... out."

"Is out now code for with Fury?" Her laugh tells me that I was right. "That's a weird fuckin' relationship."

"You're telling me." She laughs, "Not really sure if I like the idea of it. I'm not sure about seeing Lucy actually with someone."

"She's never dated?"

"Not in a long time, since..." she shakes her head, "but for some reason the two of them..."

"You don't have to say anymore." She laughs.

"You haven't been with them this week." I laugh even harder. I place the bags on the counter and she starts sorting through them.

"So, I heard that you were in on this little pool thing." She puts her head down as she giggles a little bit. I can't help but close the distance between us and wrap my arms around her body pulling her back into me. "Seems like there's a lot I don't know about you." I nip her ear which causes her to jerk to head back.

She just starts nodding her head, "Yeah... Lucy was right Brad made me into a different person. I feel like I just lost pieces of myself over the years. The free-spirited girl who would-," she pauses.

"Go to Burning Man, take acid, and sleep with her best friend." Her face reddens, causing her to look down. "Stop it, don't be embarrassed," I growl into her ear. I press my hips into her more just to make sure she can feel every inch of the erection that I have, knowing that she definitely shouldn't be embarrassed.

"Yeah." Her voice squeaks. "I lost that person that I was through years of emotional abuse." Her talking about losing herself reminds me why I'm really here.

"Let's order in," I say as she looks at me at the food that she sorts through. "We have some things to discuss... and I don't want you to strain to do both." She smiles at me and nods.

251

We wait for the Chinese food to arrive before we start talking.

We eat in uncomfortable silence for a while before I look over to her. "Bil-," her name comes out of my mouth, sadly. She doesn't look up at me, instead, she continues to stare down at her food. "Billie," the word is a little louder when she looks up at me.

"I know," her words strike me.

"You know what?" She looks down at her food again.

"I know what you're going to say." She pauses, sighs, and looks back up to me, "That I just killed my husband. I need time to process this. That he was emotionally abusive towards me for years and I need time to find myself again." Everything she says is right. Those were all things I was going to say to her and more, but if I tell her everything will it break her heart more. I don't want to look at her with emotion on my face. "Dax, if you're going to do it. Say it." Her words are strict and she means it, "If you can't say it," her voice cracks and it breaks my heart.

"Billie, we can't do this right now." I watch the water fill up her eyes. "I love you," my voice cracks.

She looks at me, "but…"

"I don't want to hold you back. I don't want you to fall into a routine and never figure out who you are." She nods her head looking away. I can't help myself when I close the distance and I want to hold her. I don't want to make her cry. I tip her head up so she looks at me. "You deserve so much more than what I have to give." She shakes her head, pushes herself out of my grasp, and walks down the hallways into her room, slamming the door. "Shit," I mutter as I stand in the kitchen, alone. I clean up the food, walk down the hallway, and knock on the door. I don't want to leave her like this, but I'm the reason that she is like this.

"Fuck off, *Khan*." The road name comes out as a sneer and I think it breaks my heart. "Go and live your life the way you want to…" I know she doesn't mean that. I sit down next to the door.

"Billie, this isn't easy for me, but I'm trying to do what's in your best interest." The door opens, quickly and I scramble up off of the floor. She's pissed now, staring at me.

"Fuck you!" She shouts at me. "Don't you think that I am capable of making decisions that are in my best interest? Just be real. You've missed your lifestyle since I've been living at your house." I know the words are being used to deflect from her own pain, but it doesn't make them sting any less. "Just go and fuck someone else since you don't want to fuck me." She stares at me daring me to say something. She knows I can't say anything back to it because if I do I'm either admitting that I do or lying. So, after staring at me for minutes that seem longer than they should she slams the door in my face.

Head hanging, I walk to the kitchen once more, I grab my wallet that I had left on the counter after I paid for the food.

Then I leave the house.

Somewhere between getting on to the freeway and exiting it my emotions turn from sadness to anger.

I'm just trying to do the best for her, not for me. If I was doing what was best for me, I would have just fucked her, cause god knows I want to fuck her. So bad, I'm trying to be good, I'm trying to be the best person that she needs right now.

When I pull up to the clubhouse I am fucking pissed. Who the fuck does she think she is? I walk through the door to the clubhouse and into the lounge area. Rox is behind the bar as I sit down, "Khan, whiskey?" I nod my head as she grabs the bottle sitting the glass in front of me and pours a shot.

"More," I mutter to her, she looks up at me, knowing that I don't drink like this, and eyes me, hesitating. I glare back at her and she tips the bottle up pouring more into the glass. "More," she looks around and begins to pour again, "Mor-" she eyes widen as I stop myself and then correct my statement, "just give me a fucking bottle," I tell her and she looks around like she wants to tell me *no*. I give her a look like *go ahead and fucking try me, you still work for me.* She reaches behind the bar and hands me the bottle with the pourer still attached, and I smile at her, "thank you." As I stand up taking the glass filled with whiskey with me.

I toss the entirety of the glass back with one gulp before I fill it back up with the bottle next to it. I feel eyes are on me as soon as I sit down on the couch. I haven't made much of an appearance at the clubhouse, especially to drink, in a couple of months, and I'm not sure any of these kids have seen me drink like this… ever. I down a second "sip" of whiskey I let my head fall back onto the top of the couch as I stare up to the ceiling.

"Khan," I hear a purr of my name come out of a mouth and I look over to it as I see Star looking at me. Wearing her classic push-up bra so her tits are so close together that there's no gap, barely covered by a low cut shirt, and short skirt. I don't say a word to her but pull her by her hand and sit her on my lap. "I haven't seen you in a while." She purrs into my ear.

"I've been busy," I tell her and slide my hand up to the hem of her short skirt.

"Too busy to come and see me." She whispers back into my ear as she turns and straddles my lap. "I've missed you." I wish I could say the same.

"I'm sorry, Star," I say as she grinds against my dick. "Lean back" I mutter to her as I pick up the bottle of whiskey and pour the whiskey right into the little divot that her tits make. She giggles as the liquid touches her skin. I suck the liquid off of her chest and lick the last little amount making sure to get all of it off her skin. She's still giggling as I lick the last droplets of liquor off of her skin. Lifting the bottle to do it again.

I feel Star being pulled off of my lap as a voice that I recognize yells, "WHAT. THE. FUCK?" at me. Every single one of the guys including Fury is standing with mouths agape at the scene of Lucy screaming at me.

"Lucy," Fury shouts at her grabbing at her arm but she doesn't take her eyes off of me. She yanks her arm away from him.

"No," she points at me and I glare at Fury.

"Lucy, you don't understand." Fury urges her. I know what he's trying to tell her. That technically she isn't allowed to talk to me like this. That this is my fucking clubhouse. I may let Fury tell me when he thinks I'm fucking wrong without beating the shit out of him, but that's only behind closed doors away from everyone. Her out in front of the entire club shouldn't be tolerated.

She's about to scream something else at me, as I get up and walk towards the hallway. I yell for Fury to follow me into the war room since it's our only completely soundproof room in the clubhouse and Lucy has every right to yell at me so I will let her. I glare at him and then glance out the door. He calls Lucy into the room and shuts the door. I step in close to Fury and look at him in the eye, "I should kick your ass for that."

"But you won't," Lucy says next to me, I turn to glare at her.

"You want to say something to me," I'm yelling now, her eyes widen maybe for the first time being afraid of me, "fucking say it. I'm giving you a chance, but don't ever disrespect me out there in front of everyone. You want to tell me I'm a dirtbag. Get in line because there are a million motherfuckers in front of you that want to tell me that. " Then I sit in my chair and I run my hand over my face, "she fucking told me to do it."

"What?" She asks me sitting down across from me.

"I told her," I pause, " I told her that, I was just trying to do what's best for her. I don't want to be the reason why she doesn't know who she is." My broken heart and the alcohol don't mix very well. I'm officially a fucking pussy.

"Khan, you have to let her make those decisions." She says to me.

"Do you know that I've been to prison?" I ask Lucy and her eyes widen,

"Khan, you can't even say that." Fury looks at me.

"I can't? Fury. Does not saying it makes it any less true." He looks at me a little surprised.

"No, but you weren't wrong in,"

I cut him off. "Does that matter, whether it was the right thing to do or not? I have an arrest record pages long."

"But you've only been found guilty-,"

I cut him off again. "Yeah, because the fucking captain of the police precinct looks at me like I'm his fucking pseudo-son." I pause, letting myself sink down into my chair and lean over letting my head fall into my hands. "She was so angry and wouldn't talk to me. She yelled at me to go fuck someone else since I didn't want to fuck her." Fury laughs, Lucy smacks him.

I glare at him, "Right, that's not funny." He mumbles.

"You're an asshole," I tell him and he laughs again.

"Khan, did you tell her you were trying to do what was best for her," Lucy asks as I nod my head. "What did she say?"

"If I thought she couldn't figure that out for herself."

"That's what I would expect her to say." She pauses and looks at me, placing a hand on my arm, "I understand what you're saying. And so does she. But she's hurt right now. Just if you guys aren't going to be together. Could you try and not to fuck or almost fuck anyone in front of me, please." I laugh. She looks over at me confused about my demeanor.

"Not gonna be a problem because apparently, your friend ruined me. That whole thing out there felt nothing." I mumble as motion down to my dick. "I haven't even fucked her yet, but after having her living in my house, sleeping in my bed, for the few weeks with a constant case of blue balls, I can't get it up for anyone else." Lucy tries to keep her laugh contained.

"You're being dramatic." She tells me.

My head snaps back to look at her, standing up I face where the two of them stand, "I was just licking whiskey off of some bitches tits who I know will blow me in front of everyone... and nothing."

When I say nothing I throw my hands out in each direction. I shout out a groan of frustration and walk out of the war room.

Before I round the corner I hear Fury say to her, "You want me to take you home, don't you?"

"Khan," Star purrs back into my ear while grabbing onto my arm as I walk through the lounge room, "now that you've got that whole thing sorted out." I pull my arm out of her grasps and continue to walk away. Making sure to grab the bottle of whiskey, I shout, "Everyone, leave me the fuck alone," and I walk out the backdoor and walk the trail back to my house. I'm stumbling up to the path as I round to the house and look at it.

"I don't deserve this shit." I wave the bottle around, I'm sure some of the liquid spills out.

"Uncle Dax," I hear Ella call to me the next morning. My head hurts before I open my eyes and the sunlight that is above me hurts my head even more. "Are you okay?" She asks me. I hear someone else approach and as I look up I see Ash walking up to me.

"What? Where am I?" I ask her as I look around me to see that I am laying in the front yard, the bottle still clasped in my hand.

"Holy shit, Prez. You look rough." He pauses and then says again, "Ella text me cause she said you weren't home. I guess she just didn't look far enough." Hints of a smirk are threatening to come out.

"Fuck off," I say to him as I lay back down in my front yard.

"Khan, get up." He says stretching his arm out to me and lifting me up. "Ella, go ahead and get in the truck. I'm going to put him to bed." He mutters a fuck as I lean all of my body weight onto him.

"You gotta bulk up kid," I'm sure my words are still slurred as he attempts to walk me up the stairs.

"Maybe you should just not drink like this anymore."

"I don't drink like this," I tell him through slurs.

"I know you don't. We were all kind of shocked to see you like this."

"I think I really fucked up with her," I tell him and he nods his head.

"Yeah, I know. I'm sorry." He pauses, "I'm sure you'll bounce back from it Khan." I sigh as he flops me onto my bed.

"That's the thing. I don't think I want to." The last few words are a mumble before I pass out.

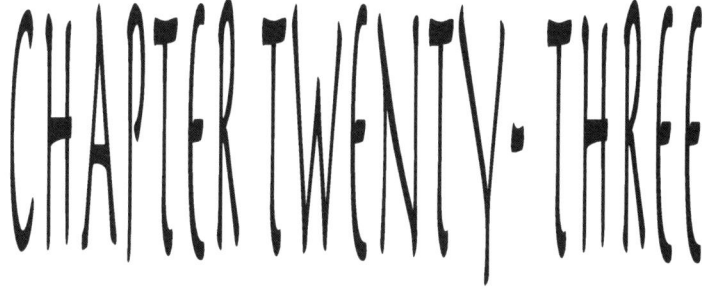

...we are going to be seeing a whole lot more of each other.

BILLIE

There's a knock on my bedroom door.

"GO. AWAY." The words come out loud and monotoned.

"Billie, if you don't open the door I'm going to break it the fuck down," Lucy calls from the other side.

"Fine," I mutter to her. Pushing myself off of my bed and opening the door. "Now, all is right in the world," I grumble out to her.

"I'm sorry, love." She mutters

"About what?" I ask her trying to play dumb. She just stares at me and I know that Fury just dropped her home so I only imagine how she found out. "Ugh, it wasn't anything. I'm fine. It wasn't even a break-up."

"Billie, it was. Even if you guys want to pretend it's not. He's pretty broken up about it as well."

"What?"

"I yelled at him tonight, in front of everyone. He was…" she trails.

"Fucking someone?" the words are strained as I say them

"No, he said uh, he couldn't."

"He couldn't?" I ask her.

"Yeah," she pauses, "fuck I'll tell you the whole story. When I walked in he had girl straddling his lap." The words hurt. And at the same time, I can't help but think about the last time that I did that. "He was doing body shots off her chest."

"I did tell him to fuck someone else," I tell her and she nods her head.

"Yeah, he told me," She brushes off my statement, "but he told me that he felt nothing. his exact words were that you *ruined him*." She uses her fingers to air quote *ruined him*.

"What?" She shrugs.

"He said that he hasn't even fucked you yet, but after you lived with him for weeks, where he had a constant state of blue balls because he wanted to fuck you, now he can't get it up for anyone else," I'm assuming she looks at my face and knows that she needs to continue to talk, "he brushed off tits and left the clubhouse."

"He should have fucked her," I mumble.

"Why are you saying that?"

"We weren't anything. We were just friends who would cuddle when they slept and make out every now and then." She sighs as she looks at me.

"It's okay to be sad. You've been through some shit recently."

"Why am I not even phased by the shit Brad did?" I ask her and she shrugs.

"Probably because you're used to him being gone." And I nod my head. Or more because I don't give a shit that he's dead. I never really loved him.

The first day back to work from the incident is two and a half weeks after Dax left my house that night and everyone is extremely nice to me. Or it may just be because it's a Friday, who knows. I walk out of my office door to hand something to Abby.

"Ash," I look at him as he's standing at the reception area.

"Billie," it's extremely awkward.

"Is Ella okay? I know you guys are usually early." Dax's big thing is punctuality for them to be late means that something is going on, but Ash nods his head, but I can see the concern on his face. "You sure, you can come in and talk if you need to," I say motioning to my office and he shakes his head no. "Okay, just know my door is always open."

"Thanks," he nods and I walk back into my office. I sit down at my computer and pull up Ella's attendance. I see that she's been signed in 4 times in the last two weeks and I become concerned every time being signed in by Ash.

"Billie," I hear and look up to see Ash standing in my doorway. I motion for him to come inside and he shuts the door.

"Is everything okay?" I ask him and he holds his arms in almost a shrugging motion.

"Relatively okay. Everything is fine with Ella and the rest of us." He pauses and then starts talking fast, "Khan's having a hard time with," he pauses motioning to me, "things." I nod my head understanding. "I think he's more confused because he keeps saying that…"

"We weren't anything so there's nothing to be upset about." He nods his head and sends me a questioning look, but I know this because it's what I keep telling myself to feel better.

"Yeah, but the thing is, I keep finding him passed out in the yard, or on the trail to the house, or in the bathtub without water in it, the bottle still in hand." I look down trying to not seem as sad as I am. I know that Dax isn't much of a drinker. Since his dad was an alcoholic he doesn't usually let himself get too carried away with it.

"Ash," I try to not sound mad or angry as I look at him. "I'm not sure what to tell you. This was his decision."

"Yeah, I know, he keeps telling me that too... I'm sorry, I shouldn't have said anything. I just figured you would want to know." He mutters as he stands up and goes to walk out of the room.

"Ash, thank you. I do want to know." My words are whispers. He nods his head

"Dax?" I call out inside the house as I open the front door, peeking around the corner. All of the lights in the house are out so I let myself in. I just need to get in and get out. I had accidentally left a few things here when I packed my things to come back home. I only noticed as I unpacked my bags at the house. I could have left them, but then I wouldn't have an excuse to come here. Even if he's working at the club. I try and shake the images of the girls all over him. I try and swallow the lump in my throat as I climb the stairs to the second floor. I look down the hall, double-checking that Ella isn't here. I know that she is most likely at the dance that the school is having for the night. Pushing the door open to Dax's bedroom. It isn't until I hear the shower running in the bathroom and seeing light from above the shower streaming into the bedroom, that I realize he is here tonight... "Crap," I mutter. I contemplate just leaving until I see the stack of clothing that is folding and stacked on the dresser. "Might as well grab them while I'm here. It would be stupid to not get them." I whisper to myself.

The few grunts that I hear coming from the bathroom grab my attention. "Great," of course I would come to try and grab my shit and he would be fucking someone in the shower. Where I'm standing I can see the shower reflected back to me in the mirror. In it I see Dax standing in the shower leaning slightly forward, but head back, eyes closed... but nothing else, the door blocks the rest

of what the mirror would be reflecting. Not being able to help myself, I take a couple of steps closer to the door.

"Fuck," he growls as I take a couple more steps and gasp. I can see his muscular ass, legs spread apart, standing in the stream of water through the glass wall of the shower, but when I look into the mirror I see that it's not anyone else who is causing the noise and I can't turn and leave. I stand watching him, his left hand on the wall in front of him, bracing himself against it, as his other hand fisting the length of his cock.

I have only seen him naked one other time, the shower shortly after I had come to stay here. Images of him having me pressed into the wall, his cock barely touching my opening, come back into my head. I hadn't had the guts to really look at his cock then, but seeing it now fully erect, even in Dax's large hands looks impressive. I let my gaze trail up his body from his erection to his face, seeing his eyes are still close I push the door open just a little bit more. He grunts causing my eyes to fall immediately back down to his movements and I can see his ass flex as he pushes his cock through this fist.

"See something you like?" His voice is rugged I can feel the blush rush to my cheeks as I look back up to his face in the mirror his eyes are ignited as he stares at me and I slowly nod my head. "Good." He doesn't take his eyes off of me, watching him until his head leans back again. "*FUCK...*" the word lingers on his lips and I can't stop myself as I pull off my shirt followed by my pants and panties at once. I pull open the shower door and I hear Dax growl out at me. "Billie, you step one foot in here..." his voice stops as he looks over at me, already standing in the shower. "Bil...." He starts

"Shut up," I mumble to him. Causing him to look at me over his shoulder. I let my hands trail down his back. Then I move to stand next to him keeping my hands on his skin as I move around his body until they touch his side. He groans as my hand slides down his torso reaching his cock. He sucks in a deep breath as my hand reaches it almost as if my touch causes him pain.

I let my hand clasp around him and make sure to match his rhythm. His growl comes out so deep that I can feel the vibrations from his cock. "Holy shit," he mutters stepping back just slightly letting his back fall against the wall. His hand falls away and mine is the only one left, working him.

His cock pulsates in my hand as his head falls back, against the shower wall. "Oh, fuck, Billie. I'm going to come." The words come out of his mouth through gritted teeth.

"I want to watch you come." My words are barely above a whisper. "You better come for me." I can feel his hips press into my hands quicker causing me to match his pace. His hands reach up to my shoulders as he grunts as a stream of cum shoots out onto the floor beneath us. He slumps against the shower wall for a second until he looks back at me.

"Why are you here?" He asks, his demeanor changes into a rigidity that wasn't there a few minutes ago.

"I left a few things here and I figured that while I was here getting them that I would bring your car back," I tell him.

His eyes smolder as he looks down at my naked body standing in front of me. His words are specific as he looks at me with a completely different agenda, "Keep the car until you get a new one. I don't care how long it takes," he then lets his mouth fall to mine as he lifts me up and his lips are on mine before I realize it. His kisses are forceful almost as if he's starving. As I feel his hands slide down my back, stopping at my ass, cupping it, then lifting me up to, and letting my legs wrap around his torso. "Awe, fuck" he groans into my mouth. The water is gone with a flip of his wrist, never breaking his mouth from mine. The shower door bangs closed as he moves me out of the bathroom and into the bedroom. He tosses me onto the bed and he crawls up it between my legs. "Fucking beautiful." He mummers as his lips kiss the inside of my thighs.

He leaves a trail of kisses up my inner thigh until he reaches my pussy. I feel his tongue quickly skirt across my opening. "Oh, my god." I mummer as I arch my back.

"Just as I imagined," he smirks back up to me, "you taste fucking amazing." His face falls back between my thighs and when his tongue sweeps inside of me a shock of vibrations course through my body that is so overwhelming I scoot my body away from his face not sure if I can take the amount of pleasure he is about to

release on me. "Oh, no you don't." He growls at me as he pulls me back by my hips, pinning my hips against the bed. "Unless you want to go, princess? Is that what you're doing? Do you want to leave?" He asks me sincerely. One shake of my head causes a grin to spread on his lips again. "Good, and what is it that you want me to do?" He asks his grin growing wider.

"What you're doing," I mutter, becoming shy. For so long in my life, I wasn't allowed to ask for things that I wanted.

He growls at me lifting his head from between my legs and stalks up my body, engulfing me inside of his. Looking down at me his eyes are dark and hooded, he leans his head down right next to my ear. "You just walked in on me masturbating and finished jacking me off," I can feel his erection begin again as he lifts his head up looking at me now. "Which tells me that you can tell me what it is you want. So, what is it again that you want me to do?" I try and wiggle away but he grabs my arms planting them on each side of me. "Princess," his word sounds of worry now, "you don't have to be afraid to say anything with me." I nod my head. "I'm sorry." His words are soft as he wraps his arms around me and kisses me gently. I feel his cock jump slightly which sets my whole body on fire again. Then I turn our sweet kiss into a hungry one. He groans into my mouth before pulling back just enough for his words to be comprehensible. "There she is. Just tell me what you want."

"I want you to lick my pussy." I look him straight in the eyes.

"Is that all you want me to do?" I shake my head.

"I want you to lick me until I come and then fuck me with your giant cock."

"Thank god." His eyes darken as he presses his mouth to mine forcefully then kisses his way down my body. Stopping at each nipple to make sure to give each one a nip, before continuing to trail kisses down my body reaching my clit and running his tongue swiftly across it.

"Oh," the exclaim leaves my mouth as my back arches. Dax reaches his hand up placing it on my chest between my tits. I have never noticed how large his hands were until this moment as if he outstretched his hand he would be able to rub both nipples at the same time.

"You," He glances up at me, tongue darts out licking my clit again, "are not going anywhere until you come." As he takes his free hand, slipping two fingers inside of me. I gasp, head pushing back against the mattress back arching as he bends one finger hitting my g-spot, licking circles around my clit. My hand tangles itself into his hair as I instinctually press his mouth exactly where I want it. I can feel a smile spread on his face.

"Oh my, fuck." I practically yell into the darkness of the house as I feel the waves of my orgasm take control of my body.

He kisses me, pulls back, "Can you taste yourself?" I nod my head, "Good," I flip him over so that he's lying on his back.

"Sit with your back against the headboard. If this is going to be it." I mutter, looking at his very erect dick looking back at me. Trying to save this image for later before I wrap my lips around his cock and slide him into my mouth.

"Holy fuck," he mutters as his hands find their way into my hair. He doesn't put any pressure on my head but wraps his hand in my hair slightly tugging on it. I let a moan escape my lips as the tugs slightly harder on my hair as my head bobs up and down on his dick taking his entire length into my mouth. "Oh, you like that?" He asks me as he pulls me up by my hair and I grin in response. "Come here." He pulls me up to him and I straddle his lap. I can feel the tip of his dick threatening to slide in as he groans and says, "Top drawer." I lean over, opening the drawer, and grab a condom out. He rips open the top and rolls it over himself.

"You better fuck me, Khan," his mouth turns up as I say the name to him and he yanks me back over to him, I instantly straddle his lap and he impales me.

"Fuck," I groan as I feel his entire dick inside of me.

"While I'm fucking you, is the only time you are allowed to call me that, you understand." I nod my head.

"You going to show me how you got your name."

"I will, I'll make it so you never forget it either." I hope not.

He pulls my head towards his, while his lips are on mine. He thrusts up into me as I move up and down his cock and he trails kisses down my chest. He takes one nipple in his mouth as he pulls me down by my hips on top of him, pushing himself further into me. "Oh, fuck," I mumble out as I force my head back up and press my lips to his sending my tongue searching into his mouth. Trying to store up enough for later.

"Fuck princess." He moans as I feel the tightening surround him and I don't feel like I can make it much longer. I feel myself release all around him and hear him follow after me. I slide off of him and lay down on the bed as he gets up and tosses the condom away into the trash.

He walks back over to the bed and I mentally make a note to remember this moment. How perfect and chiseled he is.

I understand why women flock to him.

"So?" He asks and I can't help but laugh. While I'm sitting in his bed, watching him playfully strut to me, I can't understand why we are apart I miss being here in his room, in his bed, in his arms. I push that out of my mind.

"So, what?"

He tilts his head looking at me.

"8 and 3/4 out of 10." He gasps as he tackles me onto the bed and I laugh. "I'm joking. Please, this has been the best sex of my life." He smiles, standing back up, and shrugs as if to say *I know that I know what I'm doing.* "That mouth though," I mumble to him which makes him grin.

"I'm okay with that." He laughs. "I can't say otherwise either." He laughs again. "Even better than Lucy?" He asks me causing me to glare at him.

"She should have never fucking said anything... fucking traitor," I mumble which causes him to laugh.

"Well, technically she didn't tell me, she told Fury which you can't really be too upset about I just so happen to be sitting right next to him." I roll my eyes. "So tomorrow," he mumbles out and looks at me. I nod my head agreeing with him.

"Don't yell at anyone, mostly because if you do then you have to admit that you have seen me and we know how that would go over, but the guys are worried about you."

"You talked to them."

"Fury has said a couple of things in passing but Ash popped his head into my office this morning. Said that he has had to pick you up out of the yard." He shifts on the bed for a second and then sighs.

"He shouldn't have told you that." I nod.

"I know, I kind of dragged it out of him. But I can tell that he's really worried about you. I am too." He looks at me.

And he nods then says. "You know, Lucy has talked too."

"She's such a traitor." He laughs

"You need to take care of yourself, also." He pauses "You can talk to me if you need to." I nod my head and rub my eyes as he says, "Friends?" and when I look over he has his pinky sticking out.

"Friends." I wrap mine around his.

I stand up and look at him, "I should go before the dance is over and Ella comes home." He nods his head before I stand up off of the bed and walk back into the bathroom where I dropped my clothes. He watches me dress, pulling on my shirt.

"You're killing me." He mutters as he sees that I wasn't wearing a bra earlier. Then as I pull my pants up over my ass he reaches over and smacks my butt, "I'll walk you out." I nod back to him as he slips on a pair of sweats, I grab the stack of clothes on the dresser and we walk out of the room. "Oh!" he pauses and then backpedals, "I shouldn't tell you."

"Tell me what?" I ask him and he shakes his head.

"I shouldn't, you should be surprised or everyone will know something up."

"Well, now you have to tell me." I look at him as we reach the car. He looks like he's torn between telling me and not telling me.

"I can't, unlike my brothers, I know how to keep my fucking mouth shut, but you'll know what I'm talking about when it happens." He opens my car door for me and I lean against the frame of the door as he stands in front of me so that the door is shielding both of us.

"What is Fury going to ask Lucy to marry him?" I say 100% joking and he just presses his lips into a fine line. Somehow over the last few months, we have come to be able to read every gesture that the other does.

"Whaaaaaaaaat?!?!" I shout and he looks around as I bring my volume down. "Sorry, are you fucking kidding me?" My words are just above a whisper now.

"That was my reaction when he showed me the ring."

"He already," I mutter stopping and restarting on a different sentence, "But they've only-,"

"I know, it's not my business. You think that she's going...?" and I think about it for a second. How happy she's been, how happy he makes her. And how that, for some reason, makes sense.

"If he asks, then yeah I think she will." I nod to him.

"Well, I have a feeling, if that's the case," he points from himself and then to me, "we are going to be seeing a whole lot more of each other, then." The scrunch up my nose like I hate the idea and he chuckles. "Is it against the rules if I kiss you one more time before you go?" I shake my head. His lips meet mine as he leans into me and it's not a hungry kiss this time but a sad kiss. It's a goodbye kiss. It's the type of kiss that breaks your heart as you're having it.

He pulls back and I'm pretty sure that he can see a tear in my eye, but he moves away so he doesn't have to see it. "Hold on," he says as he walks up to the house, opens the door, and grabs something that sits just inside. When he walks back outside he hands it to me. "For the gate. If you want to I can ride with you up there to make sure no one sees you." I nod my head and he gets in the passenger seat. I drive down the trail with my lights off again and before we get up to the clubhouse he jumps out and walks in front of the car. He waves me through. I press the button to the gate, slip through it, and close the gate back again. It takes every ounce of my being to not turn back and kiss him, to beg him not to let me leave. To tell him to let me stay, but I don't.

I manage to make it down the dirt road without anyone seeing me. I turn onto the main road and start to drive back to my house before I feel the tears rolling down my cheeks.

KHAN

Watching her drive out of the gate… I want to chase after her. Tell her to stay, tell her that I didn't mean what I said before. But I don't. I don't say any of it. Instead, I watch her drive away. I miss her already.

I already miss her body.

Fuck…

She doesn't deserve to be dragged into my bullshit.

She doesn't even know the half of it…

Dax and Billie's story isn't over just yet…

Keep reading for an excerpt for:

KHAN
PART II

The conclusion of Khan and Billie's story

** Note: unedited and subject to change**

CHAPTER ONE

...there just never seems to be a section to check outlaw under the interested in...

BILLIE

"-work?" I hear my date, Steve, from across the table as my attention is brought back into the current situation

"What?" I ask with a smile to make sure the he understands that I am sorry for zoning out.

"What do you do for work?"

"I'm the principal at Stenson Prep." He nods his head maybe impressed, I'm not sure. I'm really not even sure I even care. Why did nobody ever tell me that dating in your 30's is literally as fun as playing the game of life?

"How do you like it?" He asks me again, the same strained questions. I've been out a couple of times in the last few weeks and every time the same questions are asked. *What do you do for work? What do you do for fun? Where did you grow up? Do you have any pets?*

"It's okay. I love helping the kids, but now I'm usually just dealing with parents." I shrug as poke at my food with my fork. Why do I find men who have responsible jobs, now boring? There doesn't seem to ever be a section to check *outlaw* under the interested in, on dating sites... are there any dating sites for criminals I mean hell they have every other market cornered.

"What do you do in your spare time?" He makes the next dreaded mistake.

I daydream about fucking outlaw bikers. At least that's what I want to say... "Oh you know, the normal stuff." I shrug because what hobbies do I actually have?

When he drops me off at the house, he walks me to the door, and he kisses me once, it's a... nice kiss. It's not very passionate, but it's not terrible. I walk into the house and see that it's dark throughout and I assume that Lucy is somewhere out with Fury. I was not expecting to be home this early, which is probably why I feel like the kiss wasn't very good. He also made a comment about having to get up early. I put my purse down as I walk into the kitchen and I grab the ice cream out of the freezer, don't need a bowl, and grab a spoon.

I'm walking through the house with the spoon in the container. Maybe I should watch TV. Maybe I should just go to bed. I'm not really sure what I should do. A hard knock on the door brings me out of my weird "home-too-early" trance. Maybe Steve came back by to try and stay the night. Or to impress me with a better kiss.

As I open the door, ice cream still in hand, I'm somewhat surprised as I see Dax leaning with each hand on the relative sides of the door. When he looks up at me his eyes are hungry as they slowly trail up my body as if he was drinking me in. He looks at me as strands of his normally well placed hair fall into his eyes.

"You look nice." His words come out, but the intensity of his eyes doesn't waver. "How was your date?" If words could physically harm you these would have, but I don't know what to say. I sit the ice cream down on the table next to the door. He steps inside of the house, closing the door behind him, and I can feel my pulse start to race, "How was your kiss?" He asks me as he closes the distance between us.

The only thing I can think to say is, "Were you following me." His lips turn up into a grin.

"No," he leans his head down to mine, so that he is able to whisper to my ear, "I gave into my temptations and next thing I knew I was sitting outside of your house." He pauses as I feel his the tips of his fingers caress my arm, "I saw him walk you to the door." His hand skims up my arm as he pulls his head back to look at me, his next words sound pained, "Saw him kiss you," the pad of his thumb brushes against my lower lip. I can't help but gasp. "Billie," My name comes out as a breathless whisper, as his hand stops at the side of my face, tilting it up just slightly to look up at him, "tell me to leave." I know I should tell him to, but the words refuse to come out of my mouth. I can't form the strength to say them. "Billie," the way my name comes out of his mouth, the hunger that seeps through in his voice. I can't tell him to leave, I don't want him to leave. I look up at him and feel my teeth graze my bottom lip. My heart is pounding in my ears as he looks to me, eyes on fire. His head leans down to mine, "Tell me to leave."

"Stay," it comes out as a whisper and he lifts me up off of the ground as his mouth crashes down to mine. The kiss that I experienced with Steve pales in comparison to every kiss I have ever had with Dax. In his signature Dax way, his hands skirt down my back, cupping my ass as he lifts me and I wrap my legs around his waist. He carries me down the hall until we reach my bedroom. Slipping into the room, kicking the door closed, and laying me down on the bed.

He leans over top of me, "Did you enjoy it when he kissed you?" He asks me as his hands pop the button off my pants open, sliding the zipper down.

"No," I mutter as I reach for his belt, undoing it, he kicks his boots off before letting his pants fall down to the ground, and steps out of them. A hiss escapes my mouth as I feel his hand slip underneath my panties as he slips a finger inside of me.

"Good," he mumbles in my ear as he slips another finger in and my head falls back as I let a moan escape my lips. I feel the warm presence of his fingers leave me as he pulls my pants and panties down my body and he smiles. I lean up as I pull my shirt up over my head. "You went out on a date," he looks at me, eyebrow raised as he pulls his own shirt off tossing it on to the dresser and slips his boxers down his legs, "and you didn't wear a bra." I giggle, I hear him mutter. He reaches inside of his pocket and pulls up a condom, rips it open, and rolls it onto himself. "I will have to teach you a lesson about doing that." His eyes glare at me which causes me to wiggle on the bed in front of him.

I watch him as he crawls up the bed between my legs, trailing kisses up stomach, between my tits, he stops to take a nipple into his mouth and I whimper underneath him. "Fuck me, Khan." His eyes grow wild at the use of the name as he moves his mouth back to mine, forcefully crashing down to mine. I feel his arm between us as he slips his cock inside of me and I can't help but let another moan out as I feel him thrust. We're moving in a rhythm unlike I have ever had with anyone else. He's filling up every inch of me in a way that skirts the line of pleasure and pain.

He pulls back from me, pulling my hip with his until he is kneeling at me, one leg on each side of him, hand tightly grasps on my thighs as he thrusts deeper inside of me. "Holy fuck," I mumble out as I see a grin spread on to his lips.

"Shit, baby, you're so tight." He says as he moves inside of me again. I can feel my walls tightening to a point of explosion, "Fuck, baby, you're about to come with me, aren't you." I nod my head. "What?" A weak yea comes out of my mouth, "What, baby, what are you about to do?" He asks me. His hands tighten around my thighs as he pumps harder.

"I'm about to come with you." As if that was the activation word I feel us both release at the same time. Moans in unison come out as his hands loosen their grip on my thighs and he gently collapses onto me. The warmth of his body on top of mine makes me feel safe. He rolls off of me, pulling the condom off of himself and I watch his perfect, naked body as he moves across the room, into the bathroom, and discards it.

He walks back into the room and sits down at the end of the bed. I hear his sad voice come out as he whispers, "Do you want me to leave now?"

"Not yet," I mumble as I lay naked, looking over to him, "unless you want to." I see the smirk spread even from the one side of his mouth that I can see. He turns to me and climbs back up the bed, lying next to me, wrapping his arms around me.

CHAPTER TWO

...this is my hell

BILLIE

"I've missed you right here." He mumbles into my hair as he presses a kiss to my head. I smile looking up to him.

"You're the one who-," I look over at him and he presses his finger to my lips.

"I still think it's for the best and I know you think so too," he isn't wrong. "But it doesn't mean that I don't miss you and think about you, and worry about you." I lose the battle I'm fighting with myself as I move upwards and kiss him.

The sound of the front door slamming shut breaks our kiss. "BILLIE!" Lucy yells down the hall and I can hear Fury giggling behind her, "Billie, I hope you're awake, I'm coming in."

"Shit, shit, shit." I whisper to Dax as he lays in my bed, "You gotta hide." He looks at me like I'm fucking crazy, but rolls his eyes, throwing up his hands, and moves off of the bed.

"Hold on, Luce," I think to myself that Fury is most likely with her, she won't bust in if she thinks that I'm changing, "I'm kind of in the middle of changing,"

"HURRY UP!!" She yells through the door. Dax moves across the room into the bathroom leaving the bathroom light off and pushes the door almost closed. Opening the drawer, I grab out a pair of shorts and tank top sliding them onto my body. As I walk to the door I see Dax's pants, boxers, and boots on the ground, *shit*, I slide them under the bed with my foot. Cracking the door open but I'm not ready when Lucy pushes it all the way open and pushes her way into the room.

Fury follows her in, "Sure everyone come on in." I say loud enough for Dax to hear me so he's aware of what is going on.

"Billie, I have something very serious to ask you." She sits down, patting the bed.

"Lucy, what is it?" *Did she see his bike outside? Does she know that he is here with me, hiding in my bathroom?*

"Billie, you can answer this honestly. You know that I can tell when you're lying to me. And I promise that I won't get upset either way." She pauses as she looks to Fury and smiles, "Will you be my maid of honor." Oh, it's this time.

"Wha-what?" I say looking from Lucy to Fury. I can't help but smile seeing them looking at each other, completely in love.

"I know it seems kind of sudden," Lucy says as she reaches her hand over and grabs his, "but I-we know that this is right." I smile at her, "Will you the my maid of honor though?" She asks again, looking back to me.

"Of-of course." I tell her and she smiles, shrieks and hugs me.

"Um," Fury says to me as he starts, "I wanted to make sure it wouldn't be too awkward for you but I kind of already asked Khan to be my best man."

I smile at them, because even when this should be all about them, they are worried about us, and slightly because Dax is definitely standing naked somewhere in my bathroom for this conversation, "For the two of you, I'm sure we can look past our shit." I hug him.

She starts to leave and then stops, turning around, "Oh, before I forget, I'm going to borrow your straightener for in the morning, mine shit the bed this afternoon," She looks to Fury smiling, "and we're going to meet mom and dad." She starts walking towards the bathroom.

"Lucy, my bathroom is kind of messy right now, it's embarrassing, I can leave it in the hallway in the morning," assuming that Fury's staying the night.

"Nonsense, I've never seen your bathroom messy." She mutters as she steps closer. I panic trying to think of something to stop her as she opens the door and turns the light on. I'm surprised and at the same time extremely relieved that I don't see Dax standing there, stark naked. She unplugs the straightener and wraps the cord around the base.

"Billie?" Lucy says in a questioning voice as she continues to wrap the cord around the straightener but her movements have now become much, much slower, "Is there a condom in your trash can?" *This is my hell*, I just look at her and then look around, "Oh, then I guess the date went well…" She grins, "Finally getting over Khan." *If there was a cliff I would throw myself off of it right now.*

Instead I just look at her and smile, "Something like that." I'm just glad that Lucy is preoccupied with her own life at the moment.

"Speaking of him, is this his shirt?" Fury says picking up the black, much too large for me shirt, with the Midnight Syn logo on it, off of the dresser, *shit*.

"Yeah, when I was unpacking my stuff I found it. I guess it got mixed up with my things. I've been meaning to take it back over to him." I say, even shocking myself with how convincing that it is.

"I can take it back for you." He shrugs, "I know things are kind of weird between you two, right now." *If you only knew…*

I'm looking at him, with the shirt in his hand, as I try and think of a reason for him not to take the shirt with him, "I can't think of one reason for you not too."

Lucy squeals as Fury and her leave the room and she says, "We're going to go have celebratory sex now."

My bedroom door closes, I sink down to sit at the end of my bed. I barely hear the shower curtain slide back and watch a very naked Dax step out from behind it. He walks out and bathroom, sitting down next to me on the side furtherest away from the door, looks at me and says, "Did he just take my shirt?" I slowly nod my head.

The door knob turns quickly, Dax's face drops as he rolls off of the bed, and hides out of view on the other side. My bedroom door flies open and Lucy says, "Do you want to come up tomorrow with us?"

"Nah, Luce, you guys go. This is about the two of you."

"Okay, just let me know if you change your mind."

I nod my head at her, "Will do." *Please, fucking leave.*

"Love you," she grins at me and before I can say it back she closes the door. I jump up and make sure to lock the door this time.

"Good call," Dax mutters as he walks around and pulls his clothes that I shoved under the bed and pulls his boxers on. "Just in case." He slides up to the headboard of my bed and motions down to me to come up to him.

KHAN

I haven't had to hide, because I was fucking someone else, since I was like 15 and Amanda Berry's dad came home.

Right before Lucy came into the bathroom I slide behind the shower curtain that was pulled closed already.

When she found the condom, I definitely thought we were going to be caught.

When Fury found my shirt, positive that it was done. I guess that they are too preoccupied with their happiness to put all the pieces together.

When Lucy came back in, I ducked behind the bed in time.

I slide up to the headboard and motion for Billie to come up to sit with me. She holds one finger up as she gets up walking over to her dresser, opening one of the drawers, handing me a shirt... correction, my shirt. She looks torn handing it to me. I'm torn taking it. "Bil-," I whisper in a confused voice but and shakes her head and smiles, a sad smile.

"I stole it," she laughs as she climbs up the bed and lays down next to me, "I could lie and say that it accidentally got mixed up in my things, but it didn't it's the one that I would wear when I was staying there, so when I left, I stole it, but I shouldn't keep it. It will just remind me of really bad timing." I don't know what to say to that. I was the one who told her that we couldn't happen.

I sigh, "I'll leave in a little bit." As she slides into the pocket that my body makes for her.

"You can stay if you want. It's getting kind of late." She pauses and looks back to me, "How's Ella doing? I haven't seen much of her lately."

"She's good. I feel kind of bad cause I work a lot, but there is always someone there, or at the clubhouse, but she's so used to Oz leaving her alone that she's not even phased by it. She doesn't want anyone there when there are people there."

"That sounds about normal for a 15 year old." She laughs as she looks down.

The noises from the other side of the wall makes talking about Ella very uncomfortable.

MIDNIGHT SYN MC BOOK ORDER

KHAN PART I
KHAN PART II
F*CKING CHAOS
TREAD Carefully
TILL The Day I Die
BOOK 6 - TBD

ABOUT THE AUTHOR

I GREW UP ALWAYS WRITING ROMANTIC STORIES WITH A DARKER SIDE. I TOOK A BREAK FROM WRITING FOR A FEW A WHILE AFTER I WENT THROUGH A DIVORCE AND THEN DECIDED TO GO BACK TO SCHOOL.

NOW, FINISHED WITH MY BACHELOR'S, A WHOLE NEW LOOK ON THE WORLD, AND, WHO I LIKE TO CLASSIFY AS, MY REAL LIKE BOOK BOYFRIEND I HAVE THE TIME I NEED ONCE AGAIN TO TAKE ON THE LOVE OF WRITING ONCE AGAIN...

FIND ON SOCIAL MEDIA
INSTAGRAM: AUTHOR_N.TETTERTON
TIKTOK: AUTHOR.NTETTERTON
FACEBOOK: N. TETTERTON- AUTHOR